ANNIE'S VERDICT

MICHAEL GRESHAM SERIES

JOHN ELLSWORTH

COPYRIGHT

G erry's expiration date was fast approaching when he flew to Chicago to meet with me.

"Michael Gresham!" he called to me as he tramped up the jetway. "Thanks for taking the time to come out to O'Hare, man! Let's get a drink!"

We found the lounge on the main concourse and stepped inside. He ordered a martini; I ordered coffee. Before we were finished with our talk, he had ordered a second. But even with the alcohol onboard his hands shook. His eyes darted all around the lounge and back out into the concourse, looking and watching, always watching.

"I got a letter," he said under his breath. "It arrived at my office on October third. It's from a bank in the Caymans. According to the letter, the bank says I have an account with just over twelve-million dollars in it."

He passed me the letter. I studied it and nodded appreciatively.

"Twelve million dollars. Isn't this good news?" I asked.

"It would be except I didn't put the money into the account. I also don't have any Cayman Island bank accounts. But they say I do. I've only been there once in my life, nearly twenty years ago."

I wasn't sure I heard correctly. "You didn't put the money in the account? And you didn't even open an account there? But it says in this letter you have twelve million in an account in your name?"

"Exactly. That's my correct address, too. Not many people know where I live."

Now I was perplexed. "Has anyone asked you about the money?"

"Just the bank. They're recommending I move it from a straight checking account into a savings account."

"No one else has said anything to you about it?"

"Nobody has come asking for their money back if that's what you're driving at. I'm sure it's stolen, and someone's going to turn me in and ruin my political career."

Gerry was the Climate Party's nominee in the race for President of the United States. In one month the presidential election of 2016 would tally up all the votes, and we'd know who the next president was going to be. Gerry didn't expect to win; green parties never win. But he had intended to make a statement about the climate. Now he feared that some enemy was going to step forth and claim Gerry embezzled the money. His political career—and chance to make a climate statement in the election—would be ruined.

I asked Gerry, "Who would want to harm you in this way?"

He favored me with a patient smile as a professional might do with a novice—which I was, politically.

"Lots of people would want to hurt me. I'm known as a flaming liberal from New York. That's strike one. Strike two is my million enemies in fossil fuel that would love to see me crash and burn."

"What's strike three?"

He shot a look around the lounge. "That's just it—I don't know what strike three is. That's what's keeping me up nights."

"Gerry, enemies don't usually open a bank account in your name and fund it with twelve million dollars," I said. The whole concept ran counter to anything I'd ever seen in my three decades of law practice. People did terrible things to each other; giving an enemy millions of dollars wasn't one of them.

"Now look at this," Gerry said. He withdrew a second letter from his breast pocket, opened the envelope and smoothed the letter in front of me on the table. It was just a few sentences.

"So this letter is from your PAC?"

"Yes. My PAC is named GULP."

"GULP?"

"Government Use of Land Policy. GULP. I was on the board. It's where the money comes from to run my campaign."

"And according to this letter, you're being accused of embezzling twelve-million dollars of GULP funds?"

"Yes."

"There's also a demand that you return the money. Why not just do that?"

"That's what I'm thinking, too. Just be done with it."

"So, Gerry, what do you need from me?"

"I want you to arrange to give the money back in exchange for a receipt stating that the whole thing was a misunderstanding, that I didn't embezzle the funds, and that no more will be said."

"But why me?"

He took a large mouthful of his martini and swallowed hard. "I wanted someone not on the East Coast. You're here in Chicago. Plus, I've known you since our first year in law school. You were always honest and not looking to get your name in the paper at your clients' expense. I felt I could trust you, bottom line."

"All right. Today is October sixth. You want the money returned before election day, correct?"

"Yes," Gerry said, "I want the statement from them immediately. My fear is that otherwise they'll go to the media and claim I've embezzled them. If that were to happen, I'd lose ninety percent of the vote I usually get. I want to give it back before they can do that."

I considered what he was asking me to do. I trusted him--at least as much as streetwise lawyers like me ever trust anyone: exceeding caution seasoned with exceeding suspicion. But did I know that much about him? We'd attended law school together at Georgetown. He made *Law Review*; with my healthy C average, I did not. In fact, he was the editor of *Georgetown Law Journal* and wrote an incredible article his senior year supporting *Tennessee v. Garner*. That case made it a crime for a cop to shoot a fleeing suspect in the back unless there's a threat of serious physical injury to the cop. Gerry did a number on the local D.C. police for a pending shooting case in which an unarmed black teen had been used for target practice by two uniforms when he tried to run off with a quart of beer shoplifted from a 7-Eleven on G Street.

"I'm impressed you came all the way to Chicago to talk," I told him.

"Michael," he said over the double martini, "there're some very bad people after me."

"Any idea why someone at your own PAC would come after you?"

"I have some serious detractors in the PAC. The guy who wants to ruin me is Paul Wexler. At one time we were friends, but no more. Now he'd just as soon have me dead and buried."

"So what can I do to help?"

It was what he was hoping I'd say.

"I want to give you power of attorney over the bank account. I want you to give the money back and clear my name. But I've also got to protect myself."

"How does that work?"

"If they announce I embezzled the funds a day or two before the election I'll keep their damn money, Michael. Which means they'll send someone after me. They'll murder me. If that happens, I want you to make sure the money goes to my kids."

"Because you wouldn't be around to take care of them."

"Do you remember Kitty Sanders from law school? We were married for twenty years. But she passed away several years ago. My kids would be orphaned."

"I'm sorry."

"I'm scared, Michael. So scared I don't sleep. Don't eat. My hands shake. My youngest daughter, Annie, is special needs. The money *has* to go to her. Plus, there's her brother and sister. They both get a share."

I took a sip of the airport battery acid coffee. "So I'm to act as their lawyer?"

"No, as their power of attorney."

He opened his attaché case then and rummaged around inside. "I have a power of attorney right here--somewhere. Here it is. Can you read it over and sign it? I've already signed it, appointing you."

I accepted the two-page document and scanned through it three lines at a time as lawyers will do with legal documents. It was all there.

"Before I sign, where is this bank account?"

"That's the thing. I moved it all with a wire transfer this morning.

"Moved it where?"

"Avtovazbank. Moscow, Russia."

"Why Russia?"

"Because they haven't crumbled to the U.S. Government's demands that accounts of U.S. Citizens be reported by the bank to the U.S."

"You're saying it's in an off-shore account and you haven't reported it to the Treasury Department?"

"Exactly. Technically I could be looking at criminal charges for failure to report."

I passed the unsigned document to Gerry. No way I'd get in the middle of a political squabble in a national election. I was a criminal lawyer, not a politician. In fact, I hated politics and wanted nothing to do with the whole sordid mess.

"I can't help you, Gerry. I just finished up a trial in Moscow, and I was never so glad to leave some place in my life. You think we've got some terrible judges in the U.S.? You ain't seen nothing until you've litigated in Russia."

"I appreciate that, Michael. But there's no need to go to Russia. This can be done from your office here in Chicago. The withdrawal and distribution will be accomplished electronically."

Which helped to melt away my biggest complaint. "Well--"

"Please, Michael. I don't have much time. I really need this. My kids really need this!"

He handed the power of attorney back. Tears washed into his eyes, and I weakened at his distress. We had been classmates; we went way back. And I could do it without leaving my office. So, I took it and signed without comment and passed it back to him. Then we did a second one, this one for me. Both were signed originals.

"Done," I said.

"You're my hero, Michael. I'm saying a *Birkat HaGomel* for you on Friday."

"Well, thanks for that. Now what? Are you ready to see Chicago? Maybe hit a Bulls game?"

He looked at his watch. "No can do. I've got a flight out of here in forty-five minutes."

"You mean you flew all the way here just to get my signature and turn around and go right back?"

"Afraid so. My kids are back in Georgetown. I can't stop over."

We talked until he walked down the ramp to board his return flight. He'd had another martini, and I had switched from coffee to Filbert's Root Beer, a secret wonder drink among Chicagoans. He turned the corner at the bottom of the ramp and was gone.

Two days before the election, a story broke in the *Washington Post.* The story accused Gerry of embezzlement of PAC funds. What Gerry had feared was now headline news. His campaign was ruined; he got less than one percent of the vote two days later. I was sure he'd now move the money into his kids' names, which would let me off the hook for any duties I had agreed to perform in the power of attorney. I felt relieved, but I also felt sorry for Gerry. He didn't deserve to lose in a landslide when he'd been set up and played. He called me the next day after the election and said, "Now you see why I want to keep the money? I've got nothing else to lose, Michael."

"Except your life."

"Except my life. I haven't made the decision yet for that very reason: if something happens to me my kids are all alone."

"Return the money, Gerry," I said. "Your kids need you."

"Maybe you're right. In fact, you are right. I'll return it."

I thought it was all done. We hung up still friends with him expressing his gratitude to me. I thought nothing more about it.

But then Gerry suddenly flew into Chicago again, insisting I drop everything and meet him at O'Hare. We met in the airport lounge. He insisted he was going to keep the money for his kids, which put a bounty on his head.

"I've made some very powerful people very angry by refusing to return the money."

"I thought you were going to return it?"

"I can't. I'm mad as hell at what they did to me. No way am I giving it back."

"Are they threatening you?"

"Not coming right out and making a threat. But it doesn't matter: I told them where they could stuff it. Maybe I overdid it, but they killed me in the election."

"So now what?"

"Just be ready, Michael. If anything happens to me, get the money to my kids."

"That's a tall order, Gerry."

"Promise me, Michael. You're my only hope, my only friend at this point."

I sighed and shook my head. "I'll do what I can."

Just then they announced his flight.

"I've got a return flight to catch," he said and headed for the jetway.

That was the last time I saw Gerry. I drove back to my office praying he'd be okay and I wouldn't have to get involved.

I almost made it, too.

But then Gerry's expiration date rolled around.

2

Rudy was a torpedo, an enforcer, a hitman, all of these things and little else. He loved the Washington Redskins because he lived just south of the Beltway in a one-bedroom where the whole universe spoke Redskins this and Redskins that. And he loved his mother--God rest her brave and devout fish-on-Fridays soul. And Rudy hated politicians--a hard if not impossible pill to swallow for someone living in Washington, D.C. So the shooting of Gerry Tybaum would be easy: the guy was the Climate Party's candidate, a politician. Rudy would've killed him for free except he had received $50,000 for the hit. Ordinarily, Rudy would've taken his fee and headed for Boca and the horses, but first, he had one more piece of business, a piece insisted on by the man who hired him to kill the father: Rudy was also to murder Tybaum's children. The man who hired him was Paul Wexler at Gerry's PAC's headquarters.

Paul Wexler had written the demand letter to Gerry on the PAC's letterhead. It demanded the full return of the twelve million dollars which, it claimed, Gerry had embezzled. The demand letter didn't bring rain. So Wexler turned to Rudy. He had obtained Rudy's name from a *Washington Post* article announcing his release from prison. Rudy had become a legend, being released to come home after doing a twenty-year stretch for the murder of a senator's chief of staff. He met Rudy at a bar in a dangerous neighborhood in Baltimore.

Rudy would do the job for fifty-thousand dollars.

Before the hit was to take place, Wexler hired Nivea Young to follow Gerry. He had to know the whereabouts of the money before Gerry went down. Nivea Young, an ex-CIA agent, followed Gerry from Washington, D.C. to Chicago. She watched him meet with a lawyer.

Young called Paul Wexler late that afternoon.

"He met with a lawyer at O'Hare airport," she told Wexler. "They talked for only about twenty minutes, then Tybaum turned around and took a flight back to D.C."

"We need to find out what they discussed," said Wexler.

"I can get into the lawyer's office," she said.

"How do you know that?"

"I followed him back downtown after their meeting. He's in an office on the Loop, not far from the federal court at the Dirksen Building. It's an old, renovated building with suites of offices, lots of wood, stained glass skylights, the whole nine yards. He's on the second floor. I can be inside and out in minutes."

"Then do it. Get in, find Tybaum's file and copy it. Or find the lawyer's notes and copy those. Something was written down after their meeting. I need to locate that money."

"Why not just call the bank? You put the money there."

"That's just it; I put it in Tybaum's name. The bank refuses to give me any info now."

She nodded appreciatively. "I'll make entry into the lawyer's office tonight. Anything else?"

Just then, Wexler, brainiac that he was, took it one step further that most people might.

"Yes. Go through the lawyer's desk. If he has a gun, bring it with you."

"I'll have to check it on the airplane."

"You traveling under your name?"

"Please, Mr. W. What do you think I am?"

"Then there you are. Bring the gun."

"Anything else?" she asked.

"Just don't get caught."

"Please, Mr. W."

"I'm just trying to emphasize."

"It goes without saying."

That night, Nivea easily broke into the lawyer's office. She had one goal: the Gerry Tybaum file. Wexler had made it clear that he wanted to track down the money. Sure enough, she located a file smack on top of the lawyer's desk and opened it. There was one page inside. She ran the page through the office copier then sat down and read it through.

A power of attorney. Wexler would be very pleased. She continued riffling through the lawyer's desk drawers, looking for what she was guessing might be kept there. Sure enough, third drawer down, right side, she found it: a semi-automatic pistol, loaded. Ever so carefully, so as not to disturb the fingerprints and DNA clinging to the gun, she dropped it into a plastic bag, picked up the page she had copied, and left.

She returned to Washington and headed straight to Wexler. Wexler saw the gun, read the stolen power of attorney, and called her brilliant. Then he called the hitman, Rudy, and said to meet him at a Denny's in Foggy Bottom. After the coffee had arrived, Wexler passed the lawyer's gun to Rudy. "Use this," he said. Rudy nodded and slipped the plastic bag and gun into his coat pocket. That's all it took.

The day of the hit rolled around overcast and quite cold. A freeze was predicted for later. Rudy, watching and waiting outside Tybaum's office building, spied the hapless Tybaum walking up the sidewalk to the glass doors. Rudy switched on the GoPro camera mounted on his North Face coat. Wexler wanted a picture of the hit and Rudy was going to give him one--a whole video, for that matter.

It was just before six o'clock p.m., which meant Tybaum was probably working late. It was cold out, but his coat was unzipped. He was wearing a flannel shirt beneath his coat. Rudy took all this in without thinking. Rudy fell in behind him. Perhaps feeling he was being followed, Tybaum abruptly stopped and swung around to stare at his pursuer.

He immediately knew he was being followed. He broke into a run. He had known this day would come once he refused to return the money. He vaulted the railing running along the sidewalk, dropping ten feet onto a sloping driveway that terminated at a basement loading dock. Rudy followed, caught up to Tybaum, and the men struggled against each other before Tybaum again broke free, kicked Rudy in the head, and ran. Rudy recovered and then chased Tybaum up onto the basement loading dock. Gerry went tearing through the warehouse and out the other side. A path took him past the Lincoln Memorial and along the Reflecting Pool, that shallow body of water keeping the Lincoln Memorial and the Washington Monument from sliding into each other. At the near end of the pool, Tybaum made a left and began running obliquely to his earlier path. Just then, as the candidate straightened his left turn into a thirty-yard dash for the far side of the pool, Rudy closed the distance between them and, latex gloves covering his hands, he raised the lawyer's gun, aiming it from can't-miss range at Tybaum's back.

The first round pierced Tybaum's pounding heart; his momentum carried him headlong into the Reflecting Pool. Rudy then closed on the dying man and fired five more rounds into his back. Rudy was a terrific shot: the group was no wider than the mouth of a highball glass. Rudy felt proud. *Even hitmen have their standards*, he thought to himself as he suddenly turned and headed back the way he had come. He was running for his waiting car and the anonymity of the nearby freeway.

Halfway up the steps of the Lincoln Memorial, a woman turned to look, after the first gunshot. She was down on her knees, engaged in a sex act for pay with the man lurking above her, and she saw Rudy's face, which was familiar because she was a *Post* subscriber for the "men-seeking-women" section. She didn't know his name, but she'd never forget his face.

Down on her knees, the woman turned back to her work to fulfill the contract she had entered into with the man standing over her. She looked up, and their eyes met. Should we run off? Her look asked her customer. His look said it all: run off only if you want to be in breach of our contract.

So she finished with her work and, the contract completed, the man double-timed down the steps and ran to the far end of the pool and the parking lot beyond.

The woman, on the other hand, was slow to run off because, as she opened her purse for a tissue, her roll of casino quarters fell to the concrete steps, scattering twenty-five-cent pieces up and down. Those were key, those quarters, the coin of the casino realm's slots. So she calmly bent down and began herding the quarters back into her purse. She'd seen a mob hit before and such things no longer frightened her as she'd seen much worse. But there was more. She'd also fulfilled a contract with a United States senator known to her as Stanley J. Jessup, a good ole boy from South Carolina who stayed happy on hookers and whiskey and missed Senate votes.

As she bent down three steps to retrieve the last of the quarters it was then she slipped, banged her head hard against the closest step, and awoke hours later with a Capitol Cop holding a smelling salt under her nose and inquiring, "Can you hear me?"

She didn't respond right away. He massaged her hands and spoke her name again.

"I can hear you," she said. "What a dream. Someone shot someone."

The Capitol Cop spoke into his shoulder mike. "I've found an eyeball."

Down below, the FBI agents heard the news. The woman was helped down the steps and delivered to the agents for a quick round of questions before being taken to the emergency room to be checked out.

"Yes," she told the first suit to reach her. "I saw the whole thing. So did my trick, Senator Stanley J. Jessup."

One special agent looked at the other.

The murder suddenly sprouted first-page prospects. Careers were made from such stories. The agents couldn't miss the possibilities.

The first agent spoke casually so as not to frighten off this songbird.

"You're sure it was Stanley J. Jessup?"

"You want me to describe his penis?"

The agents smiled.

"That won't be necessary. We're quite confident he'll be cooperative."

Then one agent demonstrated the brains that all FBI agents

must have. "While she's in the ER getting checked out have the doc swab her mouth for DNA."

"That way we know we have the right senator," the second agent said to the woman.

"Sure," she said.

"And don't drink or eat anything until they're done."

"I already know that," she said. "The swab."

"The swab, exactly."

3

The EMT's cut Gerry out of the ice in the Reflecting Pool at the Lincoln Memorial in D.C. Pictures were taken and observations made; official reports would follow. The coroner counted six bullet holes in Gerry's back.

The Washington D.C. detectives said it was a robbery. *Sure*, I thought when the TV story played here in Chicago, *robbery indeed. That's why the shooter left the $300 in Gerry's pocket he'd pulled out of an ATM not fifteen minutes before he died.* His murder made me close my eyes and say a prayer for his soul. I'm Catholic, and that's what I do.

And while Gerry's soul was negotiating passage through heaven's gates, I began negotiating with the Russians for a transfer of the money to Gerry's kids. But before I could put things in motion, I had one big problem: I didn't know his kids, didn't have names, birthdates, Social Security numbers and so forth.

I knew I owed it to Gerry to get myself back to Georgetown and tell the kids everything and get their personal info. He'd trusted me, and I didn't have any choice but to fly out and keep my promise to him.

Later on, I learned that the police wanted to write it off as a robbery. But Gerry's daughter—Mona—insisted it had been a fossil fuel assassination. She accused the oil oligarchs of the crime. But she had zero proof of any such thing. So, the police wrote her off as paranoid and not just a little crazed over her father's death. Behind the scenes, they thought she was a kook. They thought it was just another ho-hum robbery. Except their reports all said the same thing: Gerry's wallet was found in his pocket. The $300 he had withdrawn from an ATM fifteen minutes earlier was still inside the wallet. This entry into the first detectives' report went without comment.

Ever the Curious George, I began nosing around. I called a friend at the U.S. Attorney's Office in D.C. What I learned was compelling. Whoever killed Gerry acted audaciously. Apparently, he did not expect to be arrested for he gunned him down a short hike from the White House, an area crawling with cops and federal law enforcement agents. Then I made a call to Gerry's law office to talk to his secretary. The office was closed. The recording said they were closed because they were in mourning for Gerry, to call back in three days. So I waited three days and then called again. Much to my surprise, according to the *Post*, there had been a one-eighty on the investigation: now the FBI was working the case. Which told me there was a suspicion that some federal crime had been committed in Gerry's death.

Three rings then a curt answer.

"Gerry Tybaum's office, can you please hold?"

"I want--"

"Thank you."

I was on hold, just like that. Then the voice returned.

"How may I help you?"

"My name is Michael Gresham. I'm a lawyer in Chicago. Gerry came to see me before he died."

"What is this about?"

"Gerry wanted me to do a job for him."

"What might that have been?"

A light bulb went off in my head. Gerry's receptionist wouldn't be asking me what I was doing for Gerry. No, she would have asked me whether my call was personal or business and, accordingly, directed me either to Gerry's probate lawyers or his law partners. This voice was doing neither. It was inquiring about my work for Gerry. Improper. So, I dodged.

I asked, "Who are you?"

"This is Special Agent Ames. May I get your name, sir?"

"Special Agent as in FBI?"

"Yessir."

"Why is the FBI at my friend's law office?"

"May I get your name, sir? We have the number you're calling from. Getting your name won't be that hard. It would be much easier if just told me who you are. A friendly request, sir."

"Michael Gresham is my name."

"And did you have a case with Mr. Tybaum?"

"No, we were law school buddies. I was just calling to shoot the breeze."

Suddenly the voice wasn't nearly as friendly. "You say you're a lawyer?"

'Yes."

"What kind of law do you practice?"

"I don't see how that's any of your business."

"Well, sir, let me put it this way. We are knee-deep in tracking down all leads that might help us find who killed Mr. Tybaum. Now we have your name. You can either help me out with who you are and why you're calling, or I can send two agents to your office, and we can take your statement."

"Bet me, take my statement," I scoffed.

"Sir?"

"Bet me. There's no way your goons are coming in here and taking my statement."

"Then are you saying you have something to hide?"

"I'm saying the FBI has no right to come in here and question me."

"You're unwilling to cooperate with law enforcement in your friend's death?"

"That's right. I don't usually cooperate with law enforcement in my criminal defense practice. Color me silly, but my clients would rather I didn't cooperate with the police."

"Mr. Gresham, was Mr. Tybaum one of your criminal clients?"

"No, he was not."

"Was he the subject of a criminal investigation such that he might become one of your criminal clients?"

"Not that I'm aware."

"Then there should be no problem. Please tell me why you were calling."

This came out fast. "We had a bet on the Wizards versus the Knicks. He lost, I was calling to collect."

"How much was the wager for?"

"Steak dinner next time he came to Chicago."

"Did he come to Chicago regularly?"

"I have no idea about that."

"Was he in Chicago to talk about financial matters with you?"

Careful now, Michael, I cautioned myself. Martha Stewart did not go to prison for insider trading. She went to prison because the FBI claimed she lied to them. If I lied to them about Gerry coming to Chicago and discussing the Russian bank account, I could open myself to the same kind of liability if the FBI found out I was lying. And they'd have bank statements that led them to his airline ticket and his connection to Chicago. There I was, on the other end of that trip. Coming clean was the only move.

"He came to see me just before he was murdered. He was scared."

"The main purpose of that visit?"

"Confidential. Attorney-client privilege."

"You were his attorney? You represented him?"

There we were again. Technically, Gerry was not my client. Which meant technically I was not his lawyer. I held a power of attorney, but that's not covered by the attorney-client privilege. But here's the key consideration: upon the death of the the person who gave the power of attorney, the power of attorney is at death rendered void. It no longer exists and the person who received the power of attorney no longer can act as POA.

"I'm not saying yes to that, and I'm not saying no. I'm saying this conversation is concluded."

With that, I disconnected my phone and told Mrs. Lingscheit--my receptionist--not to accept any calls regarding Mr. Tybaum or the FBI.

My hand was shaking as I struggled to replace the phone in its cradle. Damn, these guys are good, I was thinking. Just like that, in less than two minutes, the agent had me backed into a corner about to commit a serious federal crime of lying to the FBI.

The worst part of it? They weren't done with me. They'd be back. In fact, they'd probably show up in my office in the next twenty-four hours.

I was only doing Gerry a favor. I had wanted nothing to do with Russia because I didn't want to go there. He had told me there was no need for that. It could all be done by telephone.

What he didn't tell me about was that the FBI would come crawling over the phone lines and put me in a legal stranglehold. He hadn't warned me about that.

With one simple little call, I had become a name associated with my friend's murder.

Nor was I one step closer to finding out about his kids.

I puttered around the office for an hour, surfing on my computer and studying a few pending files, all the while thinking in the back of my mind about what I should do next. Then I had a quiet lunch with my brown bag. I finally visualized my next step.

I called the bank in Russia. I gave them the account number and the key code and asked for a balance.

"Yes, Mr. Tybaum," said the English speaking customer support representative. "Your balance is twelve-million USD."

"I need to transfer that money to the United States."

"No problem, Mr. Gresham. But we're going to need a fee of one million dollars."

"What? You do it electronically. There shouldn't even be a charge."

"Bank policy with U.S. citizens."

I hung up at that point, a sick feeling washing over me. I wasn't about to return to Russia. Yet I had promised Gerry for the sake of his kids.

It was too much to get my head around right then. I went into my outer office and told Mrs. Lingscheit I was ill, and I was going home. She gave me one of her patented "Ain't gonna happen" looks.

"What?" I asked her.

She answered softly. "The FBI wants to talk to you. I told them you weren't in. But they said they knew you were."

"What? How do they know I'm in?"

She pointed behind me.

I turned and saw a man in a neat business suit, hands on his knees, eyes glowing at me.

"He's the FBI. He wants to talk to you and says he's not leaving until you do."

4

Back into my office I trudged, this time with an FBI agent in tow. I was astounded at how fast they'd moved on me. Plus, it downright pissed me off. No one--much less criminal lawyers--likes the FBI in their office. So we sat down and traded stares. Then he opened a thin folder and pulled out a notepad. He scanned over it and then looked up.

The FBI agent was direct: "Mr. Tybaum's political action committee is known as GULP. It stands for Government Use of Lands and Policy. It had accumulated massive amounts of cash from climate zealots just like Gerry."

"So he had a PAC that wanted to get him elected. That isn't illegal or even suspicious, last time I looked," I said.

The agent was impassive. He'd said his name was Harold Leders and he was out of Chicago. It wasn't an even match so far, as I was still trying to recover from how fast I had gone from being Michael Gresham, relative nobody, to someone the FBI wanted to question. Agent Leders had me on my heels from the moment he identified himself.

He continued. "GULP has been very active. It's a liberal PAC with some very famous supporters on the East and West coasts. People you might see in the *Hollywood News* and *New York Magazine*. Are you following me so far?"

"I am. But so what?"

"Mr. Tybaum made a withdrawal from the PAC's bank account about one month before he died."

"And so?"

"So, it was for twelve-million dollars and change. We want to know whether he spoke to you about this before he died?"

That was twice in one day I'd heard that number.

"That number isn't part of my vocabulary. I don't talk those numbers."

Special Agent Leders stared a hole through my skull. He apparently *did* talk those numbers. He just tossed it out like Gerry had written a check for nineteen dollars, and they wanted to know about it. Ordinarily, I would have maybe discussed what I knew, just put it out there. But Gerry's mission to me had been to help his *kids* get his money, not help the FBI. Then I began thinking I'd need deposit dates and that kind of thing before I made any decision about revealing what I knew. Plus, I'd need to know what withdrawal and expenditure powers Gerry had at the PAC. Maybe the withdrawal was totally authorized by its charter, and I would be a dupe for revealing it. Worse, maybe his kids would sue me for breaching the attorney-client confidentiality law--if it even applied--if I did reveal it and they didn't get their money. Then there was Annie, Gerry's special needs daughter. Her story tugged at my heartstrings. I owed her and felt it clear down to my toes. There was a good dozen movies playing in my head, so I didn't want to say too much. Again, withholding information from the FBI.... There had to be some way out of this.

"I'm not feeling well," I told Agent Leders. I felt around on my throat and shook my head. "Hurts," I rasped.

But he wasn't moved even a millimeter.

"No go, Mr. Gresham. Nobody's leaving until we have some answers. I'll run you down to the office if I have to; I'll even put you under arrest for conspiracy if need be. But you're giving me some answers, and you're giving me some answers right now."

"Answers about what? If I knew anything, I'd answer you."

"Two days after he embezzled the PAC's bank account, he came out here to see you. Did you take control of those funds? Are you ready to turn over your own bank statements so we can confirm what you tell us?"

"Please remember there was an attorney-client relationship. I cannot talk about Gerry and his finances."

"Attorney-client?"

"Well, power-of-attorney."

He sat back and smiled grandly at me. I thought It's a ploy, an attempt to frighten me. Well, think again.

"The fact that a power-of-attorney relationship exists between two persons is itself not privileged. *U.S. v. Leventhal*, 961 F.2d 936, Mr. Gresham. I can put you in front of a grand jury tomorrow and throw you in jail if you refuse to answer these questions. There's no protection for you. Or, you can simply answer them here, today. Which is it, Mr. Gresham?"

Now, he had my hackles up with that threat. I'm almost sixty years old; threats don't much work with me anymore.

"Put me in front of your grand jury, then. I won't be coerced by your threats, Agent Leders."

He sat back, placing his hands on the arms of the client chair. He nodded thoughtfully.

"How about this," he said, somewhat calmed. "How about you bring up your trust account on your computer screen. Let me scroll through the last thirty days. If there's nothing there that looks like Gerry's money, I go away and leave you alone. Does a compromise like this work for you?"

"I'm not letting you into my client trust account, Mr. Leders. That information is privileged. I could be sued--even disbarred--if I let you in on those client confidences. Sorry, but no."

"Then I'll be gathering up the grand jury and issuing a subpoena for you, Mr. Gresham."

He stood, making ready to go.

"Oh, there's one more thing," he said, looking up from buttoning his topcoat.

"Yes?"

"Where were you the night Mr. Tybaum died?"

The question shook me. It shook me because, for the love of God, I was actually in New York the night Gerry was murdered. It was only last Sunday so I couldn't plead memory loss. I beat myself up. Think, damn it!

It was getting rough. I decided to meet them head-on. After all, I had done nothing wrong.

"Come to think of it, I was in New York taking depositions in a medical malpractice case against a drug manufacturer."

"Were you with anyone that night in your hotel room?"

The noose had just tightened around my neck. New York was too close to where Gerry was killed.

"I think I might have rented a PPV movie that night in my room."

"What movie would that be?"

"Honestly? I can't remember. I'm sure my room charge would say if you're wanting a thumbs up or thumbs down from me."

"Funny man. So, you were in the vicinity of Gerry's death the night he died?"

"How do you know it was at night when he died?"

"The park police make their rounds at sundown. No bodies were seen in the pool at the Lincoln Memorial."

"Sure, that makes sense. You know what? I think we're done here today. I'm just not going to answer any more of your questions because I don't appreciate the implications you're making, Agent Leders."

"Implications? I'm just trying to absolve you of any wrong-doing, Mr. Gresham. We know Tybaum came to see you soon after he made off with twelve-million dollars; we know you were in the area the night he was killed; we know we don't have any leads on anyone who might have pulled the trigger. It's only natural the FBI would view you as a person of interest."

I stood behind my desk. "This talk is concluded. Please leave, sir."

"Mr. Gresham, please don't leave town over the next two weeks. And please let me know if you do."

"I'm not reporting to you, Agent Leders. I'll come and go as I damn well please."

"Then, that will require we take certain steps I didn't want to take."

"Step away if you must," I told him. "Just don't threaten me and don't try to hogtie me. It doesn't work."

He finally turned away from my desk. "Goodbye, Mr. Gresham," he called back over his shoulder. "See you again. Very soon."

I didn't respond. There was no need.

I sat down and pressed my hands together to stop the shaking. I had just implicated--or almost implicated--myself in an old acquaintance's murder despite my promises to myself I'd do no such thing.

It never pays for a lawyer to represent himself in a criminal case.

Especially when he doesn't know what he's doing.

5

On my drive home to Evanston later that afternoon, I considered my quandary. The lawyer side of me wanted to protect Gerry's children. I probably had a legal duty of some sort to protect them. But the personal side of me wanted to protect myself by telling the FBI what it wanted to know so Agent Leders could direct his attention elsewhere. But...I couldn't tell even though I wanted to tell. As in all things legal, the client's needs came before mine. Which brought me to critical mass in my professional life: I no longer enjoyed practicing law. When Danny died, my desire to practice law died with her. I had been over it dozens of times in my mind and, as near as I could tell, I think I was suffering from the fact that Danny and I had started the newest edition of the law practice together and now she was gone. Anymore, the physical office depressed me. Her office was just as it'd been when she died. I couldn't even stand to open the door and look inside. Law practice? Maybe I was done and just coming to grips with that fact.

I rocked along in my Mercedes tracing Lake Michigan's

shoreline. Every now and then I caught a glimpse of the lake between the mammoth houses that were built along its shores. They were magnificent and I knew what I always acknowledged when I came home on this road: I would never own a house like that. Too rich for my blood. I just don't make the kind of money it takes to snatch one of those off the market. Of course, I mused, if I had twelve-million dollars I'd grab one in a second. Or maybe I wouldn't. Maybe instead I'd live in Florida or Southern California right on the beach. Sand between my toes. That money could buy me a lot of peace. But it wasn't my money.

Was it? Maybe no one would ever know I had access to that money. I was sure Gerry hadn't told his kids about the money even though the two older were grown and no longer living with him. He couldn't afford to have done that. And hadn't I heard somewhere that he was a widower? There wouldn't be a spouse to tell. So maybe I was the only one who knew. Just me and the board members at Avtovazbank Bank who were lying awake at night plotting how to keep Gerry's huge deposit from leaving their vault. Just me and the Russians.

I had just finished a trial in Russia, so that phrase, "Me and the Russians," left a very unsavory taste in my mouth. Never again, I had sworn. Never again would I set foot inside the Russian Federation. But what about twelve mil? Would that be enough to lure me back?

You're damn right it would.

I had to pull in for a fill-up, so I found a gas station. Ten minutes and forty dollars later, I was on my way again. It was a perverse little pleasure for me to think about the charge I'd just made on my American Express. Imagine what life would be like if it didn't ever matter to me ever again how much I charged to my card? That's what Gerry's money could mean to me. Or what if I wound up with only half of it? Maybe a fifty-fifty split with his kids? Would that be so bad?

Twenty minutes later I hit the garage door opener at my house and pulled inside my three-car garage. Verona's Range Rover was parked inside. I pulled alongside it and threw open my door.

What the hell? Thoughts like I'd been having on the way home were random and meant nothing. No way would I ever in real life abscond with a client's money. I just didn't do stuff like that.

But wait, I told myself. What if the FBI filed charges against me? What if they actually indicted me? Would it be okay in that case to use some of that money to defend myself in court? To hire a lawyer? After all, it was Gerry's money that might put me in that position in the first place. Shouldn't he be the one to pay for that problem if it ever arose? Now I was walking a very thin line between right and wrong. Now I was in that gray area that makes lawyers flail around in at least once in their careers. Now I was in that ambiguity that might get me sentenced to years in a federal prison for stealing a client's money. I stuffed my car keys in my pocket and climbed the stairs to the door that led into my laundry room and then into the kitchen. It was time to put these thoughts to rest. That money wasn't mine and there would never be a situation where I would touch a dime of it.

Never.

Not even if it got me arrested.

Really? Maybe I would need to consult a lawyer of my own about that. Maybe I shouldn't be the one making that decision at all because I was too close to it.

Maybe, maybe, maybe.

I went inside my house, hating myself and hating the practice of law. It would be good to see my partner, Verona, and allow her sweet love for me to make me whole again. To make me more than I really was.

That was something all the money in the world couldn't do.

It was love that could.

"Verona?" I called out. "Your missing person is home."

It was true; this missing person spent many long nights into the wee hours at his law office chasing justice for his clients. Good results are always the result of good research; there are no shortcuts in law. Of course there's always the first-year lawyer who stumbles across a quadriplegic case when he's writing a will for some old lady and her grandson is now married to a wheelchair due to the negligence of some five-hundred-billion-dollar railroad. That lucky lawyer with his lucky catch was never me. I've had to earn it.

No Verona. I called out again. "Michael?" she replied from a back room. I set off in the direction of her voice. This is the woman I met while in Russia on legal business. Her name is Verona Kristinova Sakharov, she's fifty-one years of age, a widow, and in Moscow she supported herself by teaching at Moscow State University. She has no children, but four brothers and four sisters, all of whom live in and around Moscow. When we met and fell in love we knew it would end when I returned to America from Moscow. But it didn't:

she came with me and we've been happy and in love ever since hitting the United States.

I located her in our bedroom, swapping bedspreads she had purchased from Amazon. I knew her *modus operandi:* one of the bedspreads would make the cut; the others would be returned for refunds. She turned from her chore and came around the bed, taking me in her arms and setting me down on the bed then sitting down beside me. "Tell me about your day," she said with a smile.

"I saw some clients, appeared on a motion to suppress-- which I lost--then met with the FBI. Seems I have in excess of twelve-million-dollars USD ready for my signature in Moscow."

"Twelve-million in Moscow? I thought we were done with Moscow."

"We are. We were. No, this doesn't mean I have to go to Moscow; this one's a power of attorney that can be done electronically. Not a big deal, except the man who gave me the power of attorney was shot and killed afterward. Which means the power of attorney is no longer good. But the Russians don't have to know he's dead, do they?"

Her eyes narrowed at me. She snuggled up closer. "What the Russians don't know won't hurt them. But does it mean you're at risk, too?"

"Not at all."

Which wasn't true, not entirely, but I really couldn't say much more than what I said because, in all honestly, I didn't know whether Gerry Tybaum's death created any kind of exposure for me or not. But I did have to admit, the thought did cross my mind after the meeting with the FBI agent. Crossed my mind more than once, in fact.

She removed her arm from across my back and crossed her ankles. She stared at her feet, shaking her head. "Damn, damn, damn. I swore once we left Russia we'd never know persecution again. Does this mean I was wrong? I'm so worried about you, Michael. And what about the kids? Are they safe?"

"Where are they, by the way?"

"At Tory Evanhope's birthday party."

The Evanhopes were our next-door neighbors. The kids were safe there, I had no doubt, and I left it at that. At some point, one or both of us would hike next door and walk them home.

"What time is it over?" I asked

"Seven-thirty."

"Time for a cup of coffee before all the fun starts when our sugared-up tribe hits the door?"

"I say let's go for it."

"Anything else?" I said, hoping against hope we might have time for quick us.

"What, time for anything else? What is this, Jiffy-Lube?"

"Actually I wasn't thinking of giving you a lube job. Something more along the lines of scheduled maintenance."

"You're nuts, Michael Gresham. Maybe later you can change my fluids. For now, we've got twenty minutes until we get the kids. Let's do coffee. Come along."

We did coffee that night. The kids made it home, speeding on sugar like meth tweakers, but after homework and story time I finally got a break from them. I love my kids--I'd go to the gallows for them in a heartbeat--but kids plus white flour and sugar are a whole other world.

Much later that night I did make love to Verona. When it was over, all thoughts and musings about absconding with Gerry Tybaum's Russian funds were released like air out of a balloon.

It was his money and his money it would stay.

I fell asleep thinking about ten-million-dollar lakefront houses and walks across Russian snow at midnight. Incompatible but somehow, deep down inside where our real secrets are stored, there was a connection between megabucks and Russia.

But as I slept I couldn't smile. The money wasn't mine. It never had been and, in fact, I didn't even want it. Annie Tybaum needed that money. Her dad had been insistent.

What I had was enough and so it would remain.

6

The next day, I called my contact in the U.S. Attorney's Office in Washington, D.C. Her name was Antonia Xiang and we had met in Russia. I had gone to Russia to defend her husband, the son of my law school roommate. After a long, hard court battle, I saved him from a firing squad.

"Antonia?" I said to her over the phone. "Michael Gresham calling."

I swept my arm across my desk, clearing a place for a clean yellow pad, something to write on because I knew Antonia would help and I didn't want to miss a thing. Like I said, anything she could ever do to help me, she would.

"My God, Michael, how long has it been since you gave us our lives back? Six months? Nine?"

"Somewhere around six, I think," I said.

"So how can I help you? What's up with Michael Gresham?"

"I'm in a bit of a bind, actually, or maybe not. Do you

suppose you could find time for me in the next day or two-- someplace away from the office where we could talk?'

"Anything, Michael," she said. "Just give me the day and the time you'll be here and I'll make it happen."

"Fine. I'm thinking tomorrow, one o'clock, on the benches surrounding the Washington Monument?"

"Works for me," she said. "Anything I should know going in?"

"Nothing I want to discuss on the telephone. See you tomorrow, Antonia. One p.m., Washington Monument."

"I won't be late," I said.

We hung up and I didn't give it anymore thought until the next day when I left my room at the Hyatt for the Capitol Mall. It would be good to see her again, a lawyer I had respected right out of the gate because she was so strong with the law and so imbued with common sense.

Antonia is the woman who stands out in a crowd. First, she's tall and quite attractive, in a tough kind of way. Her eyes and mouth say she's seen it all before and she isn't taking on any shit from anyone today, thank you very much. But there was a softer side, too, that I had seen once or twice, mostly after the Moscow case when she again could hold her husband in her arms and meet his gaze with her own. Then she was soft and accessible and, in a small way, I envied Rusty.

I found her already sitting on the long, curving bench at the base of the Monument, staring up at the obelisk. She saw me coming and immediately broke into a grin and stood up. We hugged. There would always be an invisible bond between us from what we'd both gone through in Moscow. Always.

"Antonia," I said, "thanks for coming. Especially on a cold, blustery day like this."

'Really?" she asked. "Do you want to hike across to the Wee Tavern and get in out of the cold?"

"No, I'm good. This won't take long, anyway."

We sat down on the freezing cold bench and I shivered.

Just as we were about to start talking, I noticed a man standing fifty feet away, pointing his camera directly at us. I've been around the block enough to know that police cameras have built-in directional microphones capable of picking up and recording conversations over great distances. I don't know why, but I got the very negative feeling that the man I noticed was doing that very thing: videoing and recording our conversation. What's more, he looked familiar, even from that distance. Antonia started to say something but I suddenly stood back up and put my back to the camera man and whispered to Antonia, "Don't say anything. I think someone is about to record us. Don't look behind me, either. Let's just move on."

Without another word, Antonia stood and I began leading us directly away from Mr. Camera. We walked maybe fifty paces when I suddenly spun on my heel and had a look back behind us. Sure enough, there he was, following close behind, holding his camera at chest level as he moved along. So I went directly to him and confronted him, catching him off-guard and forcing him to step back.

"What can I help you with?" I said. "I know you're following us and trying to record us." At that point I recognized him and cried out, "What the hell, Leders?"

Agent Leders was not a small man. He was built solidly beneath his Brooks Brothers pinstripes and had knuckles like an ape. So I didn't encroach on him again. But we were faced off, my question hanging in the air between us. "What?" I said again.

"I don't know what you're talking about," he said, snapping the lens cover on his camera. I'm taking pictures of this incredible monument to send my wife back home. She's never seen this before and I've tried to describe it to her--"

I didn't see her, but Antonia had joined us. "Hold on, Antonia" I suddenly exploded, "this is Agent Leders! The same FBI agent who came to my office and tried to intimidate me. Are you looking for us to sue you for our privacy, pal?"

He raised a hand and smiled. "I'm in D.C. on business, Mr. Gresham. Like I said, I was taking pictures of the monument--"

"Oh, like hell!" I cried and I lost it, moving forward, getting right in the FBI agent's face. "Now you listen to me. You get the hell out of my sight or I'll be in federal court before two o'clock getting a restraining order against you. And I'll be on the phone with your boss demanding you be fired. You don't want any of this, Leders. So back the hell off!"

The agent actually took another step backward. I was barely in control and the agent knew better than to further provoke me. Antonia then reached inside her coat and produced the picture ID all Assistant U.S. Attorneys are issued. She flashed it in the agent's face. He studied her likeness then looked up.

"You're a federal prosecutor?" he said to Antonia.

'I am. And this man you're following and trying to eavesdrop on is a friend of my office. He's a good man and I'll vouch for him anywhere. So what's your beef?"

"No beef. Just taking snaps for the wife, Mrs. Xiang."

The three of us knew he was lying, but what was the point of pursuing it? Still, I knew this wasn't the end of it. I was going to be pursued and hounded until these guys absconded with Gerry's money.

"C'mon, Antonia," I said to my friend the prosecutor, taking her by the elbow and walking her backwards, away from the agent. "Let's go someplace and talk."

Antonia shouted behind me, "Agent Leders, don't follow us where we're going or I'll be in court with Michael at two o'clock helping get that restraining order. And as a U.S. Attorney I promise you it won't end there, either. Now move on, sir, nothing to see here."

Without another word, Leders turned and drifted away, leaving us behind.

Antonia and I then proceeded to the Wee Tavern, where we stepped inside, removed our coats, and headed for the table at the very back.

It was time to find out what the feds knew about Gerry's death.

7

The lunch waitress took our drink order and left us alone. While she whipped up our coffees, we waited, studying the swag on the walls of the Wee Tavern. The owners evidently fancied the pub as somewhat Irish and themselves as curators of old photographs and random items Irish. Whatever, we were avoiding eye contact until it was time to talk. She served us and left us alone. We doctored our coffees and looked up.

"Okay, Michael, let's hear what's going on between you and the FBI."

I nodded and proceeded to impart to her, in somber tones, what had transpired up to that point. There was no need for me to swear her to secrecy going in; as friends, we were way down the road on that one. What we had, went far, far beyond the jobs we held or offices we represented. So I was free to talk and talk I did.

I concluded my history of the case with several choices,

obscene comments about the FBI agent we'd just encountered, and then sat back. It was her turn.

"So this money," she began. "It seems to me the first thing to
do is get a full account statement from the bank. I'm talking
about the complete account history so you can find out
when all deposits were made into the bank. Maybe the
money Gerry Tybaum had in Russia was money that was
rightfully his. In that case, you want to fend off the FBI no
matter what. The money would belong to his kids, and the
FBI would have to be driven away. You owe the kids that. On
the other hand, if the deposit is one lump sum and if it coin-
cides in time with the funds taken from the PAC, then you
might simply be a witness to a criminal matter. You're not
his attorney, and there's no attorney-client privilege owed. A
power of attorney isn't a real attorney, necessarily, and
there's no privilege between you and Gerry. So, yes, you can
be forced to testify before a grand jury or risk going to jail.
Which wouldn't be worth it, legally. But maybe morally you
would feel a need to protect his kids and so morally you
would refuse to talk. That would be a whole other thing,
and that would be between you and your priest. It wouldn't
be a legal matter then."

I nodded at her, sitting with my arms folded across my chest,
my head cocked to the side, not missing anything she was
saying.

"Great analysis, Antonia," I said to her. "I knew I could count
on you. But there's another reason I came here besides your
analysis, which I wanted. I'm wondering if you could take a
look around and try to find out where the FBI and the prosecutor are with Gerry's case. Gerry was shot in D.C. so your

office would be handling any prosecution that came out of it."

"I really can't do that, Michael. I would be in a world of hurt if it ever came to light that I was using my federal office to help you spy on a federal investigation. That has Obstruction of Justice written all over it."

"Yes, and to tell the truth I had thought of that. So if you think that's not something you can do I appreciate your position. Nor would I ever do anything to put you in jeopardy, Antonia. I hope you know that."

"I do," she said. "But why don't we try this." She leaned in and lowered her voice. "Why don't I check out the pending case lists in my office? Checking pending matters is something all prosecutors do maybe dozens of times a day. At least I know I do. That's one of the ways I get notice of new case assignments to my office. So I'd at least be able to do that and then we could talk it over. Something else I'm wondering about, too. How old are Gerry Tybaum's kids? Are these little kids we're talking about here who might need a guardian? Or are they adults now and able to speak for themselves. If they are adults, I'd suggest you talk to them and see what they might know about the money. Maybe their dad had talked to them at some point before he was murdered."

"That's my plan, to contact them while I'm here. The older girl and boy are probably fifteen or so years older than the youngest girl."

"Any of them connected to Russia in any way?"

"Not that I can find. Nor are they working for any federal agencies that are Russian, from what I can find out. This information might be incorrect, though, as I found out all this stuff on the Internet."

As we were talking, I was keeping an eye on the door. A lone woman had entered and taken a seat not far from us. But she was busy with her tablet, her reading glasses perched on her nose, and I thought nothing about it. As far as the FBI, Agent Leders seemed to have reconsidered following and recording us and had disappeared. Funny how flashing Antonia's U.S. Attorney's ID at federal agents can suddenly get their full attention. Hell, for all he knows, *I'm* working on a federal prosecution, and he's the one that might be obstructing justice. What's good for the goose, and all that.

"Let me ask you something," she said, ready to change the subject. "Have you ever thought about practicing law in Washington?"

I shook my head. "Not really. Why?"

She leaned closer. "I have the authority to hire four new attorneys for a Special Prosecutions team."

"In the U.S. Attorney's Office?"

"Yes. You'd be working as an Assistant U.S. Attorney. With your background and experience, I can bump you up and offer a great salary and case autonomy. Does this sound like something you'd like to try on?'

I thought about my Chicago law practice. I thought about Verona and my kids. The kids were doing well in school, and I wanted them to finish their school year in Evanston. My law practice consisted of four lawyers who were virtually handling all the cases we had. There was no reason I couldn't sell out to them. The prospect of something new--

of starting over as a young buck--hit me in the face. Hard. Plus, there was the aching hole in my heart left by Danny's death. I couldn't get her out of my mind, but I knew the law practice we operated together was no longer a healthy place for me to be. She had left too many fingerprints on that practice, and I needed to quit seeing them every day. Besides, opportunities like the one Antonia had laid out before me come along once in a lifetime--if you're lucky. I made my decision on the spot.

"Consider me in," I told her. "When do I start?"

"How soon can you get a place to live and pack a suitcase?"

"I need two weeks. I have law firm business to wrap up."

"What would you do?"

"Sell out. Since I lost Danny, I've lost all interest in the Chicago practice. It was ours together, you know. With her gone, there's a huge hole I fall into every time I go into the office. God, I miss Danny. A change would be very welcome about now."

"We'll show you starting the first of next month. That works?"

"It does."

"Then give me a hug. I'm your new supervisor."

"And a lucky man I am to get the chance to work for you. Thank you."

"Now. What about Gerry Tybaum's money? Can you wrap that up right away?'

"I'm going to contact the Tybaum children this afternoon

and see how that works. That might be another reason to be in D.C. at least part-time."

"Do you know who they are?"

"No."

"It's all in my file back at the office. Let me email you their names and addresses."

"Excellent, Antonia, and I'll do everything I can to finish up the favor I was doing Gerry."

"Great. I need you to close that case, so there's no appearance of conflict between their claim on his money and the work you'll be doing on the case for the government."

"What, I'll be working on the Gerry Tybaum case?"

"That's the plan, Michael. You know the most about it, so why not?"

Yes, why not? I'd love to nail whoever killed the man who trusted me with his children's inheritance.

That settled it for me. That and the thought of the Tybaum kids now without their father.

"Absolutely no reason why not. I'm in one hundred percent."

8

———

I t was just after two o'clock when we hugged goodbye at the Monument. She would text me about the kids' address.

Twenty minutes later my phone pulsed with the new text. Now I had the kids' info and address. I was hoping to see what insight I might get from them on the Russian money.

I called Jarrod Tybaum's listed number in Virginia. Jarrod was distant because he didn't know me from Adam, but after a few minutes of back-and-forth with me, he confirmed his address. I grabbed a taxi and headed off. Crystal City was just south on Highway 1 and traffic was light, so we made good time. The cab fare was exorbitant, but it beat a car rental and following a GPS. At least this way I could sit back with my broadband and laptop and check email and messages. I also took a few minutes to call Martin Tinsley, the number two lawyer in my practice who is also our managing attorney. I broke the news to him that I was selling out. He pushed back at first and told me all the reasons I couldn't leave the Chicago law firm I'd founded, but eventually he heard the determination in my voice, and my words settled over him, and he finally relented. He said he'd talk it over with the others and get back to me. We then hung up.

We pulled up at Jarrod's address, and I asked the cabbie to wait while I kept my appointment. He told me he'd have to keep his meter running and I told him that I'd had worse things happen to me in life than that. He smiled, and I climbed out.

The doorbell chime could be heard from the front porch, those same tones we all know so well. Minutes later the door opened.

There sat Jarrod Tybaum, wheelchair-bound, his face contorted into the best smile he could make. He checked my ID then waved me inside.

Then the tone turned friendly. "Thanks for coming," he said over his shoulder as he rolled into the living room with me close behind. "You're here about my dad. Anything my sister and I can find out about him will be great."

Much to my surprise, Jarrod had called his sister, and she was primed and ready in the living room. She was a tall woman, red dress, and low heels, with a gorgeous scarf around her throat and a beetle brooch above her heart. Her brown hair was cut short, and I guessed she was maybe all of twenty-five. I would have pegged Jarrod at twenty-five, too. Twins? Very possible.

"I'm Mona," she said solemnly and with a hint of reticence as people often do when meeting me for the first time, my scarred face and all.

"And I'm Michael Gresham."

"This is Annie, our baby sister," Mona said, walking up to a girl of about twelve who sat on the floor immersed in her laptop. "Annie is our special girl. Aren't you Annie?"

Annie gave no indication she had heard any of what was said. Her legs were crossed as she sat bent forward snapping her fingers across the keyboard. Then she looked up at me and our eyes connected just for a moment. A feeling was shared between us. I could sense her loss of her father and how sad she was: it was the same feeling I had over the loss of Danny, my wife. I didn't know how, but somehow those feelings between us connected and drew me to her. Without even thinking about what I was feeling I knew I'd do anything within my power to help her. I'm like that with kids anyway—a total basket case when it comes to a kid in need. Add-in the sense of loss she silently projected and I was hooked. At the same time I was feeling this strange warmth toward Annie, I was filled with a desire to locate and execute their father's murderer.

Jarrod maneuvered his wheelchair, snugging up beside his twin sister's wingback chair. I sat across from them and put my laptop down beside me in the chair. I had brought it along because I didn't know exactly what to expect, but it had a PDF of the power of attorney in Gerry's file, and I planned on showing that to the kids. Which I did, first off.

"Why I'm here, your dad came to see me just two days before he was killed. He signed a power of attorney appointing me as his power-of-attorney. Here's what it looks like." I held the laptop toward them, and Mona leaned forward, taking it from my hands. She sat back and held it up so Jarrod could get a look along with her.

"Okay," Jarrod said, "You're dad's POA. Why was it necessary for him to have a POA?"

I didn't deny I was no longer the POA since Gerry was dead. Why not? Because I wanted to see it through to the end, see whether the Russians might cough up the money.

"Well, let me answer your question with one of my own. Did your father ever talk to either of you about a bank account in the Cayman Islands?"

The two older children looked at each other. "No," they said in unison.

"Well, there is a bank account there, and Gerry wanted you to have the money in it. That's why he appointed me his POA, so I'd get the money to you."

Jarrod bit his lower lip and traded a look with his sister, who rolled her eyes.

"What?" I said. "Is something wrong?"

"Dad never gave us anything. We understand even his will leaves us out. Everything goes to Annie, which we fully support."

"Did he leave anything to your mother?"

"He would have, but mom died several years ago. No, his will leaves everything to Annie."

"You mean this house too?"

"No, not the house. We were all joint tenants on the house with the right of survivorship," Jarrod said. "That was because I have CP and dad wanted me to have someplace to live."

"Cerebral palsy?"

"Yes."

"Sorry. I maybe knew that, and it slipped my mind."

"So you didn't think the wheelchair was my idea of fun?"

His voice had raised a notch. I pulled back and said, almost meekly, "No, and I didn't intend anything. I said I'm sorry for your situation and I meant it."

He cooled down and backed off. "Okay, okay. We're all on edge here. So tell us about Moscow. How much money and when do we get it?"

"Let me take the last part first. You'll get it as soon as I give the bank directions where to wire the funds. So I'm going to ask you for a bank account you want it wired to. I'll need the name or names on the account, routing number, account number, and wire number. Can you do that?"

"Sure," Mona said. "Just wait here, Jarrod, I'll grab your checkbook and give him the numbers."

"Top right-hand drawer of the roll top," he called after her.

"Roger that," she replied.

Jarrod and I were left staring at each other. It was uncomfortable for me, mainly because just moments ago I thought he might take a swing at me. Annie continued with her construction on the floor. Now and then she would pause and scratch absently at a red welt on her leg.

But Mona soon returned, handing a checkbook to her brother.

"Okay, here are the names and numbers."

I had my laptop open and was ready. He recited the information I needed and folded his checkbook. "Get all that?"

"I did," I said. "Thank you."

"So back to my original question. How much are we getting?"

"Twelve million. Four million apiece."

Silence. Jarrod's face twitched. Mona studied her hands, neither one of them looked up at me.

"What are you thinking?" I asked.

"It's just that it must be a mistake. Dad never made over a hundred thousand a year in his life. He lived for his PAC, and he took the minimal salary. There are federal laws about that, you know. He wanted to comply. He constantly worried that he was going to do something wrong, so he paid a law firm to keep him on track. He must have paid the lawyers more every year than he paid himself in salary. That was just how he was," Mona said.

"I agree," said Jarrod. "He needed something to immerse himself in after mom died. His PAC meant everything to him, and he would never do anything to foul it up."

Which left me wondering. On the one hand, Gerry said the money just appeared in an account in the Caymans. But what if that wasn't the true story? What if he had embezzled it? But that just wasn't who Gerry was. He didn't do stuff like that. If the money came from the PAC, that would have been way out of character. I wondered whether he would have survived criminal charges of embezzlement had he lived? Would a case even have been filed against him? It would be a difficult case; embezzlement of PAC funds would fly in the face of everything Gerry held dear. It would all come down to the forensic banking evidence--about which I knew nothing. Yet.

Mona beat me around the corner. "Where did the money come from, Mr. Gresham?"

"I don't have the foggiest idea. I knew your dad in law school--we were classmates. But to be honest, we hadn't been in touch since graduation. In fact, I didn't even know where Gerry had settled down to work. We all went different ways. I live a thousand miles away from here."

"Why would he go outside DC for a POA?" asked Jarrod.

"Why wouldn't he choose someone closer?" Mona agreed.

"Again, I don't know. I do know he said he trusted me, but that's about it."

"Wait a minute," Jarrod said slowly. "Am I beginning to see something here? How much do you stand to make off this deal, Mr. Gresham? What's your part of our money?"

"Not one dime. He didn't offer to pay me, and I didn't ask."

"Forgive me for the stupid question," Jarrod suddenly blurted out. "I thought something else was going on."

"Not at all," I said. "I would be suspicious of any lawyer I didn't know, too. It's a huge amount of money, and in the hands of the wrong representatives it would be quite a temptation."

"But that's not you," Jarrod said, shaking his head. "You were dad's classmate, and he trusted you."

"That's about the sum and substance of it. Okay, so let's do this. I'm headed back to Chicago tomorrow. When I get back to my office, I'll deliver instructions to the bank to make the wire deposit into Jarrod's account. Then my part will be done. Fair enough?"

"Yep," said Jarrod.

Mona studied me. "You didn't answer. Where do you think the money came from, Michael?"

"To be honest, I've had the FBI in my office asking me the same thing. Their spin is that your dad's PAC was embezzled for the same amount before your money showed up in Moscow. Is there a connection? Of course. But is it all above board? It could very well be, I don't know. Don't be surprised if the FBI comes nosing around. I'd just tell them you have no idea of the origin of your dad's gift to you. You might also want to have an attorney present."

"Could you be the attorney we have present?"

The earlier discussion I'd had with Antonia about joining the U.S. Attorney's staff was a definite roadblock to my having anything more to do with the money once I was sworn in. I would have to decline.

"No, but it could be a trusted member of my firm."

"Sure," Jarrod said. "I like you, and I think I trust you. I'll trust your law partner too, I'm sure."

"Jarrod!" Mona snapped at him. "Keep that to yourself. It's impolite to tell someone you 'think' you trust them. Michael, Jarrod says things that maybe the rest of us would only be thinking. I think it's the CP talking. I'm sorry."

"Quite all right," I said. "I appreciate knowing where I stand with people who might become clients of my firm. I'll be leaving that firm, by the way. But my partners all work from the same perspective as I: clients come first above all else. You'd be in good hands with them."

I saw a sorrowful look creep across Jarrod's face. "I am sorry if I hurt your feelings, Mr. Gresham. Forgive me, please. I do trust you. I mean, I'm starting to."

"That's good to hear. All right, I think we're done here, at least for now. By the way, the partner in my firm who will be contacting you about taking over from me is Martin Tinsley. Martin is a straight shooter and the best attorney in a court-room I've ever had the pleasure of watching. You could do much worse."

We shook hands all around and said our goodbyes. Then I stooped down to Annie.

"Goodbye, Annie. Good luck with that computer."

She looked up at me and wrinkled her nose. Then she shook her head and bent back to her work. That was it.

Jarrod drew me into the dining room, where we sat at a long, oak table. There, he told me about Annie.

"She's seen every kind of doctor. No one really tells us what's going on with her. Annie has low-verbal abilities with islands of genius. With her, it's a superior systematizing abil-ity. She surfs the Internet all day and remembers every item she sees. All its details."

"So she's autistic?"

"No doctor has said that. They all say she's very low-verbal.

So we rarely talk. But when she does talk to us we're stunned at all the details she knows about everything she's seen."

Mona walked in. "Annie has an obsession with memorization of trivial and obscure information. If she ever talks to you, I guarantee you'll be astonished at what she knows. Usually about *you*. But she rarely talks to anyone."

I was leaving when Annie came into the room and fixed me with her gaze. Then I heard her say, "You're from Chicago."

I said, "I am from Chicago. How do you know that?"

"You're wearing Balani."

"Yes, I am."

"With red buttonholes. That's a trademark feature of his Chicago suits."

"That's pretty amazing you know that," I said to her. Next to me stood Mona, her face a study in shock. She was shaking her head in disbelief that the girl was talking.

"I know more, too."

"Like what?"

"I know your wife died."

I felt a slight buckle in my knees. Danny had died; she had been murdered. I fought down the urge to turn to Mona and say something about her remarkable sister. Instead, I said, "How do you know my wife died?"

"Your ring finger has a white circle around it. You've removed your wedding ring. You never got divorced because you haven't lost the sparkle in your eye that happily married people have."

I didn't push it in response. Instead, I turned to Mona and mouthed, "Incredible!"

Mona only nodded, yet in shock that her twelve-year-old sister was actually speaking to someone.

"What else do you know about me?" I asked.

"You graduated from Georgetown Law. I know that because you knew my father. Otherwise you wouldn't be here. And my father went to Georgetown. I'm guessing you were class-mates there. How close am I?"

"Guilty," I said. The girl didn't react.

Annie turned away and walked out of the room.

Mona took me by the shoulder and moved me along to the front door. She opened the door, and I stepped out onto the porch. It was snowing again and very cold. I quickly slipped into my topcoat and turned to go.

"Wait," said Mona. I turned back.

"I'm still stunned," I said. "Annie is amazing."

"Annie is a savant, Michael."

"How do you know that for sure?"

"One day she looked up and recited the breeds of house cats to me. Abyssinian, Balinese, Chartreuse, Devon Rex, Exotic, Havana Brown--the list was endless. We had her to do it again for Jarrod when he got up. Same list as what she told me."

"So she remembers what she reads on the Internet?"

"She remembers every detail of everything she reads on the Internet. She browses hundreds of pages of different websites every day. And memorizes everything on every page. It's her gift. She can tell you the cats' breeds. But if you asked her, she can't spell 'cat.' That isn't part of her gift. Nor could she tell you how many cat breeds. That's how she knew about your suit and your wedding ring. She's a profiler, Michael."

"Wow. That's amazing."

"Annie is amazing."

I finally turned to go. "Don't be a stranger," Mona called to me. I promised to come back and check in on them. And I meant it--especially Annie. I was taken by her like no other child ever, not even my own.

But the encounter left me unsettled once I stepped through the front door. The entire meeting had left me uneasy--which any lawyer would relate to, given that the funds were looking more and more like the product of a simple embezzlement. I wanted distance between myself and the problems the money was going to raise. My bottom line was that I was soon to become a prosecutor. I had no business nosing around in a potential embezzlement case. I needed to make other arrangements.

The taxicab burned through a hundred-dollar bill by the time I got back to the Hyatt Regency on Capitol Hill.

Maybe I'd be reimbursed, or maybe I'd just eat it along with the plane fare and hotel and meals.

Those plans remained to be made.

9

Two days later, Nivea Young was called in by Paul Wexler for further instructions. She was unsmiling upon entering Wexler's office at GULP as she thought she knew what he wanted next.

Wexler looked up from a pile of papers on his desk. His bushy white eyebrows knitted together in puzzlement though he was pleased to see his hire. "I received your report. You followed Antonia Xiang to the meeting with Michael Gresham? What do we know?"

"She met the man. Same name you gave me: Michael Gresham. Same office I entered before. Chicago defense lawyer, mid-fifties; widower, two kids too young for a man his age; SEP-IRA worth 2.2 million at Fidelity in a mutual fund consisting of emerging medical technologies; multiple law partners and a dozen or so support staff. Plus, there's the investigator, name of Marcel Rainford, once with Interpol and New Scotland Yard. He's now working out of London. No reason is known for that." She tossed a thin dossier on his desk and stepped back. "It's all in there."

"What did she see him about?"

"They met at the Monument, but the FBI was there attempting to eavesdrop and photograph their meeting."

"What did they discuss?"

"Unknown. I also spent time on his tail. He didn't make any calls after his flight touched down at Reagan. He just climbed into a taxi and went directly to their meeting at the Washington Monument. I followed. They were approached by a known FBI asset and moved their conversation to a public tavern nearby. I followed and got close enough to eavesdrop. He booked a return flight to Chicago and then went to see Tybaum's children. No opportunity there."

"They discussed what?"

"She wanted Gresham to work for the U.S. Attorney here in Washington."

"Who is this guy? Why the U.S. Attorney?"

Young shrugged. "He's a nobody. Maybe around Chicago, there's a certain cachet among the criminal bar who know the guy. He's been known to win a few cases. But not a heavy hitter. I followed him to his hotel and took the room next to his. I paid the desk clerk $100 to extend his phone line to mine. This allowed me to listen in on his conversations. From what I could gather out of just two conversations, he knows too much about the Russian account. We need him out of our way before he makes a play for the money with the power of attorney."

"Which is exactly why I called you again."

"Take him out?"

Wexler rocked back in his chair, thoughtful. "Yes. Make it happen."

"Done."

Then Wexler smiled. She smiled at him. They broke into muffled laughter.

"Amazing, the things you do," Wexler whispered to his field agent. "And where is Gresham now?"

"His hotel. He hasn't moved his family out of Chicago yet, so he's living out of a suitcase here in Washington."

"What plans do you recommend for him?"

"Frame him for the murder of Tybaum," she said.

"Use Tybaum's money as his motive?"

"Of course. He has the POA. It fits perfectly into that theory."

"You are on your game today," said Wexler, an appreciative tone in his voice.

"Where's the gun? Did you steal it back from Rudy Geneseo?" she asked.

Wexler smiled. "He was glad to turn it over to me. I'll have it in your locker by close of business."

"All right."

"When will you go into his room?"

"Tonight when he goes down for dinner."

"How can you be sure he'll go downstairs for dinner? What if he eats in his room?"

She smiled. "Would you stay in your room if Jimmy's Steak-house comped you a twenty-ounce porterhouse?"

"Not likely. So comp away, my dear friend."

"Done and done."

W hen she was finished with Wexler, Young returned to her room at the hotel. She then hacked into the Hyatt Hotel's computer system and accessed Michael Gresham's registration. She backdated the registration to include Christmas Eve day, the night of Tybaum's murder. In fact, she reconsidered and then had him registering two days previous to that. Might as well have it appear that he'd been in town for awhile to accomplish his mission. She made the same changes to the American Express card he had used to pay for his room. Now it was all nice and tidy, the lawyer was registered and the card imprint taken all on the same day, December 22. Even US Airways accommo-dated the ruse--they didn't know it, of course; she simply hacked their system too. How would they ever know the difference between a passenger who wasn't there and a computer system that said he had been? Like the hotel and credit card, they couldn't. None of them could. As for TSA check-in, that was a governmental arm. Their cooperation was cheap, simple, and expedient. All evidence would contradict the protestations that were sure to erupt from him when he was arrested.

At 6:15 p.m., she accessed her locker at the Langley Athletic Club. As agreed, Wexler's gym bag was awaiting her inside her locker. She retrieved the bag and left the club at 6:19

p.m. Ensconcing herself in the lobby of the Hyatt Hotel, in plain view of the elevator bank, she began her lookout for the guest of Jimmy's Steakhouse whom she knew would be coming along in the next hour or two.

Sure enough, at 7:22 p.m. the elevator whooshed open, and the lawyer stepped out and breezed by her, headed for the restaurant. Young could see the hostess greet him and then lead him away to a table. Young wasted no time heading immediately for the elevators. She jabbed her finger against the UP arrow several times. Doors parted and she stepped aboard.

Gaining entrance to his room was simple-

Using an electronic passkey. Before entering, she slipped on latex gloves and a hairnet. No reason to leave DNA behind when she was finished.

She set the gym bag down on the floor and unzipped it along its length. Inside reposed the pistol that had killed Tybaum. It had been stolen from Gresham's desk drawer in his Chicago office after Tybaum's visit. It had been used to execute Tybaum as he attempted to run away. It was encased in clear plastic. Young took care not to brush away any of the oils along the barrel and trigger and hand grips. Then-- holding the gun in her arms as you might hold a child--she turned away from the bed in search of a hiding place where a novice like Gresham might hide something like a hand- gun. Her first thought was, of course, the water tank on the toilet. The gun could remain inside its plastic wrapper, and the DNA material remain untouched, but still, there was the slightest possibility that water could enter in and ruin the whole game as the DNA washed away. So she continued looking.

Beneath the room's one long window, an air conditioner stared back at her. A thought occurred and she two-fingered the collapsed toolset from her pocket. She unfolded the screwdriver blade and approached the AC unit. Four screws later, the cabinet was lifted up and away. Around the bottom of the rectangular unit was a sheet metal skirt six inches in height. At its front side was the exact amount of space needed to hide the pistol. She laid it down inside the trough and replaced the cover. Four screws were driven, and then Young stood back from her work. Just out of curiosity she fired up the AC unit and stood for several minutes, listening to its fan. Nothing alarming about any of that. She then collected the gym bag and smoothed the bed covers where the bag had been placed while she labored.

It was time to leave.

10

M y Chicago law practice was a good twenty years old, and I had been fortunate enough that it had a good reputation and was salable.

Martin Tinsley--Marty--sat down in my office late the next afternoon to hammer things out. The key issues were how much would be paid for my interest in the law practice, what funds would be used to pay me, and how long I would continue receiving fees from our work-in-progress. In the end, we decided I would receive my partner's share of the WIP for twelve months beginning on the first of the next month, February, just twelve days away. The amount to be paid to me remained to be hashed out, but I tossed out a number and Marty said he'd talk to the others and get back to me on that. Next up was the need for my partners to take over my cases. In truth, the clients had hired me, but our fee contract reflected that they were hiring the law firm, an LLC, meaning any lawyer in our firm could take over any case and that would be allowed within the four corners of our client fee agreement. At a practical level, it meant that I would have to phone or meet with every one of my clients on my roster and seek their permission to substitute in a firm attorney on each client's case. If they refused, we would offer to withdraw from their case and give a full refund of the money they'd paid us. Over the ensuing three days I made those calls and met with some of those clients, and no one objected to the firm continuing with their defense. Which left me wondering whether my clients had somehow sensed that my heart was no longer in my work. Maybe yes, maybe no. But this much was true: to my great surprise, there were no objections and no refunds necessary. Wow, I thought, I am replaceable. It was a good lesson in ego management for me.

Mikey and Dania are my children, the greatest and toughest little kids God ever made. Danny was their mother and when she'd died the children were suddenly thrust into a single-parent home with a dad who had no idea how to mother. It had been extremely difficult, and I'd resorted to the use of counselors and Danny's wonderful mother to help us make the transition into our new way of living without Danny. So it was with great caution that I intro-duced Verona into my home and the lives of my children. Much more than a casual relationship was required, and the two of us waited until we were sure before we moved Verona from her long-term stay condo into my home. A good six months had gone by and slowly the children, and she were introduced and foundations laid. It took that long for me-- and probably her--to be sure of this new direction for my life and so the six months proved extremely important in the world of my family. Danny's mother was still with us as well, living in our guest room and providing the continuity kids need. She was there with them before and after school, helped with homework, and sometimes prepared supper and sometimes our nanny, Cindy, prepared the meal. Verona fit into the calculus of my little family with ease, and she'd established a flourishing relationship with Dania and Mikey before the first time she spent the night. After that, it was incremental so the kids could get accustomed to the idea of daddy having a girlfriend.

Now, however, there was going to be a fly in the ointment because I was going to be living in D.C. during the week and commuting home to Evanston on weekends. Everyone else would be in Evanston all week, at least until school let out, at which time I would move them back to Washington with me. The kids were a bit older now, and they understood why their father would be gone during the week. Don't get me wrong--they weren't happy with the idea, but they under-stood it was something about my job, which had at various times taken me away from home but they knew I always came home to them. We talked, and I promised that this time would be no different, that we would soon be together again full-time.

I reported to Antonia's office the first Monday in February, which was February 6, and found that I was slated to do ten days at the DOJ's National Advocacy Center in Columbia, SC, where I would receive training. One week later, I checked into my room in Columbia, where I spent the following two weeks in seminars on advocacy skills. These programs were designed for new federal prosecutors with little or no prosecutorial experience who would be responsible for the trial of criminal cases. The seminar utilized lectures, skills exercises, critiques, and trial strategy sessions. Some of it was very basic; some of it was vanilla brush-up on things I knew but had forgotten; some of it was advanced tactics in criminal advocacy that opened my eyes to how things were done in the employ of the Department of Justice. At the end of my two weeks, I flew home to Chicago and spent several days with my family. All was well, which freed me up to return to Washington on a Wednesday.

Antonia showed me around the USA's Office and led me into my office, a small, efficient room that included a window. We sat down in there, and Antonia gave me what must have been her canned speech she gave to all her hires.

"The United States Attorney's Office for the District of Columbia is unique among U.S. Attorney's Offices in the size and scope of its work. It serves as both the local and the federal prosecutor for the nation's capital. On the local side, these prosecutions extend from misdemeanor drug possession cases to murders. On the federal side, these prosecutions extend from child pornography to gangs to financial fraud to terrorism. In both roles, the Office is committed to being responsive and accountable to the citizens of the District of Columbia. Now I've said a mouthful."

"And I'll be working the local side, is that correct?"

"Correct. Your first case is the investigation and prosecution of those responsible for the murder of Gerry Tybaum. I'm making good on my promise to you that you would get first shot at the case. I know how you feel about Annie and the twins."

"That's what cranked my gears," I said. "It made me come here."

She nodded. "You probably know more about the case than I do. Come by my office after you go downstairs for your ID photo and badge and I'll hand over the file. You'll also be receiving twenty other criminal prosecutions, to start, ranging from misdemeanor cases to a second homicide case. In a month you'll receive another thirty cases in progress."

"What's the case load for someone like me?"

"With your experience? I'd like to see you at one hundred cases by the end of the year. A good number of them will be major cases. You're my go-to guy, Michael, because you have so much experience in federal courts already. Now, am I scaring you off? Any second thoughts about being here?"

"Not at all. I'm ready for the challenge, and I thank you again for giving an old dog a new start. I know it is very unusual for DOJ to hire anyone my age, but--"

"Not so fast. We don't discriminate, remember? We don't even ask ages or birth dates on hiring documents. You were hired because of your ability to hit the ground running and take on a full caseload."

"And the pay is one-twenty-five?"

"One-hundred-twenty-five thousand a year. Does that make you cringe?"

"What do you mean?"

"Well, you've been making a helluva lot more than one-two-five. I know that for a fact."

I shook my head. "You know what? I'm looking for fulfillment and getting some joy back in my life. It's been too long. This job fits that need exactly. The truth is, I'd do the job for no pay at all. That's how much I love this."

"No need for freebies. Uncle Sam can still pay his way, Michael."

"I see that. All right."

"Run on downstairs now and get your ID rolling. Then come by, and we'll issue your files."

"Will do. Thanks again, Antonia."

"Wait until you see the cases before you thank me."

"All right, then. But thanks anyway."

She smiled, gathered up her things, and left me there in my office.

I looked around before heading downstairs. The place was elemental at best. I was used to much finer digs. But you know what? The much finer digs were no longer making me happy. The new office felt happy. I was elated to be there.

I liked it already.

11

R onald Holt was assigned to the Metro Police, Second District, D.C. He was a large black man whose body type most closely resembled a grizzly bear. His face had an old look to it, widespread eyes, perfect teeth when he smiled--which was often and easily--and a mind that was always running a mile or two ahead of any conversation. He was one of the brightest cops I'd ever met, which was evident within the first five minutes of our meeting.

Detective Holt came to my office on my first full day at the USA's Office to discuss Gerry Tybaum's murder.

He came into my small office and chose the visitor's chair closest to the window. Wearing a black suit and a red neck-tie, mini-Afro and an intense look on his face, you instantly knew Holt was in law enforcement. He sat easily in the chair, one foot crossed over his knee, tapping his car keys against the heel of his boot in a Hurry-up-and-let's-get-this-over-with rhythm.

But I wasn't in a hurry. I wanted to know everything he knew.

First, he withdrew a sheaf of papers over an inch thick and pushed them across the desk.

"Police reports, counselor. We've got everything here including first on the scene, CSI, detectives, photographer, and M.E.'s report. This should get you quite a way down the road."

"Don't I already have this in the office file?"

"Most of it. Some you don't."

I stared blankly at the papers without touching them, then, "This is all well and good but suppose we cut to the end. Who do you think killed the guy?"

"If I were a betting man I'd say it was a jealousy killing. Word on the street is that Tybaum was getting in the pants of the VP's wife. But Antonia told me about the Russian money, too. But I'm sticking with the sex fun theory."

His assuredness threw me. I had come to office thinking Gerry died for the Russian money. Here was a new twist.

"The Vice President's wife? Of the United States?"

"None other, counselor. Get used to it. In the District, you'll find everyone is screwing someone else's wife, from the President down. It goes with the territory. It's part of the power madness that takes over when a newbie comes to town. See, the game here is 'How close can I get to the President?' Some try to excel at their jobs to get closer; some try to sleep their way closer, some try to get White House jobs in hopes of establishing a relationship with him."

"With President Sinclair?"

"Sure, I mean the guy's very approachable and the District's actually a small town. Everyone knows everyone else-- which is also part of everyone's power struggle. The more you know, the more powerful you become. It's a crazy place. You'll find yourself prosecuting people who will pay millions of dollars just to make their case go away. Even simple cases like shoplifting. The woman you're replacing took a five-hundred-thousand dollar bribe on a check-kiting case. The perp was some guy out of Iraq who hit town and immediately bought a condo in Georgetown, a Rolls-Royce and hired two maids and a gardener. He was spreading money around like the ice cream man. The only problem was, the letter of credit he gave to First American Bank he also gave to three other banks. Writing checks on one bank to cover another. Like I said, your predecessor took one of his checks, and it bounced, so guess what? She sued him."

"You've got to be kidding me. That's insane."

"Scout's honor. Word got out about the lawsuit, and she was canned less than a day after she filed her case. Dumb, dumb, dumb, but that's what this place does to people. Keep your nose clean, counselor, and you'll love it here. But don't ever let anyone get an angle on you. If they do, it'll take you down with everything you've got. Which brings me to the main reason for my speech this morning. Don't hand out special favors to anyone. They not only won't appreciate it, but they'll also come to expect it, and next time they come around with their hand out, they'll threaten you with blabbing about the first deal you gave them. I shit you not, that's who you're dealing with here. Be brave but be smart. You've now been warned."

With that, he smiled ear-to-ear and I saw he had a perfect smile that lit up his face like a Christmas tree. He was charming and tough and smart. That's what I came away from our meeting knowing about Ronald Holt.

We also talked some more about Gerry Tybaum.

"Word has it that you knew Mr. Tybaum," the detective said to me. His eyes narrowed as he said this as if he were about to appraise my veracity in light of what he'd just finished saying about integrity.

"He made me power of attorney on a Russian bank account. This was two days before he was shot to death."

"Why would he do that? Did you guys go back?"

"Yes and no. We were speaking acquaintances from law school, but we never hung together. I worked nights and keeping a social calendar was all but impossible for me. Gerry's dad was connected in Washington and had tons of money, from what we all knew."

"His dad's a lobbyist for the pharmaceutical companies. Or he was. Eventually he retired from that and went back to the home office where he's still the CFO. He's in on the ground floor of the company that makes Muraxin, the wonder drug for arthritis, and I guess he's made a fortune off his stock options."

This news turned my head. "So is it possible Gerry's dad's money was used to fund the Moscow bank account? Might Gerry have taken that position?"

He stopped tapping his keys against the boot heel. "No. Reason I say no is because the GULP PAC was embezzled in the same amount as the Russian deposit Antonia told me about. I have no doubt in my mind where the Russian money came from. That's even better than the sex theory, I'm guessing."

"Question about the PAC, Detective Holt. Did Gerald Tybaum have the right to remove campaign funds from the PAC and place them in a Russian account?"

"Unknown. We're waiting on the organization's articles of incorporation and so forth. We're then going to be looking to your civil department to give us an opinion on that. Why, do you know any differently?"

"I don't. I'm just wondering out loud."

"We are too. Incidentally, when I say 'we' I include the FBI agent assigned to work the murder with me. Her name is Carlotte Siragusa and she's presently on family leave. New baby. She won't be back for two more weeks, so it's just you and me for right now."

"Interesting. Would you be receptive to my riding along with you as you work up this case? At least until she gets back? I'd like to see how you conduct witness interviews and talk to witnesses and CI's if possible."

"Entirely possible. If Carlotte isn't in my passenger seat, there's no reason you shouldn't be. I'll keep you posted on the next interview."

"That's great news. It will help with my understanding of how things work in Washington. Who knows, I might even be able to help you track down Gerry's killer in the process. Thank you for the opportunity, Detective."

He brushed at the space between us. "Think nothing of it. We're all in the same boat on this side of the street. Who knows, I might want to tag along with you on trial one of these days."

"Entirely doable," I said eagerly, though I had no idea whether that would be any violation of official USA policy or not. Even if it were, he could accompany me to court, sit in the gallery, and be in on the convos during recesses and breaks from the trial. Tit for tat.

"Tell you what,'" he said suddenly, "Let's start out by visiting the scene together. I can help you get a mental picture of what happened that Sunday night and show you some detail about what we did. Tomorrow morning at eight work for you?"

"Just let me know when and where."

"I'll be here waiting when you get in. Bring coffee and donuts, counselor."

"Roger that. I'll see you at eight mañana."

He paused at the doorway. "One other thing. About Agent Leders? He came to see you in Chicago?"

"The FBI agent?"

"Yes. He says hello. He also says no hard feelings now that you're both on the same side."

"That's fair."

"He also says he ran down your pay-per-view at the New York hotel the night Tybaum was murdered."

"I would've expected no less."

"Whether you were there watching the movie? He says he's

giving you a pass on that. He's just going to assume you were in your room in New York when your movie played."

"I was."

"Do you recall the movie, incidentally?"

"No."

"Okay. See you in the A.M."

"Cool. Until then."

He stood and tossed off a friendly salute and clomped out of my office.

So. A new friend and some good advice.

I was going to like it here.

12
———

Annie's safety--and the safety of Jarrod and Mona--was gnawing at me after I met with Detective Holt. It had surfaced in my mind that I couldn't just leave them alone in their father's house with a murderer on the loose. They could be next if my thinking about the killer's motive were correct. So I paid a visit to Jarrod.

"I'm concerned for your safety, Jarrod," I said after he took me inside the house. "The people who killed your father might very well come after you kids next."

"People?" he asked. "There's more than one?"

"That's my thinking. Your father was killed over the money in Moscow. I have no doubt about that. The case has been assigned to me at the U.S. Attorney's Office to investigate. The only problem with that is time. Investigations take time and manpower, and I'm afraid that in the meantime they might strike again. I don't want to lose you or your sisters."

He wheeled himself back in his wheelchair. Then he reached

down and retrieved a glass of orange juice from the coffee table at his elbow. I was seated across from him in a blue velour wingback chair. The living room that day was in somewhat of a disarray, giving it a well-lived-in look. About the time he had taken a second swallow of his juice, Annie came wandering in. She was wearing tennis shoes with flashing lights around the soles, jeans that were probably two sizes too large for her, and a T-shirt that said *Lebowski 2020*.

"You're a Lebowski fan?" I asked her.

She came over to me and touched my hand.

"That's her way of saying hello," Jarrod explained. "You're a big hit with her if she does that."

I sat very still, waiting to see what she'd do next. She surprised me, then, by turning and backing up until she was touching my knee. She remained like that, staring straight ahead, barely breathing.

"I think she's missing our dad," Jarrod said. "Mona thinks she is, too. Maybe that's why she sought you out. Maybe you remind her of him."

Unable to restrain my love for this little kid, I reached forward and touched her shoulder. Much to my surprise, she didn't just pull away, though she dropped her shoulder like I'd put a twenty-pound weight there.

"Wow, now you are something, Mr. Gresham. That's not like Annie."

I sat back in my chair, instinctively knowing I'd responded enough for one day. Annie then wandered off and took Jarrod's orange juice from the coffee table. She drank, sighed happily, and set it back down. Then she wandered from the room.

"Where's she going?"

"Who knows? She might go out back. She loves the snow."

"What I'm going to suggest, Jarrod, is that we remove the three of you from this house until I can make this case go away."

"Go away?"

"Arrest the bad guy and make it safe for you again. That could take six to nine months."

"We can't afford to leave here, Mr. Gresham. The house is paid for; I get disability; Annie gets disability; Mona works but doesn't make all that much. We're pretty much stuck here."

Which brought me up short. I didn't like what I was hearing. The kids were not safe in their father's house, not if someone was making a play for their dead father's money.

"Did you tell me your father didn't leave a last will?"

"I might have mentioned that. But it's true; there's no will."

"Here's the deal. When your father died without a will, his assets went to you kids in equal shares. That includes the Russia money. Whoever killed your father is after that money and might very well come after you three to get the heirs out of the way."

"How does that help them?"

"Then there's no one left to challenge their request that a probate court turns over the money to them."

"And who is behind this?"

"My best guess is that it's your father's PAC."

"GULP? I don't know about that. He was always on great terms with his PAC, Mr. Gresham."

"And I can appreciate that, Jarrod. But we're talking about an enormous amount of money, and there are going to be lots of people after it. People are plotting against you three right now if I don't miss my guess."

"That scares the bejesus out of me. But there's still no way we can afford to move."

I considered what he was saying. There was no way I could do nothing while these children were murdered.

"Look," I said, "what if I supply the house? Or condo? Would you be willing then?"

"I'd jump at the chance. So would Mona. She talks about how frightened she is anyway. I think she'd love you for helping us. I know I would."

"Okay, then let me put my people to work on it. We can have you ready to move in forty-eight hours, so you should each pack a bag. Not a whole lot, just enough to make it a week or so at a time between washes."

"This will upset Annie no end. She has this place memorized. The last thing she wants is change. It's going to be especially hard on her."

"We'll just have to walk her through it," I said, interjecting myself into the "We" part of what I'd just said. Careful, I told myself, you can help, but you can't allow yourself to get too close. Then I realized how stupid that was to say. I already *was* that close. Especially to Annie.

"Well, if you can help I can have the girls ready to move by tomorrow. Maybe faster is better."

"I can do that. I'll have some people here tomorrow to move you, then."

"Who will come to help? We don't know anyone."

"I have some friends, so just relax about that."

I was already considering which of the police officers I would call on to move a load or two. They would be excellent at losing anyone trying to follow them. That was my plan, at least.

So we shook hands, and I headed back to the office. I was going to need Antonia to sign off on my plan. Time to make that happen.

I was also going to need to call up some funds from my retirement account. It was going to take first-and-last month's rent to pull this off.

Which was money I was more than ready to spend if it would save lives.

Antonia was in her office at eleven a.m. when I made it back to the office. She said she could make five minutes for me if I hurried before she had court at half-past the hour.

"I've got a solution to a problem I haven't discussed with you," I told her.'

"What problem is that?"

"Gerry Tybaum's kids. They're at risk."

"Of what?"

"Of being murdered by the same man or entity that murdered their father. They're heirs to a huge amount of money."

"And you think someone wants them out of the way so they can make a claim?"

"Exactly."

"What do you propose? Sending them to live with family?"

"There is no family. I'm willing to rent a house or condo and put them up myself. I just need to use a few cops to help me move them, and for that, I need your blessing."

She waved her hand at me. "Consider it done. You mean you'll be paying their rent?"

"I do. They have no money."

"All victims should be so lucky as to have you show up on their case."

"It's a one-and-done. I've never even attempted anything like this before, Antonia."

"That's probably because you were always repping the bad guys before."

"I'm sure that's right."

"Well, now you're learning how the vic's families feel. Not pleasant, is it?"

"No, not at all. But I'm also learning how happy I am that I crossed the street and now I'm prosecuting. I get to do real things that help people.

"Yes, well, welcome to government service. We're in a unique position to help."

"Plus, there's a little girl I'm very concerned about. Gerry's youngest is twelve, and she's special needs."

"Uh-oh, don't go off the deep end with some fatherly need to protect a victim's family. That's a common pitfall, Michael."

"I'm not. Yes, I am. She's very precious and very helpless. Nothing bad can be allowed to happen to her."

"Well, she's lucky to have you on her case. Okay, I have to run. Thanks for asking. You have my blessing."

"Excellent. I'm moving them tomorrow, so I need to get things geared up. Wish me luck."

A half hour later I was in Bethesda, looking at Zillow listings. I found a three bedroom within walking distance to the Metro, NIH, and YMCA. Mona needed Metro, so that worked. The house was also a one-level, which was necessary with Annie as she'd never lived with stairs and this was no time to experiment with her. The rent was $4100 per month--steep enough, but what isn't steep in this area? So I plunked down first and last and a security deposit. The deciding factor for me was the place was furnished as if the people who had vacated were on a year-long Sabbatical to Paris and wanted things left as they were for their return next winter. The layout was easy enough: living room just inside, kitchen toward the back, master to the right, hallway and two more bedrooms to the left, three bathrooms throughout. The backyard was fenced, and the fence offered complete blocking of views from all directions. I know because I stood in the center of the yard and slowly turned around, seeing who might see me. Satisfied it was safe for Annie, I then signed the lease. One year.

The next morning, Detective Holt and two more unmarked police vehicles followed me to the Tybaum house. Mona had stayed home from work for the move. All was ready, so each child rode with a different officer just in case anything developed along the way.

But nothing did. One hour later the kids were examining their new home and Annie was in the backyard trying to make a snowman out of too-little snow.

One of the unmarked cars and driver were left in the driveway until late in the evening when the vehicle was moved to the end of the block, where it lurked and watched all traffic coming and going until near midnight. It then left.

The next morning, I called Jarrod's cell phone. All was well; everyone had a good night's sleep, Mona was at the store picking up donuts, milk, and coffee.

So I could then turn back to my chores, relieved and satisfied the Tybaum kids were a thousand percent safer than they had been a day ago. Without patting myself on the back, I was proud of what I'd done and gave a silent prayer of thanks that I got to reach out and help some kids who were really in need.

I liked my job more every day.

13

Detective Holt met me in the lobby of the USA Office at eight the next morning. He had had another idea: that we should talk to Antonia and find out about her night at the scene of the murder. She might have seen or heard something we could use--which made her a witness as far as the detective was concerned. So we waited around until she stepped out of the elevator then followed her back to her office

"Can you run us through your Sunday night at the Tybaum homicide scene?" Holt asked her. She finished removing her running shoes and slipped her heels on.

"Uh-huh. Let me check my calendar first."

She checked her calendar and then looked up at us. "Okay, I'm going to tell you exactly like it happened. Here we go.

Sunday night I'm getting ready to watch Homeland. It's my favorite show because I used to have that lady's job.

"When you were CIA."

Exactly. Anyway, it turned off cold Sunday afternoon, and by Sunday night the Reflecting Pool at the Lincoln Memorial froze over. Then it froze solid, from what I could find out. Out comes a huge crowd to skate. Among them is a pair known as Bob and Carol. They're down at the far end of the pool, down where the lights are brighter, when they skate over a man frozen in the ice. They're shocked. They're in disbelief, so they stop and creep back. Sure enough, they can make out the whites of a man's eyes in the ice. Carol dials 911 on her phone. I was on-call that night, so after the dispatcher called out the FBI, she called me.

"Because you're the bottom-rung Assistant U.S. Attorney who gets on-calls on the weekends."

"Precisely. I'm low man on the totem pole. So I get the call."

"By the way, what area of criminal prosecution are you working?"

"I'm robbery-homicide. I'm working on the District's side of the street."

The U.S. Attorney's Office in Washington D.C. prosecutes both federal crimes and District crimes. I'm working the District side-- what we would call the state prosecutions if it were a state.

So I'm sitting there, praying the phone doesn't ring, but of course, it does. We're not two minutes into my damn show, Michael. So when it rang, I kicked myself for not turning off the phone during my show. Just kidding--I was on-call, so it was my turn to supervise a weekend crime scene. I hit the TV record button. I would let it play so that Rudolph would have a soundtrack if I had to go out. If he doesn't have a soundtrack, he's been known to howl, and the neighbors have been known to call the cops.

I knew it was an FBI agent before he even spoke. You can always tell the mouth breathers. Well, that's not fair. Let's just call it a strong feeling it would be FBI then. Who else would call me on a Sunday night when my favorite TV series and the favorite TV series of all of my friends was playing?

"Ms. Xiang, Special Agent Cowpers. I have a crime scene at the Capitol Mall Reflecting Pool. White male, deceased, approximately forty years."

"Is your scene contaminated?"

"No, ma'am. Nobody can get to the crime scene to contaminate it. It's the reflecting pool. He's frozen in the ice."

"Manner of death?"

"If the six bullet holes in his back didn't kill him then I'm guessing the ice did. He was a popsicle when we found him."

"He was frozen in the Reflecting Pool you say?"

"Hard as a rock. We're awaiting your instructions."

"All right. I'm on my way."

"Thank you. Sorry to bother you on a Sunday night, ma'am."

"It's all right."

I hung up and went into my bedroom. My cold weather gear consisted of my thick leather coat, hoodie, and heated gloves. I dressed and patted Rudolph's head. Then I took the elevator down to the parking garage in my building. In the garage, my helmet was locked on the seat of my Can-Am Spyder. I unlocked and pulled on the helmet. Then I climbed aboard and hit the starter one time. The engine jumped to life, and I counted to five while it warmed. Then I rolled up the exit ramp.

The ride from my condo to the Mall was less than a mile. Still, I was shaking from the cold on arrival. Motorcycles tend to do that to you.

The Reflecting Pool is that long, swimming-pool-looking thing along the Lincoln Memorial smack in the middle of Washington, D.C. At one end is the Washington Monument and along its side is the Lincoln Memorial. Along its edges, it's maybe eighteen-inches deep. In the middle, it's probably thirty inches, which made it all that much faster to freeze when the temperature plummeted that day.

The techs had chosen a chain saw to remove the body from the Reflecting Pool. When they had him free, a front-end-loader lifted him out still encased in ice. They stood him up. Which is how I found him when I arrived at the scene.

Ducking under the yellow crime scene tape into the glare of the floodlights, I circled him. Six small bullet holes penetrated his back, where the ice had been worked free by the techs. It was a tight group, too, the signature of an expert shooter.

I borrowed a flashlight from one of the Park Police then stood on my tiptoes for a closer look at the victim's face. His mouth was gaped open, his eyes wide in alarm, his body on its way to the morgue even before the brain knew it. To say the man's face reflected a violent end would be an understatement. Just know that six Hydra-Shok rounds on the left midline was about as dead as I ever see in my job as a government prosecutor.

I let myself down from my tiptoes and shined the light at where his heart should have been. What was left was ribbons.

A man wearing the black suit and white shirt of the FBI approached me. "I'm Special Agent Cowpers. What do we do?"

He knew me; I didn't recognize him. "Bring in port-a-heaters and fire 'em up. He'll thaw before morning. Just write it up as suspected myocardial infarction secondary to gunshot." I realized I sounded like a medical professional--which I'm not. But I do know some courtroom medicine and most of the violent ways you can pass from this life into a name printed on a funeral home card.

The agent left to carry out my orders. Then I spotted the police photographer. She was deep into her work, but I needed some extra shots. Approaching her from behind, I coughed so as not to startle her. She didn't respond.

"Hey," I said and touched her shoulder.

She spun around. "What!" she exclaimed.

"Antonia Xiang. U.S. Attorney's office." I flashed my ID, and her shoulders slumped.

"Oh," she said, deflating.

"Please snap pictures of the crowd. You never know," I whispered.

She nodded she would and then bent back to her work. But every so often I would notice her pointing the camera at the spectators. I knew it would be very rare for the perp to linger in the crowd just for his jollies, but it had been known to happen. Besides, some of these people would be witnesses, and we needed to establish their presence at the scene to head off the defense lawyer who might try to convince the jury the witness was never there.

More FBI arrived--two agents I knew well. I knew to stay out of their way as they canvassed the crowd. They would approach me later in the night when they were ready. And I would wait around for just that reason.

My job at the scene of any murder is to answer questions and guide the preservation of evidence. Usually, the questions are chain-of-evidence questions or search-and-seize questions. But that Sunday night, so far, there was none of that. I felt under-utilized and cold. My breath was white and my toes and fingers numb. For twenty minutes I just stood on the sidelines and observed the techs and agents at work. But cold, oh my God. Even swathed in my winter motorcycle gear, I was still shaking. It was welcome, then, when Jack Ames, a heavyset Special Agent, approached me with a worried look and motioned toward his car.

"Got one who says she saw the shooter," he said. "Problem is--can we go talk in my car? I'll turn on the heater."

"Lead on. I'm frigging freezing out here!"

I followed Jack. He was known for being smooth with witnesses and exploitative with suspects. He led me to his car. The government ride was a black Ford Interceptor. Black walls and dark windows, engine running, white exhaust floating up.

He clicked his key fob. The locks flew up, and we were inside. I tore off my gloves and jammed my numb hands over two dashboard vents. The heat poured out. The relief was immediate.

"Shit," I muttered.

"Exactly," said Jack.

"Okay, so you started to say something about a witness back there?"

"Yes, I left her with my partner, Abel. She says she saw the whole thing. But there's just one problem."

I looked at him, waiting. "Which is?"

"She has a warrant. FTA. Prostitution."

"Failure to Appear? That's peanuts. She told you she saw the actual shooting?"

"Yes, she was up at the Lincoln Memorial, down on her knees. She had accepted some guy's tallywhacker in her mouth. You'll never guess who."

"I give. Who was the customer?"

"Senator Jessup."

Stanley E. Jessup. North Carolina. A strict conservative with a draft deferment from 1965 when his daddy was a Congressman and didn't want Jessup getting shot up in Vietnam. He talked a lot on TV, but no one believed him anymore, especially about the textile industry, which he swore up and down was coming back to North Carolina.

In the dash light, I could see Agent Ames was smiling. He was going to enjoy dishing me the details surrounding the sexual encounter. But what he didn't know--what I was unable to tell anyone--was that six months ago I was a CIA officer assigned to Moscow Station. That job had used up all the parts of me that had once been embarrassed by blowjobs and whores. I had even done those things myself, all in the name of helping Uncle Sam dodge another 9/11. Now here was this FBI agent, thinking he might get to me? Wasn't gonna happen.

So I trumped him. "Was she sucking his dick?"

Dead silence.

Then, "Sheesh, who taught you to talk like that?"

"The FBI did, Jack. Guys like you."

The smile or gloat or whatever it was had disappeared. "Well, she did have his penis inside her mouth."

"Really? Do we have a picture of that moment?"

"We do. She shot video when he had his eyes closed at climax."

"You mean when he shot off in her mouth, Jack?"

This time his lips were pursed like he might make an important proclamation any moment.

"But it didn't come together for him?"

"Yes, she took the shot when he ejaculated."

"Hmm. In more ways than one."

"She showed me the photo. It's Jessup, and he looks like he's speaking to the angels."

"All right. Get her clear at the hospital and get her DNA swabbed. Jessup's DNA will be in her mouth if we get her swabbed before giving something to drink. Then get me a copy of the photo, take her statement, get them on my desk by morning."

He smiled this time and the air around him was drawn into his lungs. "Now we're talking," he said in a gush. "I wanna see Jessup on CNN trying to explain that shot tomorrow night, counselor. Tit for tat."

"I see. Well, let's make that happen after we get the senator's statement. We need to know what he saw, too. And get it on video. By the time he comes to his senses, he'll be denying he was ever here."

"He saw the back of his eyelids, that's what."

"You don't know that. He might have heard the gunshots and looked over."

"One question. Did she see the shooter?"

"She did. She's willing to work with the police artist."

"Good. Why don't you run on down there and take her statement before it goes stale? And then run down Senator Jessup and get him statementized. Can you do that now?"

He looked away, his face the dictionary picture for glum. I had asked him to leave the scene, which is almost like saying he wasn't needed there. Which he wasn't; the FBI crime scene techs would do just fine without Special Agent Jack Ames lurking. I climbed out, leaned back inside to thank him for the heat, then headed back to the crime scene. Jack nursed the Ford away from the curb.

I watched as one of the crime scene techs went outside the tape and returned with a small electronic device that she slipped into a plastic evidence bag with red tape across the top. Something curious there, so I tracked her down and asked about it.

"What is that, Ms. Birmingham?"

She held up the bag for me to view in the ambient light.

"GoPro."

"A camera?"

"Yes. Another CSI on the premises search almost fell over it."

"It was where?"

She pointed to a small abutment on the far side of the pool.

"There. On the ground in plain view. I don't know how we didn't lose it to a gawker. Rather a helpless crowd that wouldn't stoop to pick up evidence and compromise it with their prints and DNA."

"Maybe they're all honest and know better than to touch."

"Yeah, sure, counselor. Jeez."

She turned away and returned to her inside-the-tape chores. I turned away and was just about to go looking for another vehicle to hunker down in when I spotted another FBI agent I knew. This one wasn't a relationship built on mutual respect. Quite the opposite. It was none other than the top agent of the D.C. FBI office. She had come on-site while I was over warming my hands. She was there with two aides, lost in a discourse and probably praying the news team was shooting her good side. When she saw me return, she headed over.

"You just getting here?" were her first words.

"Nope. Been talking to Jack Ames."

"Where did you put him?" she asked, searching past me.

"I sent him to take statements."

"Now, isn't that my choice to make, where my agents spend their time?"

"If you had arrived when the rest of us did, I would say yes. But as it was, you weren't here and so it was my scene, my crew."

She smiled and studied my garb. "You're didn't ride your whatchamacallit here tonight, did you?"

"My Spyder and I are a team. He refuses to go without me."

"Cute, counselor."

"So let me ask you, Special Agent Marian. Why are you here at a nothing-shooting? Is the dead guy one of your Ten Most?"

"Actually, no. But he was the Climate Party candidate for president in 2016."

"Never heard of it. Who's the guy?"

"Gerald Tybaum. Remember? Wanted to dissolve all federal agencies except Defense?"

"I missed that. He probably would have had my vote if I'd known," I said.

"But it's on the street now. Press is showing up, and more are on the way. This will be all over the ten o'clock news."

"Well, you handle the press release and the TV comments."

"Are you ordering me, counselor?"

I drew myself fully upright and stared into her eyes. "Actually, I am." It was my scene. She would follow my instructions.

She pulled away and looked at each of her aides, who were standing apart while Special Agent Marian spoke with me. They didn't appear to have heard my reply. Marian's image was intact.

"I planned on talking to the press, counselor. It's part of my job."

"That's good. And tell them we haven't been able to positively ID the body yet."

"Which will give us time to notify next-of-kin."

"Exactly. No one wants to hear about her husband's murder on News At Ten."

She smiled and nodded, turning away. Without another word to me, Marian was gone, floating back to the scene with her entourage in tow. I decided it was time to check in with Jack Ames's partner, Marty Longstreet. I'd tell him where Jack had gone. Marty was a junkyard dog, and if anyone could turn up some eyeballs, it would be him.

I found Marty on the other side of the yellow tape talking to a man with a briefcase manacled to his wrist. Now what? I wondered. I approached Marty but then stood respectfully aside while the conversation progressed. From what I could hear--and it wasn't all that much--the briefcase man was a pharmaceutical rep who'd been at the White House to offload some samples with the White House Physician. After he had left the White House, he happened to stop by the Reflecting Pool. Agent Longstreet was trying to understand why a salesman would come to the Reflecting Pool after dark. But the more the conversation progressed, the more I realized the man was half of an adulterous meet-up. He wasn't willing to come right out and say that because his wife would eventually find out. So he was hemming and hawing and convincing no one that he had only wanted to see the Lincoln Memorial after dark. Oh, yeah, right.

Unsatisfied with the man's explanation of his itinerary, but running out of time, Agent Longstreet cut to the chase.

"Tell me what you saw, sir."

"I told you, I was standing right over there in the shadows. I wasn't paying any attention to the people coming or going until I saw the man come running past me. I swear, I could have reached out and touched him. Coming right behind was a man with very pale skin--it looked like his face was glowing in the dark. He was running like a track star. He was catching up to the guy. So I kept watching. Right about where that photographer is standing, the first guy suddenly stops and throws out his hands, like he wants to surrender. The other guy stops maybe ten feet away, pulls a gun out, and starts blasting the first guy in the back. The first guy falls into the pool and floats face down. The shooter walks over and fires several more times. Then he pulls up

the hood on his parka and walks off. I was stunned. I didn't do anything."

"Wait. You saw the guy go in, you dialed 911, but when the cops arrived the pool was frozen with the guy in it?"

"Not exactly. After it had happened, I left. But then I came back when I was on my way home."

"Why did you come back?"

"I realized there were video cameras everywhere. I realized they had my picture and could ID me. I didn't want anyone thinking I had something to hide, so here I am."

"Was the guy still in the water when you got back?"

"It had been hours. By then it was solid ice. I watched a young couple arrive and put their skates on. Once or twice around and they stopped. The guy whipped out his cell phone. I guess that's who called 911."

"You mean you didn't dial 911 earlier?"

"Not exactly, I didn't. I wasn't supposed to be here, officer. My wife is gonna divorce me when she finds out."

The agent ignored that.

"How long were you gone?"

"Four, maybe five, hours."

"Where were you?"

"I was meeting with a customer. When I came back, it was all ice."

"The pool."

"Yes."

"You know, Mr. Wintergreen, I'm finding some of this hard to believe. If you were meeting a girl--or even a guy--here, why don't you come right out and say that? We're going to know sooner or later."

Wintergreen staggered sideways and reached out to Longstreet for balance. It was only then that I realized he'd been drinking. Agent Longstreet's hand shot out to steady the guy. Longstreet continued with his questions, patient and plodding like the FBI at its best. I just happened to have stumbled into the interview of a key eyewitness. So I had what I came for--a case I could leave in good conscience at that point. I stepped up and whispered in Longstreet's ear: "I sent Jack to take a statement. He'll be back."

Then I located Agent Marian and told her she had the scene. I told her I was getting ready for trial tomorrow and had to skip out. She gave me a sideways glance, clearly believing none of my whopper, but nodded that she understood. I turned and walked off before anything further was said.

The ride home was a deep freeze. The temperature on a moving motorcycle is a good twenty degrees lower than the air temperature. I was a popsicle when I got home and got my ride put away in the basement.

Heading for the elevator, I suddenly stopped. I listened carefully as I had heard something that alerted me. There, I heard it again.

Rudolph was barking and crying. Something told me I was going to find a very frustrated policeman outside the door to my condo, trying to get me to come to the door so he could make the dog shut up.

But when I got up to my floor and stepped off the elevator, there was no cop, and I couldn't hear my dog.

I approached my door cautiously. It wasn't like Rudolph to just suddenly break it off and stop with the howling.

There had to be someone inside who'd done something to him. Maybe they were waiting now to do something to me.

I slipped the key in the doorknob and turned.

This was nothing to a CIA agent who had killed very large men with just her hands.

Who needed to stop and call the cops for protection?

The shithead inside my condo, that's who.

14

A ntonia Xiang to Michael Gresham (Cont'd)

When I stepped inside my condo, I was ready to bring it. All the lights were off except the entry light. I moved in and switched on the living room light. Rudolph came creeping up, his tail wagging.

Then I spied my husband, asleep on the couch. Rusty was home. He later told me that he spent the day being debriefed on yet another CIA case--something he had to do to receive his full severance package. He had sleepily driven home and here he was, sound asleep and snoring like a locomotive.

I went to the couch and sat down beside him. I tweaked his toes through his socks. The snoring continued. I leaned down and sniffed. Reeking. Drunk as a Russian on Russian New Year.

"Hey," I said softly. "Hey, Russell!"

Deafening snoring.

I tweaked toes and tickled. No sign of revival. So I went down the hall to the linen closet and returned with my mother's down comforter, the one on her bed when she passed on. I carefully unfolded it and dropped it down over Rusty. He didn't react--nor did I expect he would. My guess was that he had given notice at work--he had finally decided to leave. He had probably done just that and then proceeded to go out and get rip-roaring drunk.

And that's just it: Rusty never drinks. Maybe a beer after he's mowed my mother's yard. But usually not. So what happened today evidently had a huge impact. Which I knew it would at some point. Which was the reason I'd offered to call in sick for him and let him just send a letter of resignation. Rusty wouldn't hear of it. Wanted to say goodbye to his friends at the Agency.

I left him snoring away on the couch. In the bedroom, I was getting undressed for bed when I heard movement behind me. My startle reflex caused me to jump. I came down in a fighting stance. Rusty's eyes widened. His hands shot out. "I'm unarmed, Anty. Honest!"

Evidently, the down blanket was too hot.

"Go jump in the shower. You smell bad."

He ignored me. Instead of washing off the cocktail lounge, he undressed and crawled into bed on his side and was immediately gone again. But I wasn't. I was wired from what I'd seen and heard that night. So I pulled up a book and cracked it open. Two hours later I was sound asleep with the nightstand light still on, the book on my chest, and my neck cramping up from the two pillows under my head.

I looked over. No Rusty. I jumped out of bed.

I rushed and turned on the hallway light.

"I'm in the kitchen, Anty," he called out without too much of a slur. So I went on in and sat down across the table from him.

"You resigned?" I asked.

"Sure as hell did. Signed their NDA, signed a dozen other forms. Turned in my ID and guns. The whole nine yards. Arno said they'd pay me for accumulated vacay time next check."

"Well, I'm glad you did it."

"I told you I was going to, Anty. Didn't I tell you that?"

"You did tell me that. Hey, do you want some eggs to go with your cereal?"

"Hell, yes. I'm starved."

"The two times I've seen you drunk you were starved then too. Most people puke their guts out after a bender. Not you, you eat."

"Put any bad guys away today?"

"No, it's Sunday. Only the CIA works on Sundays."

"It's like any other day to the spooks."

"Didn't I just say that? How do you want them, scrambled or scrambled?"

"Neither. I'll have mine scrambled."

"Hey, there's a good choice. Why didn't I think of that?"

"Know what I'm gonna do now, Anty?"

"No, what are you going to do now?"

"I'm going to open a bait and tackle shop."

"In Georgetown? That sounds promising. You can service the people who dare to fish the Potomac."

"Hey, don't laugh. The tidal waters have Striped Bass, Largemouth, Smallmouth, Shad, Catfish and even Snakehead. But I'm sure you already knew that."

"Actually, no, I didn't know that. Bait and tackle sounds perfect. I can see we'll be set for life, Rusty."

"Thought you'd like the idea. But I need seed money. Do we have any savings?"

"We've got a few thousand in checking and maybe five in savings."

"Really? Where does our money go?"

"Ask me that tomorrow if you're still interested."

"Tell me about tonight. I'm guessing you got called out."

"Some guy got shot and fell into the Reflecting Pool."

"Shit, tonight? Was he frozen?"

"Harder than a mackerel--speaking of fish. Yes, he was frozen stiff. They had to cut him out with chainsaws."

"Shit, who did it?"

"Shot him? Some guy with a GoPro camera. Six rounds. Nice tight group. Reminded me of your groups."

"Well, I've got an alibi tonight. I was in several Georgetown watering holes. Someone even tried to pick me up."

"Really? Was she successful?"

"Yes, but I chickened out. Well, she asked me if I was single and I

told her about my beautiful wife waiting at home. It was a deal breaker."

"Rusty, here. Eat this."

I scraped the scrambled eggs onto a small plate and slid it across the table. He dug in with his cereal spoon.

"Know what else happened today?"

"No, what else happened today?"

"I called a guy from the Post. *I'm going to spill the beans about what happened in Moscow."*

He meant how the CIA had disavowed all knowledge of him when he got himself arrested for shooting a KGB agent. The CIA disowned him after he got caught. Rusty would still be in jail if it weren't for his father's law school roommate, you, Michael Gresham. You saved Rusty's life. Some other people too. Evidently Rusty wanted to make a deal out of it in the papers. I knew I'd talk him out of it tomorrow. No sense in both of us getting fired.

That's right. Rusty had been fired from the CIA, and I knew that. Drunk, he turned it into resigning, but I knew better. His cover was blown, he was useless to them anymore, and that left him with a huge hole in his resume when the next potential employer asked where his fifteen years went. As of tonight, he was virtually unemployable.

But the CIA knew that. That's why Rusty had a check in his shirt pocket made out to him from some business in Weehawken in Jersey. It was a CIA front, of course, but the check was real.

One million dollars, payable to Russell Xiang.

I removed the check from his pocket and slid it partway under the toaster.

He looked at me and sadly shook his head.

"I got paid. I got fired."

"I know. Let's get you to bed. I want to spoon you."

"I love you, Anty."

"Eat your eggs."

15

W hen Antonia had finished up, we thanked her and moved back to my office. "Michael," Holt said to me, "you probably need to go over my story, too." I agreed and once we were back in my office Holt poured himself a cup of coffee and sat down across from me.

Then I said, "Can you just give me the twenty-thousand-foot view of the night you got involved with the case?"

Sure. Mamie was in the kitchen frying up a pan of hush puppies when the call came. I was on the floor in front of the TV, trying to watch the Bulls-Wizards game while my kids beat up on me. They're little and spend every second I'm home trying to get up onto my back for a ride down crocodile river. Anyway, I pulled my phone out of my pocket and said hello.

"Ronnie, Andrea here. We've got an ice man at the Mall."

"Oh no. I just got home."

"Oh yes. But out of honor to your schedule, I'll just go tell the

DCPD to fish the guy out and put up barricades, that we have to finish dinner before we can get involved. I'll do that, dickhead."

"I'm on my way."

"Wait out front. Be by in ten."

Andrea Washington was my partner. Six years we'd been together in robbery-homicide. She was an excellent partner too. I pushed the little guys off my back and headed for my coats in the hallway. "Got to run out," I called to Mamie. "Most I'll be gone is three hours!"

No response.

"Did you hear me?"

"Yes, yes, yes. Quit with the yelling, Ronnie. I heard you're going out. Another crime scene, I'm guessing. Or you've got a CI on the hook, and you need his statement preserved."

"Something like that. Dead body in the Reflecting Pool."

"That's a cold dip in the pool."

"Worse than that. The guy's frozen in the ice."

"Pool froze over?"

We had come together in the hallway, halfway between the kitchen and the front door. We hugged, and I kissed the top of her head. "All right. Don't wait up. Stories for the kids tonight, yes?"

"I'll do my best," the mother of my kids promised. I was the story-teller, not her."

Then I was outside on the street in front of our house, waiting for Andrea to swing by and get me. Five minutes and lots of arm flapping later, here she came. The Chevy crawled up, and she leaned across and pushed open the passenger door.

"Hey, Andy. Que pasa?" I said as I climbed inside.

"Not much, if you don't count Mr. Ice Cube."

"You've been to the scene?"

"Only briefly because I was in the area. Then I called you and left there and came here."

We pulled away from the curb. The heater was going full blast, and I removed my gloves. Rubbing my palms together seemed to help against the cold.

"Any ID on the guy?"

"Yep. His name's Gerald Tybaum."

"I've heard that name. Bring me up to speed, Andy."

She swung a U-turn at the end of my block and came back past my house at thirty-five and accelerating. We were in a hurry now.

"Tybaum was one of the candidates for president this last time."

"Really? I'm sure there's a big story behind this crime."

"I'm sure. I've already talked to someone who said Tybaum was connected to funds missing from his PAC. How true that is, I don't know."

"What's his PAC--I'm sure I don't know."

"Tybaum's was named GULP. It was set up to collect campaign contributions and build a war chest for his election."

"Seriously? You can't make this stuff up," I said. My last year or

two the cases I was assigned all seem to have a little crazy in them in some form or another. "Why are we called out? Don't the Fibbies have this one?"

"FBI hasn't declined or accepted yet. So we're as official as they are. Course, their CSI, is working it up, not the District's."

"They've got the better crime lab like night and day."

"We've got a bunch of clowns with baggies and Polaroids in the District."

"True that."

We rode on in silence the rest of the way. The case seemed to have the potential for something more interesting than a love triangle or drug soldiers turfing it out. The thought of a large sum of money missing from a political committee was very welcome in my repertoire of unusual cases, of which there was, that night, maybe one, maybe not one, depending on whether the FBI accepted the case or declined the case and left it for us city cops.

We arrived at the scene and studied the FBI CSI's evidence flags spread through the area where spent shells and other detritus of the crime had been found. We examined the footprints in the snow (photographed), GoPro camera (tagged and bagged), most of a cigarette with a very slightly burned business end, and minutiae that would amount to nothing related. Then we talked with FBI Special Agents Jack Ames and Marty Longstreet. Ames then disappeared to take a statement. We next spoke with Assistant U.S. Attorney Antonia Xiang and got the wide-angle view of the case. She was dressed in a motorcycle insulated coverall, gloves, and hoodie beneath. While I spoke with her, Andrea fiddled with the evidence cart, and I noticed her removing the GoPro camera from its bag which wasn't yet sealed, though I couldn't say why not, maybe so someone other than the CSI could study the images on the camera. Then she called me, "Ronnie, come see this."

"I joined her at the evidence cart. She held up the camera. "Watch this." She played the video on the camera for me. It was roughly the running match between the killer and Tybaum as they made their way up the Mall and ended at the Reflecting Pool. There is some heavy breathing and some shouting, then six distinct explosions as the gun ends the chase. We then see Gerry pitch face-first into the pool, watch the view sweep around in a 180, and then see the concrete apron rushing up to meet the camera as it evidently falls to the ground and is abandoned, probably because it's dark and hard to locate, coupled with the excitement of the moment and the need to flee. Then Andrea plays it again. This time, I notice an anomaly. There are several seconds of a view of a large yellow tabby cat lying in the sun on a kitchen table. You know it's a kitchen table because there are silver salt and pepper shakers and a napkin holder.

"Okay," I said to Andrea. "I see the cat, but so what?"

"The cat belongs to the shooter. The kitchen table is in the shooter's kitchen."

I reached and took the GoPro in my own hands. I assessed its weight at maybe eight ounces. I looked at its back side. Metadata but nothing else, no initials, no serial, nothing there.

"Okay. I've looked it over," I said. "Nothing says cat and shooter to me; nothing says kitchen table."

Andrea grinned, which she rarely does, as Andrea, on the job, is all business and not much given to smiles and niceties.

"I know, I get it. But here's the logic of what happened. The shooter was trying out his new GoPro at his kitchen table. He has

a cat that fights him for custody of the table top. The shooter pressed the right button, and a brief video was shot featuring Felix the Cat."

"How sure are you about this?"

"Maybe fifty-five percent."

"I thought so. But let's start with the notion the cat and table do belong to the shooter. Where does that leave us?

"She thought for a minute. Then, "We need to canvass the local stores that sell this GoPro. We need to take it in and see whether they can trace its serial number to a name. That name will be our shooter. Then we go by the shooter's residence and try to confirm the table-cat binary clue. With me so far?"

"Wow, you're good, Andy."

"You're just saying that, but it's nice, Ronnie. So, where do we start? Which photography outlet?"

"Back to my house. We'll grab my laptop and run some searches. Then we can be ready first thing in the morning."

Andy drove us back to my house. Mamie was still up, but the kids were in bed, and that was very welcome. Andy and I adjourned to my home office inside the laundry room, just enough room to fit a desk and two folding chairs. I then fired up my laptop. Several searches were run. I learned some about GoPro: that it is hugely popular and enjoys being sold from hundreds of outlets in the greater Washington locale. We selected three major stores from Google and decided we'd go to Best Buy first thing tomorrow morning.

We then joined Mamie in the family room. She muted the TV and turned around to face us. "Don't be shy, Andy. There are leftovers in the refrigerator and ice cream in the freezer."

"Is there any coffee?"

"No, but I can have a pot ready in two minutes," I said.

So I hopped on it.

We talked for a good hour, then, mostly about family and kids, but also about yellow tabby cats and sunny kitchen table tops.

Mamie and I had the same exact setup in our kitchen. Except we had no cat, so that cleared me of the crime.

That, and the fact I hadn't buried six Hydra-Shoks in anyone's back.

Not in years.

16

Antonia said solemnly, "Michael, can I ask you for a huge favor?"

"Sure," I said. "You need to borrow fifty-thousand? No *problemo.*"

"I'd appreciate it if you'd call Rusty and talk to him about coming on board as your in-house investigator. He needs a job, and a call from me might work wonders with him.

"That works for me. I need my own in-house because Tybaum isn't the only case I have. As you know."

She blinked hard. "I'm sorry for the fast case-load. We needed an experienced prosecutor, and in you, we have lots of confidence. Not only did you get a lot of cases you also got a lot of hard cases. You do need someone like Rusty, so I don't even feel guilty."

"Agreed," I said. "All warm bodies welcome."

So, that night I called Rusty, and we agreed to meet. He

would come to the Hyatt, and we'd have a sandwich, just the two of us.

The thing is, Rusty Xiang is my son by impregnation of his mother during one wild night while her boyfriend was in the hospital. Henry was my college roommate, and Mai Yung had been his girlfriend. One night when Henry was hospitalized, Mai and I slept together. I've dumped this fact in the confessional at Our Lady of the Constant Sorrows many, many times. Next slide, please. Here's one of our baby boy, Russell Xiang. The boy who was lied to about his father until six months ago in Moscow when it came out during his jury trial that I was his dad. We hadn't talked since, because I'd promised his mother I would leave things alone. But now that it looked like my son was having troubles, I just couldn't stand by without trying to help him. Especially not since Antonia had asked me to help.

The Article One Lounge was the hotel's bar and grille, a place where you could grab a beer and a sandwich and not have a big deal on your hands. I thought it would work best because, unlike a real restaurant, it didn't require an hour-long commitment while several courses came by. The Article One was sandwiches and appetizers, which gave either of us the opportunity just to get up and leave if it got uncomfortable. Rusty must've known why I was choosing it; he didn't hesitate in agreeing to come.

He came in at seven-fifteen wearing blue jeans, desert boots, and a GU sweat-shirt.

"You attended GU?" I said when he climbed on the stool next to me.

"Yeah. Ph.D. Computer Science."

"I don't know why but I thought you told me in Russia that it was software engineering. Someone told me that."

He ordered a glass of draught beer.

"Well, someone was wrong. Software engineering was what I did at the Company."

"Are you allowed to tell me that?" I asked. "Isn't that a national security thing?"

"Not with my own father, it's not. Screw them."

"Still hot about the CIA disavowing you in Russia?"

"Wouldn't you be?"

He took a swallow of beer.

"Yes," I said, "I would be. Mad as hell at them. But that's politics. The government was trying to embarrass the Russians into nuclear disarmament talks. It couldn't afford to be embarrassed by your spying."

"So be it," he said with the wave of a hand. "I told them *adios*, so I'm way down the road on that one."

"Good for you."

"So what's up? Is this how we start the father-son bromance?"

That jolted me. I hadn't expected that kind of sarcasm. Or maybe I had. Whatever; it jolted me back on my heels.

"Look," I said, trying to recover, "this can go however you want, Rusty. As for me, I'm open to being your friend. I also want to talk about a job opening for you. That is if you're interested."

"Friends is okay. Let's leave it at that."

Another swallow of beer.

"What about the job thing?" he added.

"I'm in the U.S. Attorney's Office here in D.C. now."

"Yeah, I think Antonia mentioned that."

"I'm going to need an investigator, and so I thought about you."

"How much does it pay?"

"I'd say a hundred to start."

"That's more than I was making at the CIA."

"I've got a feeling you'll be worth every penny."

"Well, Anty's been on me to get a job."

"Antonia's right. It doesn't help anyone to avoid life."

"Who said anything about avoiding life? I've been applying to law school. But to tell the truth, that's not a good fit for me. I think I like the undercover stuff much better."

"It seems to fit you, Rusty," I said, alluding to his time at the CIA.

"It did," he sniffed. "But that was then, and this is now. When do I start?"

"Monday? That too soon?"

"Nope. I'll get a license and be ready to go."

"No need for a license. You'll be a sworn officer."

"Whatever; I'm available, Michael."

"Michael it is. Works for me."

"Sure, me too."

We had our sandwiches, beat up the Wizards and complained about the Redskins, and said good night right after. We were both relieved to call it a night. It had gone quite well, however. I now had a grown son in my life.

Something I had wanted ever since he was born. But something I had left alone.

Full circle, coming up.

17

A nnie wasn't alone in her vision, her uncanny ability to profile people. She had profiled me and shocked me by what she saw. But, I was also thinking about her and what I knew about her. My reason for doing this was simple and somewhat selfish: I wanted to break through and talk to her, back and forth, dialogue, share our thoughts and feelings. Why? For one thing, I already loved her sweet spirit. But there was an even deeper reason: I wanted to see what was inside of her. I wanted to know how she worked; I wanted to speak to the source of her genius. She was, when it was all said and done, my enigma machine. I'd never before felt so drawn to another person. But drawn in a good way—I only wanted good things for the child, and, to determine those things, I needed Annie to talk to me.

Like I said, I was also thinking about her while she had profiled me.

How to make contact with the low-verbal Annie? Logic wasn't enough. Visceral feelings and smells and sounds wouldn't do it—no need to bake her birthday cake; it would pass by unnoticed. Same with music: she didn't seem even to hear it, explained her brother when he and Mona and mental health practitioners had tried music therapy. Didn't even move one facial muscle. So that left me with what?

For one thing, I was anything but knowledgeable about what I wanted to do—to make contact and carry on a conversation with Annie. I had no special degrees, and I'd never been confronted with the situation before. However, there's a certain willingness in being a rank amateur like I was: nothing had been tried, so there were no defeats.

I thought about her and thought about her some more. Then I remembered something Mona had told me. Something about the memorization and recital of all cat breeds. Cats? Was that random or were cats something she thought about? Maybe even something she wanted to touch, to feel, to hear.

So the word jumped out at me over and over: cats.

Annie had a special connection to cats, I reasoned. They were the one thing that Mona seemed to guess maybe brought her great joy, maybe even completed her, if that was even possible, I didn't know.

I couldn't call her up on the phone and invite her to an event that might change her. I couldn't call her because I knew she wouldn't talk to me on the phone; I had to go to her house in person to have any chance of getting through to her.

I called Jarrod and made a date to see her. I showed up exactly on time, and Jarrod ushered me inside.

She was home, he said. First, I drew him aside and explained what I had in mind.

"I would love to call Annie my friend. Which means I want her to talk to me."

"Why is that?"

"Because she is a unique, beautiful person and I would like to show her my world."

"Wow. That resonates."

"Good. I'm glad it does."

"So what can I do to help?" Jarrod asked.

"Let me take her to a public place I have in mind. You can come too, Jarrod, to keep your eye on her."

"That makes sense. Yes, I'll come, too."

"Let's meet in my car. I'll go outside and start warming it up."

Five minutes later, they emerged from the house, Jarrod and Annie, the girl rushing ahead, dancing out to my car and its interior warmth. I helped Jarrod and put his wheelchair in the trunk of my car.

Our destination was the Greater Washington Animal Rescue and Adoption Center. We arrived thirty minutes after we left Annie's house, traffic being quite heavy even though noon hour was just past. We arrived without a word having been spoken the entire way. I parked, turned off the engine, and turned in the seat to face Annie, who was riding shotgun.

"Annie, we're going inside to see some animals. Would you like that?"

At some point on the drive over, she had lapsed into a behavior I'd seen before, the rocking up and back, up and back, arms wrapped around herself, making low moans in her throat. When I spoke to her, she said nothing back, and she made no other response. So, my attempt reinvigorated with the impossibility of the task, I went around and helped her out of the car. Then I pulled Jarrod's wheelchair from the trunk, and the three of us went inside.

Up to the young woman behind a chest-high counter. She was reviewing pink papers spread before her but looked up and gave us a warm smile as we approached.

"Hi, I'm Nellie. Dropping off or picking up today?"

"We're here to see the cats," I said. Do you happen to have any today?

She gave me a look like I had a hole in my head. "We always have cats, sir. Let me page someone. Cynthia, to the front desk. Cynthia!"

Minutes later, a high school age girl not much older than Annie came in through the back door. She was wearing jeans and a T-shirt, over which she was dressed in a rubber-ized apron that covered her front from waist to chin. It said, "Got Cats?" across the front in teal letters. Our person, I could see.

"They want to view the cats, Cyn," said the young woman behind the counter. "Are you free?"

"I am," said Cynthia. "What are your names?"

"I'm Michael, and this is Annie. Annie is very quiet today and probably won't have much to say."

"I'm Jarrod. I'm a bystander."

"Okay, good, well, follow me."

We did. We followed her back through the rear door, then another, then along a fifty-foot bank of cages on either side that was populated with dogs of all descriptions, colors, and breeds. The racket—barking, howling, and crying—was deafening. We hurried inside, but Jarrod paused at the entrance. Jarrod opted out of following us into the dog area when he saw the wood plank walkway facing him. "I'll be in the main office," he said, then disappeared.

Cynthia, Annie, and I hurried through the dogs and exited at the far end. Cynthia shut the door behind us."

Then she turned to me. "What kind of cat are you looking for?"

I motioned toward Annie. "Why don't we walk through and view them," I said. "We can see whether Annie reacts."

"Sure, I'll go slow."

She began a slow saunter between the cages teeming with cats on both sides of the narrow walkway. Cynthia was in the lead, then Annie and then me. We hadn't gone three steps before Annie suddenly dropped into a squat and thrust her fingers inside a cage. We could see she was trying to touch a big yellow tabby cat. She looked up at Cynthia then at me. "What's his name?"

I was stunned. Annie had spoken!

"Whatever you want to call him is fine," Cynthia said. "What names do you like?"

"Frankly."

Cynthia looked at me. I looked at Annie. "Do you want to take this cat home with you?"

"What for?"

"To take care of. To play with. To love."

She ignored me, instead moving over while Cynthia bent to the task of collecting the cat out of its cage. She helped it out and then placed it in Annie's arms. Annie's face lit up. I'd never seen any expression there before. And I mean none.

But there you had it: she was smiling and petting her cat with two fingers. Then the whole hand was involved.

"Frankly," she said to the cat. "Come with me right now."

"Shall we take Frankly home?"

Annie, petting the cat's back, nodded. "I want to take him home."

"Do you like him?" I asked, trying to elicit some feeling from her.

"He's a good cat," she answered.

Then she turned to me. "Do I get to keep him, Michael?"

There; it was done: she had called me by my name. I was in.

"Yes, Jarrod told me you could have a cat. I agree, so here we are. Let's take Frankly up front and see about getting him checked out and paid for."

With shots, neutering, and city fees Frankly cost $225. I paid with my visa and we—there were four of us now, counting Frankly—hurried back out to my car. Again, the wheelchair went into the trunk after I helped Jarrod into the back seat.

Annie and I piled inside. By now, I noticed Annie had snuggled Frankly inside her coat and zipped up. Already she was protecting him—she knew what to do without being told. I made a mental note of that.

Then we drove home.

Once we were back in the living room and Annie was watching Frankly swatting at the curtain that faced out back, I asked Annie whether she loved Frankly.

"I love Frankly. And I love Michael Gresham. My friend."

That was all it took. From then on, we were on speaking terms, Annie and I.

We have remained conversant to this day.

And Frankly is still with us.

So are two more rescues that have come to live with Annie and Frankly.

18

A day after we spoke, Detective Holt did call me. In fact, he said he was on his way to talk to Senator Jessup, did I care to ride-along? Yes, I said. So off we went in his unmarked SUV.

Holt wheeled his vehicle into visitors' parking beneath Senator Jessup's building. It was on H Street, not far from the Hart Congressional Office Building on 2nd Street. As I walked from parking to the elevator, I noticed the detective purposely move his arm against his shoulder holster. Evidently, the weight was right, which meant the gun was in place. Checking it was an old, old habit for most detectives I'd been around. They all said the same thing about it, that they couldn't imagine the day when they would retire and no longer be married to a gun carried concealed. Holt fit the mold perfectly.

Upstairs in the elevator we went. The FBI desk had given Holt the senator's address on the eighth floor. We got off at eight and turned right. Down the hall to the end, then right again. At #836 we stopped, and Holt rang the bell.

I could hear someone on the other side of the door. The peephole changed color.

"Who's there?" called a man's voice.

"District police officer, Senator. Crack the door, and I'll badge you."

The door opened on its security chain. Holt flipped open his ID wallet and badge and extended them through the opening.

"All right, officer, stand back."

Holt pulled his arm out and stood back while the door closed and then fully opened.

The senator was dressed in a silk robe, black slippers, and was puffing a white pipe. The smell of apple tobacco filled the air. Clouds of smoke hung throughout the living room. Holt shot me a look and rolled his eyes. His look that said he'd never been in the residence of such a high government official before and he was not just a little cowed by the whole experience. I reminded myself to buckle up, that the guy was only a U.S. Senator who could get both of us fired with one phone call.

"Ron Holt, District Police," Holt said as we waited to be asked to sit down.

"And I'm Michael Gresham," I said and leaned and extended my hand, which Jessup shook. He then indicated we should sit down. "I'm the Assistant U.S. Attorney on the Tybaum case."

"This must be urgent if it couldn't wait till office hours tomorrow," grumbled the senator. He crossed his arms and tossed his head back and gave Holt an up-and-down look. "All right, sit down, gentlemen. You're making me nervous looming over me. You say you're a police officer?" he said to Holt. Then, to me, "And you, I don't get why you're even here. You're not an investigator."

"Do I pass muster, Senator?" Holt asked with a big smile.

"You know, actually, you don't," said Jessup with a sour face. "My first impression? You're a pretender."

"A pretender?"

"Listen to me, son, it's written all over your face. You're after someone's job. A higher-up. You're a pretender to someone's throne. Find that fits you pretty well, doesn't it?"

I studied Holt's face. I could tell he was thinking of someone in the detective bureau. Maybe his boss?

"I don't think that's a good fit at all, no. I don't want anybody's job," Holt proclaimed. "I don't even want the job I have now, Senator, but I have to eat."

The senator laughed. "Nice repartee. But we both know you're lying through your teeth, son. But all right, we'll just leave it at that. For now."

"Senator Jessup, we're investigating a shooting at the Reflecting Pool. We have word that you were there and may have witnessed it. The FBI talked to you already, but we have several follow-up questions."

"I thought I made it clear to the FBI that I didn't actually witness anything. Except I did hear gunshots. But I saw nothing. I can't help you, gentlemen."

"We have a witness--a young woman--who said you turned

your head after the first shot and saw the rest of the shots being fired. Would she be wrong?"

"She would be. Who is it you're talking about?"

"You weren't engaged with a young woman, to put it nicely?"

"Well, yes, I was there. I was showing a visiting constituent the Capitol grounds. But I'm totally unaware of any shooting."

"Senator, before we let you get too far down the road with some lying-to-the-police thing, I'd like to show you a video. It was taken that night by a young woman."

Holt held up his cellphone and clicked a play button. The young hooker's video played. Jessup in his living room watched Jessup at the Lincoln Memorial stuffing his penis in and out of the mouth of a topless young woman while Jessup's head bobbed about somewhere above, his eyes rolled back in his head. It confirmed every John's fear: video had been rolling. The shot was a selfie. Or, more accurately, a two-sie. Jessup viewed the video, viewed it a second time, and blinked hard. "I-I-I--," he froze up, speechless.

Then the senator regrouped. His eyes opened wide, his shoulders flexed, and his hands reached for Holt's cellphone. Holt pulled it away and gave the senator his best smile.

"No, no, no, Stanley E. Jessup. Government property. Besides, I can just shoot you a copy. Now about that promotion at work you were saying I wanted.... Just kidding! No, this video won't be used to extort you, Senator, but it will guarantee your accurate re-telling of what you saw that night from the Memorial's stairs while the girl was performing her duty. Now, first up, did you witness the actual shooting?"

"Never looked in the direction of the Reflecting Pool."

"I don't believe you, Senator. You were both able to see the pool off to your left, her right. You didn't look over after the first gunshot?"

"No, I didn't."

"Is your hearing compromised, Senator Jessup?"

"No, why?"

"Because the killer emptied his gun in the victim's back. And you're saying you didn't look over after the first shot and witness the next five?"

"I didn't. How else can I say it?"

"Well, why didn't you look over?"

"Detective, have you ever had your penis in the mouth of a beautiful topless woman?"

"You know, I think I'll be the one asking the questions, Senator. Let's focus on you."

"Well, I'm about done. I may need to call my lawyer if there's anymore."

"We can do that. I can take you into custody as a person of interest and drive you downtown right now if you'd like. Then you can call your lawyer from the comfort of your own cell. After the photographers finish up with you, that is. We always grant some accessibility to photographers when we have a big name like yours. Would Mrs. Senator be opposed to seeing your picture in the paper along with an article describing what you were doing?"

"I might have looked over, but I'm not sure. That's why I can't come right out and say I did."

"What might you have seen?"

"I might have gotten a pretty good look at the guy with the gun."

"Can you describe him?"

"Not him, I can't. But I can describe the clothes he was wearing."

"Sure, go ahead."

"He was wearing dark pants and a heavy ski jacket. It was freezing out."

"Did you by any chance know the guy you saw?"

"That's a little more difficult. I couldn't swear to that."

"Couldn't or won't?"

"It wasn't an unfamiliar face."

"So tell me about this not unfamiliar face. Is there a name that goes with it?"

The senator let loose with a long sigh and collapsed back against the couch.

"Yes."

"Give me the name, please, Senator."

"All right, but you didn't hear it from me."

"I can't agree to that."

The senator shrugged and a cagey look passed over his face. "Then I don't quite recall any name."

"No, let's not play around here, Senator. We're being serious now."

Jessup deflated. He opened his mouth and roared, "Damn!" Holt and I were both surprised at the intensity of his voice and his utterance.

"So who was it?"

Jessup shook his head. "You're not gonna believe it."

"Try me."

"It was Vice President Jonathan S. Vengrow."

"The vice president of the United States?"

"Yes."

"And you would swear to this under oath?"

"Yes, but only if there's no other way."

"Is there another way?"

"Can't I just tell it to your grand jury and not have to go to court?"

"That's a possibility."

"If it comes out that I was there with a prostitute it would ruin me."

"It would ruin just about any guy with a wife. Or a guy with constituents back home who believe their senator is all about good deals and marshmallow roasts."

"Well, especially this one."

Holt looked up from his notes. "Why especially this one?"

"Because the guy the vice president shot was someone I knew."

"Who might that have been?"

"Gerald Tybaum."

"Why would that matter?"

The senator let loose a long sigh. "Because there's a connection."

"Between who and who?"

"The dead guy and Vice President Vengrow."

"Tell me about the connection, please."

"The dead guy was screwing the vice president's wife. That's common knowledge on the Hill. Is that connection enough for the MPD?"

I remained frozen in my chair, my eyes fastened on Senator Jessup. Holt was nodding and--I had to hand it to him, given what we'd just been told--keeping his cool about it.

"Will you leave now?"

"Yes, we will leave now. You've been very helpful."

"You're going to keep my name out of it?"

"Yes, I am. At least for now."

Senator Jessup's face lit up, then fell. "That's as good as it gets, I know. I know. Here's the vice president of the United States murdering the Climate Party's presidential candidate for banging his wife and there I am, my dick in some girl's mouth, witnessing the whole thing. Your elected representatives at work to make your life better. Holy hell."

"One thing, Senator. Someone has to ask, and it might as well be me because it might have to do with what you saw."

"Go ahead. It can't get any worse."

"Here we go. Did you climax?"

"I did."

"Yet you were watching the murder as you did?"

"No, I tore my eyes away."

"Where were you looking?"

"My eyes were shut."

"You had just witnessed a murder, yet you turned away and shut your eyes?"

"Tell the truth, Detective. Wouldn't you if you were climaxing?"

Holt shuffled his feet and stood up from his chair. I followed suit.

"Well," said the senator, a small smirk playing across his face. "Wouldn't you shut your eyes?"

"I'm asking the questions. Thank you, Senator."

Senator Jessup nodded slowly. "Then I'm taking that as a 'yes.'"

I said, "You'll be receiving a grand jury subpoena so we can preserve your testimony as the jury considers charges against the shooter."

Jessup had regained his footing and didn't let up. "I asked a question, officer. Wouldn't you shut your eyes too?"

Holt pulled me out of there, and we headed for the elevator.

Holt was still shaking his head as the door whooshed shut behind us on the elevator. Then the absurdity of the scene lit up a smile across his face.

"Yes," he said to the CCTV camera in the elevator. "Yes, I always close my eyes! Mr. Gresham?"

"Don't drag me into this."

He laughed. "You're already in it. Up to your chin and rising."

19

Rusty Xiang read Michael's report of his meeting with Jarrod and Mona Tybaum. When he finished, he still had a half-dozen unanswered questions, so he phoned Mona and made an appointment to meet her at a coffee shop. He was starting with her because of the constant rumor of something existing between her and the vice president--something that startled Michael Gresham and got his immediate attention. He wanted to wrap that up first thing and lay it to rest or if it turned out to be important, he wanted to follow up on it.

They met at The Coffee Bar, located at the northeast edge of downtown on S Street. The place was virtually bursting at the seams when Rusty arrived and began looking for a young woman in a green baseball cap. Then he located her-- it had to be her--alone at a two-chair table further inside. She was busy texting and didn't look up when he entered, so he approached slowly, intending to avoid a startle.

"Excuse me," he said, "but are you Mona?"

She looked up, biting her lower lip. "Yes, I am. Mona Tybaum."

"Good. I'm Russell Xiang. Can I join you?"

"Please do. I think I know what you want, but maybe not."

"Would you like coffee?"

"I'm coffeed out, tell the truth. Maybe a bottle of water."

He left and returned with a bottle of water and a large bold coffee for himself. He passed her the water, pulled out the empty chair, and settled in.

"How can I help?" she asked.

"Well, as I told you on the phone, I'm an investigator for the U.S. Attorney's Office. I'm assigned to Michael Gresham's team. I understand you've met Michael?"

"I--we--have. Nice man."

"Can I be blunt here?"

"Please do."

"I'm looking into your father's murder, Mona. In the course of doing that I've heard a rumor repeated a few times. Without intending to insult you, please let me tell you what I've heard." Without waiting for her assent, he continued. "People are saying you are or were having an affair with the vice president, Jon Vengrow. I'm here to get your response to that rumor."

"Jon and I are in love. At some point, we'll be married. Probably after he decides what to do about the 2020 election when President Sinclair's second term is up."

"Meaning you'll hold off until Vice President Vengrow decides whether to run in 2020 for president?"

She took a long swallow of the water then wiped her mouth with a napkin. "Exactly. Jon's career is the most important thing to us right now. That needs to be worked through."

"So in the meantime--how can I put this delicately--in the meantime do you intend to continue with the romance?"

"Only with great discretion. I'm young, Mr. Xiang. I can wait a few years, and it won't matter all that much. In the meantime, I'll have as much of Jon's love as he's able to give and that will satisfy me. Great men require significant nurturing. That's what I feel like I'm doing with Jon, nurturing him and nurturing his career."

"Nicely said. Jon's lucky to have you."

"And I, him. It's a two-way street, Mr. Xiang."

"Rusty, please."

"All right, Rusty."

"Which brings up my next question. I know Michael Gresham made you aware of the Moscow money and the amount, which is staggering. But I'd like to ask you whether you have any idea where that money came from."

"No, I don't. Long story short, my father was very circumspect about his finances. All we ever knew was that he had enough money to take excellent care of us and to pay for the best education we could get. He was fantastic that way. But where did twelve-million dollars come from? I have no clue, Rusty."

"Did he ever talk about his business or how he got his money?"

"As I said, Dad was very circumspect. So the answer is no, he never mentioned a word about such things. At least not to me. You should talk to my brother, too. Jarrod might have a totally different answer for you."

"I plan to do just that. Next question: who would want your father dead?"

She sat back in her chair and brushed the hair off her forehead with her hand. "Don't I wish I knew. I've wracked my mind and honestly have no answer for you because I knew you'd be asking. Maybe the fossil fuel industry? Would that make sense since dad was a climate change fanatic?"

"Makes sense to me. Any names you remember your father ever mentioning? Names of people who were fighting him and his campaign?"

"There was one, Paul somebody. Wexler? Does that sound right? Does that ring a bell for you?"

"Not really, but I'm pretty new at the Washington scene, so not much would ring a bell for me. Tell me what you know or have heard about this Paul Wexler, please."

"He's someone who was once a lobbyist for coal or oil--I don't know, exactly. Then he went all green. An opportunist. But he seemed to be someone who was always in dad's face whenever he commented publicly about climate change. It would be fair to say the guy was a climate change denier, is my best guess. I'm probably saying too much about him; I don't remember all that much."

"Paul Wexler. You're sure that's his name?"

"Yes. I'm good with names, Rusty. I'm quite certain that's the man dad mentioned was always cutting back on him trying to make him look bad. Trying to destroy Dad's position on climate issues or fossil fuels. I think he wanted to be the Climate Party's nominee."

"Now think carefully. Would you have the impression from listening to your father that this Wexler would be someone who would like to see him out of the picture? Maybe even dead?"

She didn't hesitate. "Positively. He was a mean SOB to my father. I've never seen or met the man, but I hate him for all the uproar he caused in our house at dinner time. We heard about him just about every night. Paul Wexler. That's his name."

"All right, I'll make Wexler my next person of interest."

"Will you let me know what you find out?" she asked, all innocence.

Rusty looked at her, fixing her with his firm gaze. "I can't do that. This is law enforcement business, and I can't talk about it outside our office. Sorry, Mona."

"Sure. I understand."

There was a break, then, while she idly turned her water bottle around and around and Rusty stirred his coffee with a wooden stirrer. Finally, Rusty looked up and smiled for the first time.

"Guess what? I've forgotten the rest of my questions."

She returned his smile. "Guess what? I'm glad. I don't like thinking about the people who wanted to hurt my father."

"I'm sure you don't. Nobody would blame you."

"So when are you going to talk to Jarrod? You are going to talk to Jarrod, aren't you?"

"In about thirty minutes. Right here where we're sitting now."

She smiled again. "Smart man. Two birds with one stone and all that."

"One last question. Is there anything else about what's happened that you feel might be important for me to know?"

"I have a question."

"Go on."

"Is Jon Vengrow a suspect?"

Rusty caught himself. How should I answer that? Yes, everyone is a possible suspect at this point? He decided that honesty was the best policy just then.

"Truth is, Mona, the way I work, everyone's a person of interest until I clear them by nosing around. I try not to assume things about people. As Billy Blaze said in *Night Shift* with Henry Winkler, 'When I assume things I make an ass out of you and me. 'Ass-u-me'--get it?"

"I've seen that movie. I love it. All right, then, is that it for me? I need to get back to work."

"Yes. Thanks for your time."

"No need to thank me at all. You're looking for the person who murdered my dad. I'm always available to help, Rusty."

Then she was gone. Rusty refilled his coffee, leaving his top coat lying across the table to save it as he went through the coffee line.

When he returned, waiting at the table was Jarrod Tybaum, whose photograph had made its way into the Tybaum murder file and who Rusty immediately recognized, given that the notes had him wheelchair-bound, as was the person pulled up to his table.

"I knew it was you," Jarrod said as Rusty returned to the table. "Only a cop would come into a place like this without a laptop or at least an iPad."

Rusty smiled. He already liked the young man. He held out his hand, introduced himself, and took a seat.

When they were settled, the men exchanged pleasantries but only for a few minutes as Rusty was anxious to move along, especially now that he had the name of Paul Wexler to work with. This also presented the first order of business with Jarrod, clearing this name.

'Tell me about Paul Wexler," Rusty began. "Mona had quite a bit to say about him."

"I can imagine. Mr. Wexler took up a lot of air around our family dinner time as Dad would review with us what was going on in his life."

"You say 'with us.' Does that include your mother?"

"She died after many happy years with my father. Then, Dad was mother and father to us."

"Did he ever have romantic involvements that made their way into the home?"

"As in sleepovers? Or nights away? Not at all. Our dad was all about family and doing the right thing for his kids. He always walked the straight and narrow."

"Which makes him sound like someone who would never embezzle money from his PAC."

"Never. I cannot even put 'theft' and 'Dad' together in the same sentence. He just didn't do that kind of thing."

"Tell me about this Paul Wexler person. Was he a physical threat to Gerry Tybaum?"

"Maybe, I don't know. I've never met the man although I feel like I know him intimately. At least I feel like I know his dark side because that's the side that was always in conflict with our father. Long story short, the guy was and is an asshole."

"Maybe. But is Wexler someone who would murder your dad?"

The son scoffed and said, "You have any other suspects in mind?"

Rusty didn't answer at first. Then, "What do you know about Vice President Vengrow?"

"What do I know or what have I heard?"

"Either. Both."

"I've heard my sister and Vengrow are an item. I know that he's a married man and I would hate that for my sister if it's true. I also know he's a very greedy man, someone who wouldn't hesitate to take whatever he wanted from someone else regardless."

"Would he steal money from your father's PAC?"

"Unknown. Probably not."

"Would Paul Wexler?"

"Unknown. Maybe yes."

They talked on for another ten minutes, and then Rusty asked the open-end question, "Is there anything else you want me to know about your dad or his murder or the PAC money or anything else?"

"Yes. Who is Michael Gresham? I know he's the power of attorney on our dad's Moscow account. Can he still do that now that he's working as a prosecutor? Isn't there some conflict of interest? I'm suspicious of everyone, even the people who bend over backward to help us."

"Conflict of interest? Probably so. But if there is, then his removal would mean removing the one man who has authority over that money and can bring it home to you and Mona without a whole raft of legal problems set not only in the U.S. but Russia too. I'd back off that right now if I were you. And you didn't hear that from me."

"Okay, I'll shut up about it. I don't have any other questions or comments I guess."

"How are you getting home?"

"Same way I got here. Metro."

"Can I give you a ride? Just in case?"

"Just in case what?"

"In case you were followed today. I'm betting you weren't, but if you go with me, I can at least watch your six."

"My six?"

"You know, your backside. Make sure someone isn't tailing you."

"I know it's bad. I guess I just don't want to admit it."

"Who's with your younger sister today, incidentally?"

"We called Mr. Gresham for a name we could call to watch her. He said he'd come himself."

"What? She's with Michael Gresham?"

"Yes, she's taken to him now. She touches his hand every time she sees him. Which means she's crazy about him. It's her way of communicating."

"I know. What's wrong with your sister?"

"Which one?"

"The little one."

"Not a damn thing, Mr. Xiang. Put it in your book. Not a damn thing."

"Okay, sorry. I overstepped."

"Your mistake."

"Yes. I won't ask again."

"Good. Then I won't have to not answer again."

"Deal."

20

"Mr. Gresham, closed circuit TV cameras line both sides of the Reflecting Pool. As well as all monuments and tourist sites in Washington."

"Okay," I said. "But we're only interested in the Reflecting Pool."

"That's not all," Rusty said. "We also need both ends maybe a hundred feet away."

"Can do," said the custodian.

Rusty and I were meeting with the Capitol Police custodian of video files. She quickly located that Sunday night and brought it up on the screen of one of five computers for police use in her viewing room. Rusty and I took a seat at the first empty carrel and began fast-forwarding through the video beginning at five p.m. the night Tybaum was murdered. It was Rusty's first week on his new job, and we were both relieved to have before us a task that would limit the need for us to make casual conversation. The father-son thing never came up.

The video rolled along. Five p.m. to six p.m. showed nothing of interest. Then at 6:06 p.m. we got our first view of Gerry Tybaum running into the camera's view. Gerry was wearing a winter coat, waist-length, with the collar turned up, and pants that looked like black dress pants. He was wearing no hat and no gloves, which Rusty said might indicate he lost his hat during the chase. Another possibility, a need to check the route from his office to the pool.

Gerry came into view running directly toward the camera, and back behind him, you could just make out a figure running and pointing a gun at the fleeing Gerry. Then the shooting began, and Gerry staggered hard to his right and pitched forward into the reflecting pool. Now he was face-down and unmoving. The shooter trotted over and emptied his gun into Gerry's back--which, Rusty said, will be viewed on the autopsy workup with its entry angles on the bullets that killed the man.

We replayed the video, this time in slow-motion. We noticed this time through that the person pursuing Gerry was male, about six-foot, older, but because he's close behind Gerry, we're never afforded a good view of his face. He was also wearing jeans. We replayed the video and this time stopped it several times where we tried to run facial recognition apps on the face. But they came up inconclusive, so we were left without video help as to the shooter's identity.

We ran it yet again. This time we noticed that the shooter's coat was flapped open and he was wearing a belt with a buckle like the large, oval buckles worn by modern cowboys. Rodeo winners receive them, and they can be quite large, though this one was of the smaller variety. We then focused down on the buckle, trying to find some identifying characteristic there that might confirm someone's ID later on down the road as we investigated.

"Can you make it any clearer?" I asked Rusty, who was running the keyboard.

"Let me try. This system is new to me, but I'll get the hang of it."

He tried several keys, finally finding a combination that enhanced the image the closer it got to a full-screen view of the buckle.

"'Effingham 2010,'" Rusty murmured, reading the inscription on the buckle. Below it was a religious cross with a figure hanging from it, a crucifix.

"What do we know about Effingham?" I asked.

"Where's the VP hail from?"

"Illinois," I said.

"Effingham's in Illinois, I believe," he postulated, at the same time as he ran a Google search. "Yes, here it is, Effingham, Illinois. A tiny county, maybe twelve thousand souls unlucky enough to have been born there."

"Why do you say that?"

"Ever been to a small town in the Midwest?"

"Passing through," I said.

"Hold your judgment until you know more," he told me with a wink. "Now, where's our vice president from?"

He again ran a Google search, the term under study being

the VP's name. Then there it was, sure enough, he was raised on a family farm in Effingham County, Illinois.

"Bingo," he said. "The smoking gun. Your vice president is looking very guilty right about now."

"That or someone's wearing his belt," I said.

He looked up. "That's random."

"My mind works that way. We must cross off all possible explanations before we charge anyone with a crime."

"Thinking like a lawyer, Michael. Now let's figure out the cross."

He searched again. "That was easy. There's some kind of giant cross, the Cross at the Crossroads, along the Effingham road. The Google photo looks exactly like the one pictured on the buckle. I think we're getting quite warm here, Michael."

"I think you're right. As long as it's Vengrow wearing the belt."

"Yes. That must be examined."

"So how do you do that? Break into his closet and examine his belt rack?" Rusty gave me a frown. "Okay, just kidding. But it is something to think about."

"Not at all. When we narrow this down, we'll get a search warrant and track it down. My guess is he's never thought to get rid of any article of clothing that might ID him from that night. Look at this shot over here, by the way, if I focus down on his coat."

I watched the computer enhance the part of the coat he was talking about--the left side, just above the heart.

"North Face," he said.

"I see that. So now we've got something to corroborate the belt, a coat with a brand name on the breast. This guy was not too keen on police methods when he fired his gun."

"For sure. I think we're going to crack this case early on. Then we have to consider political ramifications, too, don't we?" my son asked.

"Such as?" I asked--fishing for his take on the issue.

"Well, you don't get to charge the sitting vice president with a murder rap every day of the week. There's got to be lots of roadblocks on the way toward putting him behind bars."

I genuinely did not know. D.C. was a whole new ballgame to me and I had lots to learn and knew it.

"We just have to be a hundred percent perfect, that's all," I said. "He will have the greatest defense team in the history of criminal defense arrayed against us."

"He will. What about us? Have you ever prosecuted before?"

He knew my weak spot, not that he was working on it. But it did deflate me for a few moments.

"I've never prosecuted before. I was always defense. But I've been up against thousands of prosecutors and have learned all their tricks. Now those tricks are mine. Does this help put you at ease?"

His eyes raised up from the computer screen. "I didn't mean to insult you. Just looking for information."

"No problem. It will be my case when we go to court. We might get some help on pre-trial motions, that kind of thing, I don't know. But the case is all mine, Rusty. Your wife gave it to me."

He snorted. "She gave me this job, too, I've got a feeling."

"No such thing. All she did was tell me you were looking. Your résumé is unimpeachable, Rusty. You have all the skills I need. So think nothing more of how you got here. Let's both concentrate on how we're going to remain. I happen to like it here so far and want to make a good impression."

"I don't know, but I've got a feeling that sending the Vice President of the United States to prison will get you a way down that road."

"Funny boy. Yes, it will. You, too."

We continued with the video files, trying to locate the shooter on another camera or witnesses that might have seen the shooting. So far we thought we had isolated two witnesses, one of whom the police talked to at the scene and the other being the prostitute discussed in the police reports. Jessup would be number three, but he was trying to keep his face off the front page, so he denied all knowledge. It was then that we decided to visit the scene.

Rusty drove us to the Lincoln Memorial. We parked and walked. We surveyed the area, with Rusty pointing out various points of note to me. One thing we discussed was the trees alongside the Reflecting Pool. Running along the north and south sides of the Reflecting Pool, the tree-lined walkways provided pedestrian and bicycle access to the Lincoln Memorial from the Washington Monument Grounds. We walked the length of the pool, talking and trying to understand where the parties might have been running from and how they'd met. We finally decided--guessed, really--that they had met in the parking lot to discuss the vice president's wife and Tybaum's involvement with her. Most likely there were heated words, and a scuffle broke out. The VP pulled a gun and Tybaum ran off with the VP in pursuit. Why would the VP have had a gun with him? Maybe for self-defense, maybe because he was actively planning on shooting Tybaum even before he left home that night.

"Okay, so here's the sixty-four-thousand-dollar question," Rusty said as we walked alongside the pool.

"Shoot."

"How did the vice president get away from the Secret Service that night?"

"Shit, that's right," I said. Now it was beginning to make a great deal less sense that the shooter was the VP. "Crazy thought, but do you suppose someone might have been masquerading as the vice president to throw us off?"

"Why would anyone do that?"

"Easy. Because the VP has a motive—Gerry's boinking his wife. So...could it be done to make it appear like the VP did this? What would it take?"

"Someone who obtained the requisite belt buckle, someone who knew the VP's from Effingham?"

"Yes. Plus, the North Face coat."

"Knowing that the CCTV would be recording them."

"And knowing where the CCTV cameras were located. You

notice, he never looks directly at a camera and his face is never clearly shown. I'm thinking we've got a pretender, someone taking on the clothing and manners of the vice president. Vengrow himself would never be able to shake the Secret Service. I think we're compelled to look elsewhere."

"Fair enough, but we don't rule him out altogether. In fact, I think we approach him and tell him what we have. I think we confront him, Michael."

"Then confront him we shall."

"Good. Now let's talk about the evidence for a minute," Rusty said. "What physical evidence do we know about?"

"We know there's a GoPro camera that was dropped or discarded at the scene."

"Fingerprints?"

"Interestingly enough, no. But the owner might have been wearing gloves, which would not only leave no prints but maybe even rub off earlier ones."

"Okay. Any video found on the camera itself?"

"The shooting is seen from the shooter's perspective. My guess? Someone was paid to shoot Tybaum and part of the deal was evidence of the shooting. That's what the camera was being used for. Otherwise, why bring a damn camera to a murder scene where you're the perp? It makes no sense."

Rusty nodded and seemed to take this in. He mulled it over, quiet and thoughtful as we walked along.

Then he said, "Anything else in the video? Anything off-scene that might tell us something?"

"There's a big yellow tabby cat on the first few seconds of video. Lying on what must be a kitchen table. My guess is that the shooter was preparing the camera or fastening it to his clothing and didn't realize he was filming his surroundings. But the frames are quite clear."

"Dumb question, but is the cat wearing a collar? Anything identifying?"

"Don't know. That's one for you to check out."

"Roger that," said Rusty. "I'll do that when we get back."

"Okay. So there's the camera and maybe the cat. Anything else?"

"Physical evidence includes six Federal Cartridge Hydra-Shok rounds removed from the victim."

"Slow, very destructive round. There's disagreement whether it's any better at self-defense that your basic hollow point, but I'd prefer not to go there. Let's just say that someone knew what he was doing when he chose the Hydra-Shok round. It's a very conclusive vote when one round strikes a human being."

"How many votes are six rounds?"

"Those aren't votes, Michael. Six Hydra-Shoks is a verdict."

"I'm sure you're right."

"Now what else can this scene tell us?"

"Let's locate Camera 24 North. That's the video we were watching at the police station."

"Good thinking. I've got the schematics for the video setup on my phone. Let me take a minute."

While Rusty checked his phone, I continued looking around, taking it all in. Then I walked up to the end of the pool at the bottom of the Lincoln Memorial stairs. I looked in and saw it was maybe three feet deep toward the middle. Shallow enough to freeze hard and fast but deep enough to accept a grown man's body. Suddenly a shiver racked up my spine, and I imagined what Gerry Tybaum must have been feeling as he came running across the exact point where I was standing. It could only have been pure terror for him. I pulled the collar of my topcoat tighter and turned away from the pool. Rusty pointed at the end of the pool toward an almost unnoticeable camera mounted alongside the pool and walkway.

"That's twenty-four north. The camera that saw it all that night."

"Make sure we've got great photos of the layout and good stills of the camera setup, okay?"

"I've included that in my notes, Michael."

"Then let's get out of here. I've seen all I need."

Rusty gave me a searching look. "Is it hard for you to visit a murder scene?"

"You bet," I said. "It always has been. What about you?"

"Naw. In the CIA I was the murderer. A piece of cake, this."

"It's your cake, then, my boy. Enjoy it."

21

P resident Hubert S. Sinclair had watched his Chief of Staff squeeze the Girl Scouts time slot and the American Agriculture's time slot so that he now had gained thirty-five minutes for the President's meeting with the FBI and District Police.

Sinclair sat behind his desk in the oval office and crossed, uncrossed, then recrossed his feet at the ankles. He hated to admit it but he had to: mysterious meetings with law enforcement had always frightened him, beginning with his first days on the job as a county prosecutor, where his worry was that he would fall short and allow a guilty man to walk free. Today he felt the same generalized anxiety as he had felt even back then: what good ever came from meetings with law enforcement? When you came right down to it--

The intercom on his phone interrupted his inner monologue.

"Mr. President, I have Special Agent Ames and Detective Holt to see you. Should I bring them in?"

"Yes, please do," replied the president even as his palms were dampening with fear. I'd rather meet with Putin than the freaking FBI, he thought. At least with Putin, you knew what you were getting. But the FBI--ouch! That could come in so many different packages that he would need to be on his best game for the next thirty minutes. Plus, to make it much worse, he knew what it *could* be about and if it were--if it were about the Vice President's wife's dalliance with Gerald Tybaum--then Sinclair stood to be embarrassed by his vice president. And embarrassment was the kiss of death to any politician. Sure, let them find your sperm on some aide's dress, that might get you impeached. Infidelity was a career-killer: infidelity cost big stars their careers, cost them elections, and would never be forgotten by history. It was his vice president's infidelity, true, but it could run off onto Sinclair himself. His hand shook as he reached for the humidor and retrieved a plump Cuban cigar. They were *de rigueur* again now that Cuban relations were normalized. But he only spun it in his fat fingers without tooling away the wrapper. Smoking was illegal in all federal buildings. Which included the White House and its Oval Office, which reminded the president no man was above the law, not even the tobacco addict inhabiting the world's most powerful office. A random thought ran through his brain, a glimpse into the possibility of having the vice president's wife taken down--by some anonymous gunman, maybe. He immediately shook that off and wondered whether he was losing his mind.

The door opened.

"Mr. President, Jack Ames of the FBI and Ronald Holt of the District Police."

"Come right in, Gentlemen!"

The two cops took client chairs across from the president at his desk. Everyone settled in.

"So," said Sinclair, "what's up?'

"Mr. President," Special Agent Ames began, "we've got a situation on our hands. A dire situation."

"I'm all ears."

"Long story short--your opponent from the Climate Party--"

"Gerry Tybaum, damn shame."

"We have a witness who will swear it was Vice President Jonathan S. Vengrow who was the gunman. He says he saw your vice president execute Mr. Tybaum."

"No! That wouldn't be at all possible."

The potential uproar and coming rancor all but capsized the president's emotional state. The room swam before his eyes. His pulse shot up; he had to unbutton his collar button and loosen his tie. "My great God," he muttered.

"Well, Detective Holt here took the statement of Senator Jessup. Long story short, he just happened to be visiting the Lincoln Memorial and witnessed the whole thing."

The breath caught in Sinclair's throat. "Jessup? What in God's name was Jessup doing at the Lincoln Memorial?"

"Meeting a prostitute," said Agent Ames.

"Getting a blowjob," added Detective Holt, always keen on putting the icing on the cake, so to speak.

"No!"

It was too much. "Give me ten minutes," said Sinclair, and waved his hand at the northeast office door used by the two men. "Just go back out and wait while I make some calls, please."

The men obeyed, hurrying into the president's secretary's office outside the Oval Office and quietly closed the door behind them. President Sinclair checked the clock facing him on his desktop. Ten minutes.

Sinclair picked up his phone and dialed 1. The line was answered instantly.

"Jon Vengrow, Mr. President. Do you need me to come down?"

"I do. Come through the Rose Garden and use the east door."

"I'm on my way, sir."

Two minutes later the two men were facing off across Sinclair's great desk. Sinclair met his vice president's gaze; the vice president seemed to be cool and relaxed. So Sinclair launched in.

"Gerald Tybaum was shot down several weeks ago Sunday night."

"I know, I know. Damn shame. I always liked Gerry," said the vice president, speaking solemnly as if appearing at the wake.

"Hold on. It gets bad. Two cops are waiting outside. They're saying they've interviewed Senator Jessup, who says the man he saw shoot Gerry Tybaum was you, Jon."

Vice President Vengrow all but stood up from his chair. "Me?" he cried, drawing it out.

"That's right. Jessup was at the Lincoln Memorial when he saw the gunman chase Tybaum up to the pool and shoot him. He says the man with the gun was you, Mr. Vice President. I wanted to hear your side of this before I proceeded with the cops because I know they're going to want to arrest you and bring my whole administration crashing down. Tell me it isn't so, Jonathan."

Vengrow spread his hands. He stared at the desktop. He stuck a finger in one ear and swirled it around. His jaw jumped as muscles formed silent words. He was developing his answer.

"I have an ironclad alibi."

"Great! Great! Go ahead, Jon."

"I was home watching *Homeland*."

"You were--you were watching TV?"

"Yes. The show was about an agent operating in Pakistan."

"And how--and how is your watching a TV show an alibi? Was there someone there with you who can corroborate your story?"

"Indio had been called over to her mother's. She was ailing, and you know how Mrs. Grant can get."

"I do, I do," Sinclair said, though he had no idea how the vice president's mother-in-law "got." "What was she like?"

"Ailing." He made a sweeping motion across his abdomen as if that should be explanation enough.

"Did she go to the hospital? Was a doctor called in? How do we prove Indio's whereabouts?"

"Ask Mrs. Grant, I would say. She could confirm her daughter's visit."

"Whoa, whoa up, Jon. This is getting off-center. We're trying to prove your whereabouts Sunday night, not your wife's and not your wife's mother's ailment. Help me with sorting you out, please."

"No one was around. Secret Service has their office up front in the Observatory. I was clear back in my bedroom."

"You have your own bedroom?" asked Sinclair. It was the first he'd heard.

"I do. Privacy and working late. I need my own area."

"Got it, got it. So you were back in your office, and the Secret Service was up front. Are you able to leave your office and get outside without the Secret Service knowing? I think I know the answer without even asking."

"No, there's no way that could happen. They've got all the exterior doors covered, as well as the surrounding grounds."

"Sure, sure. So, what happened next?"

"I watched *Homeland*."

"Do you own a gun, Jon?"

"I do. It was the weapon I carried during the First Gulf War."

"A handgun?"

"A semiautomatic."

"And where's that gun now?"

"At home in my desk."

"Is there some way we can have it tested to prove it hasn't been fired in a long time?"

"That won't fly. I was out shooting the day before, Saturday."

"Shooting at what?"

"You know," said the vice president evenly, "gun range targets."

"So any tests would show it had been fired recently?"

"Affirmative. That's not a solution."

"Then you tell me. How do we overcome Jessup's claim you pulled the trigger on the gun that nailed Tybaum?"

"One thing the police will want to do is test my gun against the bullets pulled out of Gerry's back."

Sinclair alerted. "How do you know they came from his back?"

"I think I read that in the paper, didn't I?"

"I read the same paper. I've got it right here. It doesn't say anything about where he was shot. Newspaper stories usually don't tell those details. So, how do you know they came from his back?"

"I think I heard that Mr. Tybaum was running away when he was shot from behind. Maybe that's it."

"That's not in the article either."

"Well, then, screw it. I don't recall where I got it. I just know what I know, that's all."

"Maybe it's because you pulled the trigger? Work with me now, Jon. I can help you if I get all the details."

"It wasn't me." The VP's voice was small and seemed to arrive from a great distance.

The President sat back and picked up the Cuban cigar. Without a word he rummaged through his desk, looking for his BIC lighter. Once he had that in hand, he flicked the igniter and lit up his cigar. He blew a dense plume of smoke across the desk.

The president turned the cigar and studied its lit end. "Sons of bitches--I'll smoke in my frigging office if I need. And I need it now."

"No thanks, Mr. President."

"No thanks? I don't recall offering you one, Jon. I know you don't partake."

"That's right; I don't. Indio wouldn't let me in the door if I came home reeking of Cuban tobacco."

"Her loss. The First Lady says she enjoys the smell."

The vice president looked askance at the president. He couldn't imagine a wife saying she enjoyed the odor of her husband's cigar. It didn't fit into any wifely tropes he could dredge up.

"Jon, why don't we do this? Why don't we ship you overseas for a week and see if I can douse this fire? Let me see if I can work my magic to make this go away."

"All right. Whatever you want, Mr. President."

"We need you incommunicado for a few days; that's all, Jon."

"All right. You thinking maybe Asia?"

"No, those Asians are too jealous of who gets to host who. I'm thinking Eastern Europe."

"Won't that stir up the Russians too much?"

"Well, you've got a point there."

"What if I go into hiding at Bethesda Naval Hospital and we tell everyone I'm gravely ill."

The president's face lit up. "That I like. Yes, that works. Then I've got you close by while I work this out."

"I'll talk to Dr. Monks today. He can admit me and put me under quarantine."

"Take plenty to read, Jon. We all know you get restless. And Jon, just one more thing. It's no secret that Gerry Tybaum has been sniffing around Indio. Is any of that stuff I've heard actually true? Was she carrying on an affair with our dead friend?"

The VP looked injured. It was not a subject the president enjoyed pursuing. He had his suspicions about the VP's wife, but he'd never said anything, never considered it his place to speak up.

"She might have seen him a few times. She's admitted that to me."

A few times? Thought Sinclair. I heard it was a raging wildfire.

"How did that affect you, Jon?"

"Did it make me crazy? No, Mr. President. We haven't been in love for twenty years. She doesn't give a damn who I see and the feeling's mutual."

"I didn't know. Sorry to hear it's like that."

"Just doesn't matter anymore, Mr. President. Hasn't mattered for so long I forget. We're married because I need the votes and she enjoys the benefits."

"Tell you what, Jon. Your name is all over the street as the shooter. Lots of people think you shot Tybaum because of his liaisons with your wife."

"I know that. It kills me, sir."

"We want the prosecutor on Tybaum's case to finish up his investigation ASAP because it's going to clear your name. Your need that, I need that, the administration needs that, the country needs that."

"I hear you, sir. We need an indictment brought against someone besides me."

"Right. So let's keep our eye on the ball and let's be sure the investigation goes smoothly. I'm putting you on that, Jon. You ride shotgun for the prosecutor. If he needs anything, make sure he gets it. If he wants you to testify then, by all means, do so. Just be careful."

"Don't forget, Mr. President, I used to work for the U.S. Attorney myself. Of course, that was twenty-five years ago, but I still know the game."

"Excellent, Jon. Still, watch your step. I'm counting on you to do this right."

"Thank you, Mr. President. I'm all over it."

"All right. Why don't you head back out the way you came and I'll get the cops back in here? I just wanted your side of things before I went ahead with those boys. I knew you'd have something for me that made sense."

The vice president stood and solemnly shook hands with the president. Then he ducked out into the Rose Garden and disappeared. The president had Yolanda bring the FBI agent and detective back into his office.

"All right, men, I've made some calls, asked some questions."

"I'm sure you have lots of sources," said Special Agent Ames.

Sinclair stared him down. My sources are none of your damn business, he thought.

"Anyway, I'm comfortable in saying Senator Jessup's got his wires crossed. The shooter was not the vice president."

"So you're giving us the green light on speaking to the VP and getting him cleared?" asked Detective Holt.

"That's doable. But not quite yet. The vice president has been ailing. He's being admitted to Bethesda for testing and observation as we speak. There's no hurry is there?"

The last part was said with a menacing tone. It said there better damn well be no hurry. Both men agreed instantly: there was no hurry.

"So. What else we do know about the shooting?" Sinclair asked his visitors.

"Not much else," they said in unison. "Nothing further."

"Good. My time's up with you fellows. Give Bethesda a call

in five days. Maybe they can update you on the vice president's condition then. But I don't want you disturbing him while he's under the weather. You feel me?"

Both men agreed; they understood to back off for awhile. It was political, and all three men knew it. But no one was saying so. The president needed time to rally, and the cops had to do as he said.

Within reason, at least.

22

Detective Holt was waiting in my office the next morning.

"Michael," he began, "it's time to talk to Bambee."

I looked him up and down. "That sounds like a hooker's name, Holt."

"Bingo. She's the girl who was at the Lincoln Memorial with Jessup."

"Oh, yes, she's in the police reports. Why no statements yet?"

"She went into hiding after the shooting. A CI just turned her up for us."

"Where is she?"

"The good thing is, she's still here in D.C. The bad news is that she's lawyered up and won't speak without her mouthpiece present. She's also shopping her story to the *Enquirer*."

"So much for Jessup's career," I ventured. "He can kiss his Senate seat goodbye."

"He's still got almost a year left in his term. He's a 2018 candidate."

"This story will be on the front pages at least until then. Hell," I said, "maybe you should run against him, Holt. The seat is there for the taking. Move the family, get residency, throw your hat in the ring."

Detective Holt snorted. "Yeah, right. I wouldn't be an elected official coming to this town no matter how much they offered to pay me. I like to be able to sleep at night. Plus, I don't like spending time in the confessional. No, let's leave that to the real whores."

"Whoa, those are pretty strong words."

"You're new here, Mr. Gresham. The day will come when you'll be using similar words when you talk about our Congress."

"I'll put that on the back burner. So, how do we talk to Bambee--what's her real name?"

"Evelyn Adelphia. She's a cheesehead from Milwaukee originally."

"Do I need to call for an appointment?"

"Done," said Holt. "I've got us talking to her at her attorney's office at ten o'clock. So clear your calendar, counselor, this one's going to be interesting. She just might put the vice president away once and for all."

"I'll withhold making any judgment on that until after we've talked to her."

Her lawyer turned out to be a well-known Washington mouthpiece by the name of L. Jamison Hubbard. He officed at the Watergate with a nest of several other attorneys known collectively as Espinoza, Hubbard, Sharpe, and Howe. So off we went, Holt driving. We took I-395 South and then Maine Avenue to Virginia Avenue. All along the way, I kept thinking of Vice President Jon Vengrow, planning how I would approach my questions with Bambee this morning to lay a foundation for what I'd be asking the VP. It all depended on how far the witness was willing to go.

She was waiting with her lawyer Hubbard in his conference room when we arrived, and we were shown right in. Hubbard introduced himself to us and then introduced his client, Evelyn Adelphia. He was a man with a military bearing and blond crew cut; she was a woman who, I guessed, was probably ten years younger than she looked, even with a modicum of daytime makeup applied. They sat on one side of the long, expansive table; Holt and I arranged ourselves on the other.

"I'd like to record this," I began, nodding to Holt's tiny recorder. "Any problem with that?"

"I have a huge problem with it," Hubbard said icily. "You're going to subpoena her for your grand jury, why should you record this informal conference? We'll be talking in generalities here, right?"

I looked at Holt. I wasn't aware that it was just a conference; I thought we were there to take a full statement.

"Attorney Hubbard," Holt said, "when you and I spoke I was quite clear we wanted to take your client's statement. But the counselor here is convening the grand jury next week, and we'd be glad to put your client's name at the top of the list."

Hubbard knew he had no right to attend her grand jury

appearance, so he evidently decided he'd rather get her story hammered out while he was present here with her than at the grand jury, where he wasn't. So, he relented.

"I don't remember it that way," he said, "but let's let you go ahead and record and see how it goes. But if I get uncomfortable I reserve the right to discontinue at any moment, period."

"Of course," I said. "You always have that right."

"All right?" asked Holt of Hubbard. "Do I switch it on?"

"Switch away," said Hubbard and he rubbed his hands briskly together, eager to do battle if it came down to that.

"And we are rolling," said Holt.

"Good morning," I said, "my name is Michael Gresham, and I'm an Assistant U.S. Attorney assigned to investigate the death of Gerald Tybaum. Today I'm sitting in the D.C. law office of L. Jamison Hubbard, attorney for Evelyn Adelphia. Joining me in the room this morning are L. Jamison Hubbard, Evelyn Adelphia, and Ronald Holt, a detective with the Metropolitan Police Department of the District of Columbia. Today I'll be asking questions of Evelyn Adelphia, and she'll be giving her answers under the watchful eye and ear of her attorney, L. Jamison Hubbard. I want to make clear that while this is not sworn testimony under oath, it is still a serious offense to tell an untruth to an officer of the law during an official investigation, which this is. Questions so far?"

"How long am I going to be here?" asked Evelyn.

"Maybe thirty or forty minutes. That should be plenty," I said. "Now, please state your name."

"Evelyn Adelphia."

"Ms. Adelphia, what is your usual occupation?"

"I work for the federal government at the Treasury Department during the day. At night I work as a female escort."

"At night are you freelancing or is there an employer you answer to?"

"Freelance. I have a website."

"As a female escort, what are your usual activities?'

"I accompany men--and now and then women--on social outings, parties, things like that."

"Any other services performed by you?"

"Male companionship is the main one."

"What about physical relationships? Any of that?"

"You mean am I screwing my customers? Yes, I have sex with some of them. If they pay enough."

"Is prostitution legal in D.C.?"

She smiled at this one and then nailed me. "Only if you're a member of Congress."

None of us could suppress a smile. Holt even laughed.

"On the night of January fifteenth of this year were you with a client of your escort service?"

"You mean night, evening, or day?"

"What, there were three different men?" I asked and immediately regretted it. She was only trying to answer correctly. "Sorry. I'm talking about anytime on that Sunday."

"Yes, I had been asked to join Senator Jessup that afternoon."

"That would be U.S. Senator Stanley E. Jessup?"

"Yes."

"How did Senator Jessup come to call on you?"

"He had used me before."

"How many times previously?"

"Maybe twenty, twenty-five."

"Did he pay you for these meetings?"

"Yes, one-thousand for the full day, five-hundred for a half day."

"Was January fifteen a full or a half day?"

"Half. He called me after noon that day. I don't usually work on Sundays, so I had an opening. Because he was a steady I worked instead of taking all day off."

"Did you have occasion that day to visit the Lincoln Memorial with Senator Jessup?"

"Yes."

"What time?"

"About six o'clock."

"Why the Lincoln Memorial, if you know?"

"He had a thing about sex in public."

"What's that?" I said, my head jerking up from my note-taking.

"He liked to have sex in public places. It's a fetish some men have. Weird, but hey, he's paying, so I don't argue."

"You don't argue with their fetishes?"

"Nothing to embarrass them. I want my customers to feel safe and comfortable with me. Men can be very strange. The senator's was public sex."

"Did you have sex with the senator at the Lincoln Memorial?"

"I did, about halfway up the steps. There are eighty-seven steps there--I counted them one time before when we did it there."

"This wasn't the first time you had sex with the senator at the Memorial?"

"We did it there maybe a half dozen times."

"Where else have you had sex with the senator?"

"EOB, Capitol, across from the White House. And there's more."

"Did anyone ever spot you having sex with the senator in public?"

"If they did they didn't come forth. No one ever told me or confronted us."

I studied my notes for a moment. Then, "Describe the sex act you were engaged in with the senator on January fifteen."

"BJ."

"Pardon?"

"Blowjob. I was giving him a blowjob."

"This would be on the steps of the Lincoln Memorial?"

"Yes."

"Why there? Any idea?"

"Senator Jessup is from the South. He hates Lincoln, he said. So he wanted to have sex on his stairs."

"He told you this?"

"Yes."

"While you were having sex with the senator did anything unusual draw your attention away that night?"

"A gun went off. I looked over. I saw a man shooting at a man who was floating face-down in the water."

"The water, meaning the Reflecting Pool?"

"Yes. I didn't see it, but I remember thinking the first gunshot probably put him down in the water. Then I watched him shoot several more times, standing over the guy and firing at him while he floated."

"Could you see a man in the pool? Wasn't it dark?"

"There are lights. I guess I saw more like a form of a man."

"So your mind guessed it was a man you were seeing?'

"I suppose so. I don't claim to know how the mind works, sir."

"I appreciate that. How about this: you tell me if this is fair?

You saw the man shooting at a form in the water, and you thought it looked like a person floating there?"

"That's fair. That's what happened."

"And what happened while you watched the shots being fired?"

"The senator ejaculated in my mouth."

"The senator--with your help--culminated the sex act?"

"He climaxed. Went off in my mouth."

"All right. Did you happen to see whether the senator was looking over at the shooting too?"

"I did. He was watching and coming at the same time."

"His eyes weren't closed?"

"Oh, hell no."

"And how do you know this?"

"I looked away from the shooting and looked up at the senator. I wanted to see whether I should continue."

"He gave no indication you should stop?"

"The opposite. He grabbed the back of my head and pulled me closer to his penis."

"Did you and the senator discuss what you'd seen?"

"No. He immediately zipped up and double-timed down the steps. Then he double-timed in the direction of his car. I was left standing there. I didn't know how I was getting home since he brought me."

"Did you talk to anyone that night about what you saw?"

"Yes, the police talked to me."

"Why were you still in the area when the police arrived?"

"I hit my head and knocked myself out. Then they woke me sometime later. You've got to remember, Mr. Gresham, the place is swarming with Capitol Police. They're everywhere. I'll bet they were on the scene in less than two minutes."

"That fast?"

"I was passed out. I'm just guessing."

"Did you have a line of sight of the shooter's face?"

"I did."

"Did you recognize the shooter?"

"I did."

"Can you tell us the shooter's name?"

She stopped and looked at her lawyer for guidance. Then her lawyer stood up and said they were going out into the hallway to discuss her answer. I told them to take their time. It's very common for a witness and her lawyer to take a break and leave the room to discuss testimony. Happens just about every other time I'm taking a deposition. So I was neither surprised nor upset when it happened that day. Detective Holt paused his recorder and leaned back, his hands clasped behind his head. He looked over at me.

"So what else is new, Mr. Gresham?" he said with a sort of sly smile.

"Besides locating a witness to the murder of Gerald

Tybaum? Besides the witness identifying a United States senator as her date at the time and place of the shooting? Is that what you mean?"

"I know. She's going to make a terrific witness."

"Ingénue," I said. "She comes across with all innocence and honesty. Even with her startling story."

"Yes, she is very likable."

"Agree one-hundred percent."

The witness and her attorney then reappeared and took their seats. Holt switched the recorder on, and we were rolling again.

"Ms. Adelphia, you just took a break from the recording with your attorney and went into the hallway, correct?"

"Yes."

"Please tell us what you discussed out there?"

"Objection, attorney-client privilege," said Hubbard with a biting tone in his voice. "Don't answer that, Evelyn."

"Withdrawn," I said. "You were going to tell us the identity of the man you saw doing the shooting. Please tell us now who you saw."

Without hesitation, she said, "I can't be sure who it was, and I don't want to guess."

"I told her not to guess, Mr. Gresham," Hubbard interjected.

"What else did he tell you?" I asked.

"He told me--"

"Objection! Attorney-client privilege," Hubbard cried out.

I fixed him with my eyes. "Nonsense. You just waived that privilege when you said you told her not to guess. Please let her answer my question."

"Don't answer that question, Adelphia," said Hubbard. "Gentlemen--and lady--we're done here today. I'm ending this interrogation."

"Well," I said, "you have the right to do that. Counselor, this statement will be reduced to writing. Will you allow your client to sign it and attest that it's her statement?"

"Hell no. She's not signing anything."

I looked casually at the attorney on the other side of the table.

Then I nodded. It was no time to throw my weight around. Which was a new weight, the weight of having the full force and authority of the U.S. Government behind me while I conducted the investigation. I had promised myself that I wouldn't bully and I wasn't about to start then.

So I let it go, and we broke up the meeting.

Once outside, in the reserved parking where Holt had left his unmarked car, he unlocked the SUV then caught my eye across the top of the car just as we were stepping inside.

"That was terrific," he said. "Nicely done."

"That was nothing," I said. "Wait until I get her before the grand jury and make her give up the shooter's identity. That's when it's going to get fun."

"Hmm. Do you think she knows who it was?"

"Oh, she knows all right. Did you see her hands shake when she went to take a drink of her Starbucks? Shaking like a leaf."

"I noticed that."

"We've only just begun, Detective Holt. Now take me back to my office, please. I need to get ready to meet the GULP CEO."

"We're on our way."

23

R udy had staked out the Tybaum house three times to no avail. Meaning no one came or went and no one answered the door.

"They're moved out," he whispered to himself as he gave up the third time, put his car in gear, and went rolling off in search of the missing heirs. One thing he knew for sure: he knew where Mona worked and he was going there just then. He would follow her to wherever she was living now. Which would lead him to the others, ninety-nine times out of a hundred.

He arrived at Kricket Enterprises at half-past four in the afternoon. The building was located on a secondary street in Northwest D.C. It was a tree-lined street but it was serviced by Metro buses, which is how he guessed she would be getting home.

Sure enough, at five o'clock, just as he was lighting a cigarette off the ember of one he'd just smoked down almost to the filter, she came out of the building and pulled her collar tight around her throat. She was wearing gloves and he was close enough to see they were made of green wool. He didn't move his car as she walked along the block, down to the south end of the block, where she took a seat on a bus bench. Ever so slowly he eased his Lincoln along the curb to where he was less than fifty feet from her. She was reading on her phone and never looked up. *Easy*, Rudy thought. *Not paying any attention to her surroundings just like everyone under thirty in America.*

Rudy kept a watchful eye out the windshield and out the back window using the mirror. Then he saw the bus come lumbering up the street, swaying from side to side on the crowned road. It drew abreast of him and he turned to avert his face. One never knew. Then it stopped at the corner and he watched Mona climb aboard. *So, is it really going to be this easy to locate the family's new digs?*

He planned the assassination of Mona Tybaum. To begin, he wanted no witnesses. Which ruled out the bus stop at either end of the route. It also ruled out the Kricket Building. Would he end up just entering their new residence and murdering them one-by-one where they lay sleeping? But surely they would be under the watchful eye of a police contingent. He was certain there was a grand jury meeting and searching for his identity already; which most likely would mean there was also police protection.

Finally, two bus changes later, they arrived in Bethesda. She was let off on Elm and began walking the long block to the next street, which was Beech. At Beech she turned north and walked up to the front door of the third house on the left. It was a friendly-looking little house. From the exterior he could see the living room at the front window on the right side and on the left side were the bedrooms and maybe a basement below, he wasn't sure. At any rate it looked like windows somewhat above ground and windows at ground level. Maybe a story-and-a-half. From the end of the block he watched as she disappeared inside the house.

Now to sit and make sure she was at their home, that she wasn't just there to visit someone.

From six-thirty until eleven-thirty when all windows were dark Rudy sat in his Lincoln and waited. He called Wexler to report in.

"I think I've got the house," he said without introduction over the phone.

"Good. Where is it?"

"Not over the phone. I'll wait here until sun-up so I know for sure."

"Have you seen anyone else come or go?"

"No. And I haven't seen any cop cars, either, marked or unmarked. Which kind of puzzles me. Wouldn't they have the cops watching Tybaum's kids like hawks once they figured out the hit was about money? Wouldn't they know we'd come after his heirs next?"

"You never know. Cops and government lawyers can be quite competent and they can be dumb as rocks, too. I'd like you to stake it out for another day just to be sure of everything. If you decide you've got their home, call me. We'll make plans. Do you understand me, Rudy? I don't want them hit prematurely before we know for sure what we have. Hear me and act accordingly."

"Got it. I'll just settle in for another day. Then I'll call you."

"I'm out."

Rudy ended the call without another word. He hated that he'd been told to hang out at the house for another full twenty-four hours. To him, it was quite obvious he'd found the new house and it was quite obvious he could kill them all there at one time. All he needed was a door key and a silencer for his Glock .40. But he reconsidered and had to give Wexler a point when a cop car pulled up at seven a.m. and a uniformed officer climbed out and rang the doorbell. He spoke with Mona only briefly before climbing back into his vehicle and driving away. Fifteen minutes later, Mona reappeared, walked out to the sidewalk and began her trek a block over to the bus stop. She was dressed in a long black coat, unbuttoned up the front, and what looked to Rudy like a pantsuit beneath. Her shoes were half-heels and clacked on the sidewalk as she made her way up to Rudy then passed by without so much as a glance his way. He then pulled around the block and slowly drove up the street. He pulled over just less than halfway to the end and waited until--sure enough--the woman appeared again. This time she stopped at the bus platform and ducked under the small rain cover. Ten minutes dragged by before the bus came. Rudy watched her climb aboard and watched the bus then recede back down the street and drive out of view at the corner. She was gone.

So he pulled back around the block and this time went beyond the Tybaum's temporary house and pulled into an empty drive then backed out so he was again facing the house. It was hard staying awake, he found as he settled in for the long watch, but he knew it was going to be worth it.

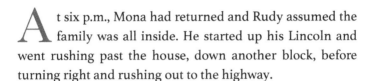

At six p.m., Mona had returned and Rudy assumed the family was all inside. He started up his Lincoln and went rushing past the house, down another block, before turning right and rushing out to the highway.

He needed a silencer and he thought he knew where he might find one.

Across the river in Arlington, just as he drove down off the bridge, Rudy turned right, drove up two blocks, then made a left turn. He pulled down three store fronts to a window that said, in large gold letters, PAWN. He parked in the side lot and hurried inside.

"Raul here?" he asked a burly white man behind thick bulletproof glass.

"Raul!" called the burly man down the length of the display cases full of pawn. "Window One!"

A Hispanic-looking man wiping his hands on a shop towel appeared out of a private room at Rudy's far left. He saw Rudy but remained impassive even though he knew the man quite well.

"Yes?" he said through the aluminum speaker embedded in the glass divider between the two men.

"Forty- caliber Glock. Silencer."

The man's eyebrows knitted together. "That'll cost you."

"Not a problem."

"Five grand. I can have it here in one hour."

Rudy pulled a gangster's roll of hundreds out of his pocket. He counted off fifty bills, pushed them beneath the glass, and said, "Count it."

The man riffled quickly through the bills, counting. He then turned and ran the bills through an electronic counter. Same total: fifty.

"Done," said Raul. "Come back in sixty minutes. Leave for now."

Without a word, Rudy turned and walked out of the store. Out on the sidewalk he looked both ways. A restaurant across the street caught his eye. *Fernando's* said the blinking sign in the window. Dodging two oncoming cars, Rudy danced across the street and entered the restaurant at a slow walk so as to not draw attention to himself. A woman holding a plastic-sleeved menu to her breast approached and motioned for him to follow her. At the table she set down a plastic drinking glass of water and ice. She then turned, went behind the counter, and returned minutes later with a bowlful of tortilla chips and smaller pot of salsa. Laying her offerings before him she said, "Take your time."

He ordered a green chili relleno and a cheese crisp with a bottle of Dos Equis. The food was passable and the beer was refreshing. In fact, he decided to have a second, something he almost never did when he was working a job. But he had an hour to kill and he didn't want to pass the time outside the pawn shop sitting in the parking lot while running the engine to stay warm. The second beer was nursed for almost thirty minutes. Then he stood up, walked to the register, and asked for his check. He paid up and shrugged into his North Face coat and stepped outside. Snowing again.

Back across the street he dodged, this time going straight inside the pawn shop and walking directly to Window One.

"Raul!" called the burly white man. "Your customer is back!"

Again Raul entered from Rudy's left, this time carrying an object wrapped up in a yellow shop rag. He placed it on his side of the bulletproof window and unwrapped the shop rag. Rudy stared at the silencer. "Pass it through," he asked the proprietor, and the silencer came sliding from beneath the window. Rudy picked it up, turned and stared through the instrument into the outside light--gray as it was--coming in the front window. He turned the item as one might turn a kaleidoscope for effect. Evidently satisfied with the silencer, he nodded to Raul and pocketed the device.

"Come back," Raul said.

"You can be sure of it," Rudy replied on his way to the door. "*Adios.*"

"*Adios.*"

Rudy drove slowly back to the Tybaum house. There was no hurry; the hit wasn't until after midnight but before dawn.

The two Dos Equis beers had left him drowsy. Sitting behind the steering wheel, his head propped against the window, he shut his eyes. Just for a minute--he thought. Four hours later he jerked awake. Something had hit his car. He scanned around 360 degrees. Then there, off at his four o'clock, he saw the body of a large man. He was holding a baseball bat on his shoulder and now was walking around to the driver's window. Rudy rolled down the window and looked up. The silenced gun was resting on his lap under a newspaper he'd brought along for that purpose. The man leaned down.

He was brawny and he wasn't smiling.

"That's my house back over there," the man growled at Rudy.

"I see. How can I help you?"

"Why're you parked in front of my house?"

"It's a public street, mister. I can park here for a week if I decide to."

The man reared upright. For just a moment Rudy was afraid the bat was about to come crashing back down.

But it didn't. Instead, the man leaned down again and pointed the thick end of the bat right at Rudy's head. "No, son, that ain't the way it works around here. You can't park here for a week. Not even for a day. We've had burglaries and we've had muggings in our neighborhood. Our watch group is online; we've got shit going down every day. So you're gonna have to leave or I'm gonna have to think of some other way to convince you."

Staring straight ahead, Rudy flexed his jaw, trying hard not to be aggressive. "Tell you what," he said. "What if I pay you to let me stay here just awhile longer?"

"How much longer?"

"All night."

"Why would you want to do that?"

Rudy's mind was racing. The man knew what he looked like. If the Tybaum kids died that night, the man could pick Rudy out of a lineup in a hot second. And he knew it. His cover was blown, the hit was off, he'd have to think of some other way of getting the job done.

"All right," Rudy replied. "I guess you're right, I guess I wouldn't really want to."

"That's right."

"So I'm going to leave now. I won't be back. I'm sorry I bothered you tonight."

"Don't come back," the man said, waggling the bat menacingly at Rudy.

Rudy felt the heavy gun in his hand, made heavier and even more deadly with the silencer mounted on its muzzle.

"I won't be back," he finally said, relaxing his grip on the gun. "I'm done here."

"You are that."

"No need to be a tough guy," Rudy said back, his hackles suddenly raising up.

"No tough guy, friend. Just a man with a family. You know what else? My wife has your license number. Anything happens around here, you're the first suspect on the cops' list. Got me?"

"Sure. But don't worry, I'm already gone."

Rudy downshifted the idling Lincoln, nodded at the man and raised his window as he began rolling away.

"Damn it to hell!" Rudy cried under his breath as he accelerated on down the street. He pointed at the Tybaum's house as he rolled past. "You're very lucky, my children. Very lucky."

Then he was at the corner and turning right and gone.

But he wasn't finished.

It had only just begun.

24

Vice President Jon Vengrow was widely known as a private man who kept his own counsel. He was rarely seen in public except for Rose Garden events where the president announced some new tax cut or new treaty with a trading partner. So when I called his office and explained who I was and that I wanted to speak privately with him, my request was summarily rejected. I thought maybe they didn't realize who I was, so I tried writing a letter to him explaining that his name had been mentioned by a witness in a criminal case I was investigating. Again, nothing but a stonewall.

I decided I must be trying the wrong approach.

So, I convened a grand jury and issued a subpoena to the VP. It was served on him by a U.S. Marshal on March 2 by leaving a copy at his office with his legal counsel, who stepped up and said they would accept service. So be it. The subpoena's appearance date was March 9, a Monday, at 10 a.m.

Next up was Vincent Tirley. I made an appointment to speak with the treasurer of Gerry Tybaum's PAC. I wanted to discuss the missing 12 million dollars and see whether we could begin to understand exactly what had happened and how the same amount of money was deposited in a Russian bank and whether any of it was related to the Gerry Tybaum murder. The FBI had taken a statement from Vincent Tirley previously, and I had his statement, but I wanted more. So Mr. Tirley agreed to meet with me--but only after I let it drop that I was convening a grand jury and that he could tell his story under oath to the grand jury if he didn't want to speak to me. He elected the one-on-one with me in the privacy of his office.

I arrived at Tirley's Foggy Bottom office on Tuesday morning and was immediately provided with coffee and a seat in a small conference room. Tirley didn't keep me waiting but joined me just minutes later, a second man accompanying him, a man who I knew would be his legal counsel. Introductions were made, and a court reporter commissioned by Tirley's lawyer set up her tripod and cracked her knuckles then nodded, ready to proceed.

"I'll want a copy," I told her. "Any problems with me getting a copy of her transcription?"

Tirley shook his head.

"Good, then," I said, and took a seat at the table.

I didn't waste any time. Tirley was a slight, pasty-faced man, early fifties, whose pinstriped suit was perfectly tailored to fit his body and whose fingernails reflected the dull light in the conference room thanks to their coat of clear polish.

I launched right in, acceding to a standard question-answer routine because that's what I do whenever a court reporter shows up. I thought it fit the mood and the staffing quite nicely.

"State your name," I said.

"Vincent Richard Tirley," came the reply.

"Mr. Tirley, what is your business, occupation, or profession?"

"Chief Financial Officer, Government Use of Lands and Policy. It's a PAC."

"Also known as GULP?"

"I think some people are fond of that acronym, yes."

"Tell us the nature of GULP's business."

"We are a political action committee. Our charter provides that we may do any and all fund-raising as we choose where climate policies, legislation, and elections are involved. We work hand-in-glove with the Climate Change party."

His face brightened as he told me this. Evidently, he was proud of the work of his PAC and his cheerfulness convinced me that he believed in its mission.

"Are you acquainted with Gerald Tybaum?"

"I am. Or was. Mr. Tybaum founded the Climate Change party and served on the board of GULP."

"As a board member of GULP, what were Mr. Tybaum's responsibilities?"

"Hiring and policy. All new hires went through GULP's board of directors and all policy matters, and campaign supports were debated and voted on by GULP's board. Sometimes those debates were quite heated too, I might add."

"I'm sure that's true. Especially in today's political climate and environment where giant masses of the Arctic and Antarctic are melting away."

"Exactly."

"As a member of GULP's board did Mr. Tybaum have access to GULP's checkbook?"

"Could he write money out of our accounts? Is that what you're asking?"

"Yes."

"No."

"Recently I was visited by the FBI in connection with a meeting I had with Mr. Tybaum. The FBI indicated there was likely a connection between Mr. Tybaum and funds reported to be missing from the PAC. Can you enlighten me about this?"

"We were embezzled to the tune of just over twelve-million dollars and change. The embezzlement was investigated by the FBI under federal PAC laws."

"Please state what you told the FBI about the missing funds and Tybaum's ability to move those funds himself."

"Pretty much what I've told you, that Gerry Tybaum didn't have access or signatory authority on any of our cash accounts."

"Did you give your opinion regarding Tybaum's involvement in the embezzlement of GULP?"

"I did give my opinion."

"And what was that opinion?"

"I told them I believed Gerry Tybaum had no way of obtaining control over any of our accounts or monies. I still don't see how he might have. Plus, we have no idea where the money went or wound up so we can't even formulate an educated guess as to any role Gerry Tybaum might have had."

I realized then and there that the FBI hadn't advised GULP and Tirley that Tybaum's Russian bank account had received a deposit of almost the exact amount that had been embezzled. I decided, moreover, that they weren't going to learn about this possible connection from me. So I moved on.

"Can you share with me any notions or theories you do have about the disappearance of GULP campaign contributions?"

"Yes, I believe our money was moved from our account to some other account by someone within the bank. Not from our end."

"What bank was that?"

"Charter Bank and Mercantile of Boston. All of our accounts are with Charter Bank."

"Did the FBI investigate Charter Bank?"

He looked at his attorney at this point, who did a small shrug and a nod. Go ahead, answer.

"The FBI investigated, but we haven't been told anything they found out. We're as much in the dark now as we ever were."

"Mr. Tirley, I've never dealt with a PAC before. But twelve-million dollars is a trainload of money. Would that be a lot for any PAC? If you know?"

"I've worked for several PACs. Twelve-million is at the top end of what I've seen. But remember, there's a zillion climate activists out there, Mr. Gresham. Everyone's in on it now. The only ones who don't realize this yet are your current administration in the White House. They still want to drill, baby, drill."

"Without getting into the politics of climate change and the polarization of people because of it, can you tell me whether Gerald Tybaum had any detractors who might have wanted to see him dead? Any that you're aware of?"

"Only about twenty-million executives working for the fossil fuel companies. Hatred for Gerry ranged far and wide. Petroleum hated him, so did coal, even certain people in Congress whose campaign financing relies on coal and oil barons writing huge checks. They hated him too. Yes, there was a world of hatred for Gerry out there."

"What about more personal relationships? Are you aware of any one person who might want to see him dead?'

"Not really. Well...maybe I shouldn't say this."

"Say what?"

"I know Gerry was reportedly boffing the VP's wife. So maybe the government wanted him dead. I'm half-kidding, sir. I don't know this, and I really shouldn't have repeated it. It's just a rumor. But everyone around the Beltway knows about it."

I smiled at him. "I'll put that down as pure guesstimation. Not to worry."

"Thank you."

"Had you ever seen Gerry and Mrs. Vengrow together?"

"Oh, no. Gerry would never have been that open and notorious. He was a gentleman."

"So this connection between Gerry and the woman is just hearsay?"

"I think that's right. I'm feeling terrible about myself for repeating that rumor just now. Nobody knows anything about anybody else. It's all hearsay and guesses."

"We've talked about detractors who might want Gerry dead. And we've talked about an alleged affair he was having. Can you think of anyone else who might've wanted Gerry dead?"

"No, sir. The whole climate thing is a hornet's nest. There are millions of people on both sides of the issue. Any of them might have a grudge. It looks like an all-but-impossible case, Mr. Gresham."

"All right, I'll remember that. Do you have any questions for me, Mr. Tirley?"

"Yes, do you have any idea what might've happened to our missing money?"

"No," I lied. "No idea."

I then thanked him, and we said our goodbyes.

Part of being a good prosecutor, I had just learned, was keeping a straight face when telling a lie.

But I had been a defense lawyer since forever.

The lying skill was one I already owned.

25

The Vice President was anxious to sneak out of the hospital to keep a rendezvous with his lover. However, the Secret Service insisted the official vehicles be used—flashing lights and all. If he agreed to that, they would agree to look the other way—as usual, the unspoken gentleman's agreement between the errant husband and his armed entourage. So, he grudgingly agreed—which spoke to the desire he felt for the young woman.

Mona Tybaum was always anxious when meeting the Vice President. Low profile and clandestine was out of the man's reach, as the second-in-command of the U.S. Everywhere he went it was long black cars, lights and sirens with Secret Service escort, squad cars and police motorcycles. It was very little different from the motorcades typically seen when the president comes to town.

On the same day Michael Gresham was meeting the GULP CEO, Mona was attempting a meet up with the VP. Their plan was for him to go the Georgetown Good Egg restaurant, be seated, get up and go to the bathroom, and then disappear on down the hallway and out the back door to where Mona would be waiting with her Subaru SUV. It was all going as planned until the VP pushed open the rear restaurant door and an alarm sounded. Someone was using a protected doorway. A sole security officer was first on the scene and just managed to see the Subaru speeding away down the alley with two figures in the front seat. The Secret Service officers behind him pushed him roughly aside and began shouting into their wrist mics for vehicles to be brought around to give chase.

But it was too late. By the time the motorcade squad cars came around the SUV was long gone. And no one had a description as the security officer alone had seen the receding vehicle, and he was not a car buff. Meaning he had no idea what make or model he was watching squeal off down the alley. Nor did he get a license number. "I don't think it had a license plate," he told the Service. They gave him pained expressions and moved away to begin searching by air and along surface streets driven randomly by a large force of Washington D.C. Police. As a Service lieutenant said to the men he commanded, "This could even be a kidnapping by a foreign power."

Which was horrifying even to consider.

They had lost the vice president in a small strip mall restaurant, and already the media was swooping in with their TV cameras and microphones, taking statements and descriptions from anyone who'd stop and talk to them. Finally, the president himself was notified, and he wanted to know who was in charge and whether Service had enough staff to locate his Number Two.

Inside the fleeing vehicle, the VP's hands were all over

Mona as she drove, rocketing around corners and shooting down back alleys. At last, they found a parking space at the far end of a root beer drive-in, and she parked but left it running for the heater. The loudspeaker demanded to know their orders, and she responded they'd like a burger, fries, and two chocolate malts. "Coming right up," was the reply. "Will this be cash or credit card?"

At just that moment, Mona felt his hand on her neck, and the vice president was pulling her face over to his. He landed several kisses on her mouth and ears and managed to slip one hand through the buttons on her silk shirt and began massaging her ample bosom. Mona moaned and put her head back. Her knees parted beneath the steering column and she shuddered when her lover slid his hand up between her legs and touched her panties.

Which was the exact moment the food arrived and the waitress on roller skates shouted and motioned to put down the window and pass a credit card out to her. Mona shook herself back to reality and fumbled through her purse, finding a card floating loose inside following that morning's purchase at a Starbucks where she had been hurried to exit the line and hadn't been able to put the card back in her wallet.

Neither the vice president nor Mona noticed the black Lincoln that had followed them to their location. It had been waiting at the far end of the alley when Mona had pulled in from the other end. It had waited and fallen in behind her when she came tearing out of the alley and squealed onto the street, making a screeching right turn almost on two wheels only. She was busy steering and accelerating; he was busy with his hands roaming her body hungrily, his lust blinding him to anything outside the Subaru.

Now the Lincoln nosed in behind them, having gone past and turned around and returned facing directly to the street. There was a reason for the maneuver. Which was this: he would be leaving in a hurry.

In a quick, fluid move, Rudy Geneseo came out of the Lincoln and came up behind the waitress, who was running Mona's credit card through her validator. No one saw him as he swung the large gun out of his inside coat pocket and thrust it forward, placing the muzzle just behind Mona's left ear. A second later her forehead and brain tissue was spattered across the windshield, the waitress had fainted, and the vice president was sitting with a line of blood across his expensive white shirt and crying unintelligibly, "Ahh! Ahh! Ahh!"

The gunshot was silenced, but there were witnesses.

Rudy casually returned to his vehicle, tossed the gun on the passenger seat, and lowered himself into the driver's seat. He carefully put the car in gear and rolled out to the sidewalk. Blinker flashing, he made a legal and careful right turn and melted away in the heavy traffic.

The vice president's door flew open, and the man staggered up against the car next to Mona's. He rapped his knuckles against the window glass and instructed the driver to dial 911. She did and handed him the phone. He gave instructions, reporting the homicide, and was told by the dispatcher to move away from the car, go inside the restaurant, and wait in the restroom until Secret Service came for him.

The vice president did exactly as he was told.

When the Service arrived they found him seated on the porcelain lip of the toilet, the ring up behind him pressing against his back. His trousers were down around his ankles, and he was weeping and shaking without letup.

The story made the news that night. The TV reporters had a world of questions but few answers.

They promised to update their viewers at ten o'clock once more was known.

That same night was hell night at the Tybaum residence. Jarrod was inconsolable, and his pain and weeping caught the notice of Annie, who reacted violently to her brother's emotions. She destroyed the dolls in her room, pulling arms and legs out of torsos and dumping the disarticulated limbs into the hallway toilet, which she repeatedly flushed until the water was leaking out into the hallway.

Police and Annie's psychiatrist came to the house. Gerald Tybaum's sister was flying in from Berkeley where she taught law at Boalt Hall. It was a long night for everyone; finally just after two a.m. Annie fell asleep and was carried by her psychiatrist into her room and settled on her trundle bed.

Tomorrow would be a long day, and so far there was no responsible adult in the house, not with Jarrod still in shock. A social worker arrived. A priest followed. Detective Ronald

Holt appeared and began putting together the pieces as to what had happened that day.

Tybaum's sister arrived at the house just before noon and very capably took charge.

Jarrod came out of his shock and began looking after Annie, who by the morning was her usual, detached, uninvolved self.

Ronald Holt called Michael Gresham, and they talked. Holt did as instructed by Gresham, calling the Naval Observatory and demanding an appointment with the vice president. The operator advised him the vice president wasn't seeing anyone.

"Bullshit," snarled Holt. "He'll see me, or I'll show up with a SWAT team and take his ass to jail."

The appointment was made shortly after.

But the appointment went by the wayside as Michael Gresham was suddenly unavailable.

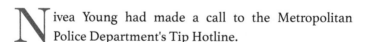

Nivea Young had made a call to the Metropolitan Police Department's Tip Hotline.

She gave them Gresham's hotel, room number, and location of the handgun. She said she was calling from a payphone. Why was she calling? Because he had jilted her and she wanted payback. He had bragged about killing Gerald Tybaum and had told her he was leaving the country and she couldn't go with him. After he had promised to take her along, he had gone back on his word. She was furious, she exclaimed before hanging up. She hung up the pay phone and yanked open the phone booth door. Only then did she remove the latex gloves, stuffing them into her pants pocket. She swiped the hairnet off her head and climbed into her truck.

She pulled her RAM half-ton out of the Texaco parking lot and accelerated eastbound, toward the river.

26

Special Agent Ames, Detective Holt, and I met in my office the day after Mona was murdered. We discussed what we knew about the vice president and Gerry Tybaum's death. And Mona. For openers, we knew that Gerald Tybaum's shooter was wearing the VP's belt buckle--or one exactly like it. Plus, the North Face coat, which wasn't determinative except to a minimal degree. And we knew the VP had a motive--Tybaum's affair with the vice president's wife was embarrassing and painful for Vengrow. But we agreed that Vengrow had had nothing to do with setting up Mona's murder, and this fact cleared him, in my mind, of any connection to Gerry Tybaum's case. Why? Because it would be a one-in-a-million occurrence for Vengrow to want Gerry dead and someone else to want Mona dead. It was much easier to accept that whoever wanted them dead was the same person.

I said, "Mona's death has changed everything. Four eyewitnesses saw what happened. The vice president is obviously in the clear. So we need a new suspect."

"Michael," Special Agent Ames said to me, "you're clearing the vice president on Gerald Tybaum's death too?"

"Of course," I said, 'unless he steps up and confesses to it. We're not going to theorize about two different shooters going after Gerry and then Mona. It's the same person. The FBI can clear Tybaum on this one. You can tell them you got that straight from the U.S. Attorney's Office."

"Will do."

I continued, "Now we need to start thinking about motive. I'm thinking of possible reasons why someone would want the senior Tybaum and his daughter dead."

"Plus, there's the question of the son and the younger daughter," added Holt. "They're at risk now too, at least in my book. I've got them under protection right now twenty-four/seven. Two officers are always on the premises."

"Good," I said. "Now here's something I've been looking to plug in. Two days before his murder, Gerry Tybaum visited me in Chicago. He had me sign a power of attorney that gave me authority over funds in a Russian bank account."

"What funds?"

"I believe they are PAC funds. The deposit is twelve-million dollars."

"I interviewed the CFO at GULP," said Agent Ames. "GULP is a PAC, and he didn't think Gerry Tybaum had any way of accessing their funds."

"I know," I said. "Now, there are lots of people who would want someone dead for that amount of money. And Gerry told me at the time that there were some very powerful, very evil people after him."

"Any names?" asked Ames. "Any clues at all who he might be talking about?"

"No."

"Did he have any theory about any missing money?"

"No. But if the money was PAC money, we start right there."

"Makes sense," both men agreed. "So. Who's the CEO?"

Ames opened his file and checked through his interviews.

"Man by the name of Paul Wexler," said Ames.

"Paul Wexler," I said, trying hard to remember. The name was very familiar. Then I remembered my meeting with Jarrod and Mona. They had both mentioned Paul Wexler. As I recalled, there was also bad blood between the two men. My suspicions went up. "Paul Wexler's name came up when I spoke with Jarrod and Mona. There were significant problems between Gerry and Wexler. The GULP CEO was a thorn in Gerry's side, according to his kids."

"What was that all about?" asked Ames.

"It sounded like Wexler had at one time been in bed with the oil and gas industry."

"Good grief. How did he wind up at GULP? Aren't they tree huggers?"

"Not entirely," I said. "I've been nosing around. There are competing interests inside GULP. Gerry headed up the environmentalists in the group; Wexler represented the interests of Big Oil. But Gerry had the upper hand because the PAC was the baby of all the environmental groups. That's where the 'save our home' money went for the protection of the planet. All of that. At one time there had been spin-offs into oil and gas, but for the last two elections it had all been about solar and hydroelectric."

"So, we've got two guys who are opposed in their energy positions. Does that translate into the murder of one by the other?" said Holt. "How does that work?"

"I think it at least opens a door we need to pass through," said Ames. "But I still fail to see why Tybaum would steal all that money from the PAC that funded his run for president."

I nodded. "I don't have that much trouble with it. There is authority to the effect that PAC money inures to the PAC's candidate. Gerry might have thought the money was his, earmarked for a run in 2020. So he pulled it out of the PAC for safekeeping overseas where Wexler couldn't get to it."

"Works for me," said Ames. "So what do we do with this?"

I said, "We start calling people before the grand jury and start getting stories pinned down. Then we put our heads together again and see where we are when we come up for air."

"Who's up first?" said Holt.

"Vice President Vengrow. Then Senator Stanley Jessup," I replied. "He deserves no less than to be one of the first in line."

"Agree," the two cops said in unison.

"I thought the vice president was cleared," Ames said at that point. "Why are you taking his testimony?"

"Because he was at the scene of his lover's murder. And it was reported he was at the scene of the father's murder. We need to dot the i's and cross the t's."

That afternoon, I gave my paralegal a list of folks to subpoena for the grand jury. Then I began drawing up lists for the documents portion of the subpoenas so the witnesses could bring documents too.

Somewhere in the midst of all this, I called my house just to check in.

Verona picked up my call on the second ring.

27

"Verona? Michael here. How's everyone?"

Her voice was immediately warm. "Everyone is great. The kids and I were talking about you over supper."

"Really? Are they getting along without having me around every night?"

"The FaceTime calls are helping."

"Good. I'll keep them up."

"Definitely. They're doing better than I am, Michael. I miss you. Are you in your hotel room?'

"I am. I'm going over some new files and getting ready for some motions tomorrow in court. It's never-ending, the files coming my way. I'm all but underwater already."

"How are you liking prosecuting?"

"I love it. It's very organized and very methodical. I didn't realize how much I enjoyed painting by the numbers. I mean we have an answer for everything in our DOJ manual.

Which greatly relieves pressure on us so we can prosecute and always know we're operating within DOJ guidelines. Venture outside of those, however, and you do so at your peril. Long story short: it fits me to be here. Now, how is your green card application coming along?"

A short pause, then, "It would be much easier if we were married. Now, wait, before you answer. I'm not saying this to get you to marry me, though I'd probably jump at the chance. I'm saying it because the steps are much easier if an alien like me is married to an American citizen. But it will be great to get the card and be able to work again."

"So you're still thinking of going back to teaching?"

"I am. My diplomas and post-graduate documentation are all gathered. I just need the damn card at this point."

"Listen, I've got a mess on my hands, and I'm going to have to cut this short."

"What's going on?"

"One of my victim's daughters was murdered. I'm on my way over to her house right now."

"Okay. Well...goodbye, then."

I could tell from her tone she was troubled. I said, "Well, I think we need to discuss--"

Just then there was a loud pounding on my hotel room door. I told Verona I had to answer, set the phone aside, and went to the door and pulled it open.

Only to be greeted by three uniformed officers and two men--armed with wallet badges--demanding entrance. I stood aside and told them to come right in. One of the street clothes cops took me aside as everyone else filed past us.

"You're an AUSA, correct?" he said to me.

"Yes."

"Please show me your ID."

I slipped my U.S. Attorney ID out of my pocket and opened the wallet. "Here we go. What is all this?"

"Search warrant."

He held out a single sheet of paper filled with writing and signed at the bottom with a fancy signature. I glanced over it and knew immediately that something had gone wrong in my life. It looked to be a valid search warrant, and I seemed to be on the wrong end of it. I stepped back and went over and hung up the phone without another word to Verona. The same cop followed me as I did this. Then I turned back to him.

"Okay, I'm an Assistant U.S. Attorney, and you can trust me with the story behind the search here. What gives?"

"Mr. Gresham, we've received an anonymous tip that there's a murder weapon hidden in this room."

"What? That's insane!"

Just then two of the uniforms removed the inside cover from my air conditioner. One of them swept his hand down inside, and I watched as he pulled out a gun wrapped in plastic.

"Who would hide a gun wrapped in plastic," I said to the plainclothes officer. I realized I was already making my argument to a judge. No one hides murder weapons wrapped up in plastic.

Unless he meant to keep it away from water. Which is a common event inside air conditioners as water condenses and is carried away by the drainage system. Water, in my air conditioner, a gun inside my air conditioner. Suddenly the plastic made a lot of sense.

The plainclothes officer nearest me told the uniform to leave the bag unopened and to put it inside an evidence bag. Then he turned back to me.

"We're going to need you to come down to the MPD and talk to us, Mr. Gresham. I'm guessing this can all be straightened out in an hour or two."

I sighed and began looking for my shoes.

Thirty minutes later, I was escorted from reserved parking into the MPD building on Indiana Avenue NW. Inside was a discolored tile floor and the standard tan walls and ancient windows of old buildings. I was steered along to an interview room consisting of a table and six chairs--three on each side--, and I was told to take a seat. I asked whether I needed an attorney and the plainclothes officer said he didn't think so.

For almost thirty minutes I cooled my heels, waiting for whatever. Then, much to my surprise, there came a friendly and familiar face: Ronald Holt walked in wearing jeans and a sweater. On his feet were running shoes. He looked like he had come here in a hurry without much thought to wearing the MPD detectives' suit-of-the-day. But it was great to see him, and I almost wanted to give him a hug.

"Michael," he said, taking the seat directly across from me. "I see you've been swept up in something here."

"Can you help me understand what the hell's going on Ron? Where did the gun come from in my room and--"

"Whoa up, Michael. Don't say too much until you hear what I've got to say. I don't want you inadvertently implicating yourself in something you're not a part of. Fair enough?"

"More than fair. Thanks. So, what gives?"

"Evidently the MPD received an anonymous call. From a woman. She told our front desk that they could find in your room, hidden inside the air conditioner, the gun used to murder Gerald Tybaum. So that's where we are with this."

"Good God! Has anyone examined the gun?"

"I have."

"Are there prints?"

"There are. Those have been lifted and fed into the database. Unfortunately, the gun has your prints all over it. Now, whether the gun was used to kill Mr. Tybaum remains to be seen. We won't know that until tomorrow when the examiners come in and do some studies."

I leaned back in my chair. I was stunned. This was happening way too fast, and I could find no handle any place to grab onto as it slid past me. "What kind of gun is it?'

"Smith nine-millimeter."

"That's what I own."

"With a Hydra-Shok load."

"That's what I use. Self-defense rounds. This is astonishing and upsetting beyond belief. Wait, does Antonia Xiang know about this yet?"

"Antonia has been called, and she's on her way here. She'll have answers for you. I hear she stands solidly behind her assistant attorneys."

"She does. I can't help but remember, she hired me, and now she can fire me, too. Something's terribly wrong here, Ron. Somebody has set me up."

"Well, you probably shouldn't say anything more to me right now. Why don't we wait until Antonia gets here and then maybe we can make a plan?"

"What kind of plan?"

"A plan to get you out of this. We all know you didn't kill Tybaum. But we've got a compelling piece of evidence in the gun, and we have to deal with it. There has to be some explanation here."

Holt went out in search of two coffees, and again I was alone in the interrogation room. The CCTV camera glowed red as it recorded my every move, my every breath. He wasn't gone five minutes until Antonia came rushing in, fit to be tied, an angry spark in her eyes.

"Michael! Someone is trying to frame you!"

"Exactly. But I have no idea who."

"Well, the first thing to do is figure out why. From 'why' we go work our way back to 'who.'"

"Okay."

"Why would anybody want you charged with the murder of Gerry Tybaum, Michael?"

"Because of the power of attorney. Someone doesn't want me around that money."

"Who would have an equal claim to the money, the FBI?"

I rubbed my hands together, considering what she was saying.

"No, I can't see the FBI in competition with me. I've talked to Agent Leders twice since I hired on with the U.S. Attorney and I've told him everything I know about the money."

"Is it still in Russia?"

"It is. The Russian bank wants the holder of the POA to show up in person to sign the account transfer paperwork. They say there's too much risk just to do it electronically. I don't blame them."

"So you've got to go to Russia. Or someone else is going to use this as an opening to install themselves as the proper entity to move the funds."

"How would they do that?"

She sat back and held her arms out expansively.

"Well, for example, if Tybaum's PAC decides to make a claim for the money it'd be nice to have you locked up and out of their way."

"I met with Vincent Tirley, the CEO of GULP, a few days ago. He didn't seem to me like the kind of guy who would try to frame someone. He was laid back, well-spoken, and seemed honest and fair."

"What else?"

"Two things. One, he told me the bank used by GULP is based in Boston, the Charter Bank and Mercantile of Boston. He indicated there might have been something fishy about them. Two, he brought up an alleged relationship between Gerry Tybaum and the vice president's wife. We've already viewed on CCTV some personal articles of clothing owned by Jon Vengrow and worn by the shooter on the video. But Ron and I aren't convinced the shooter was Vengrow. We were working from the assumption that the shooter was someone who wanted the police to think it was Vengrow."

"Misdirection."

"Yes. Oldest trick in the book."

She sat back and crossed her arms. She stared at the ceiling, lost in thought. I just waited while she put together whatever it was she was going to say.

Then she began. "I'm not clear on what to do with you, Michael. We all know you're being framed, but we also have this big red flag of the gun. We need to dispose of that issue before you can come back to work at the USA's Office."

"How do we do that?" I asked.

"There is the rub. I honestly don't know. But I believe I want to put Rusty and Holt together working on the whole thing. I believe they've got the tools to resolve this without much delay."

"So someone's keeping me away from investigating Tybaum's murder and the case of the twelve-million dollars just by planting a gun on me?"

She pursed her lips thoughtfully. "See, that's what I'm afraid of. It might not be just a gun. It might turn out to be the gun that shot Tybaum six times."

"A gun taken from my office desk in Chicago?"

"That's easy enough. Anyone can make that happen."

"So there's the gun, and there's the money."

"Michael, there's the POA and the huge pile of money in some Moscow bank. These things easily add up to motive. You had a motive for shooting Tybaum."

"You don't believe that?"

I could feel my grip on reality starting to slip away.

"Of course I don't believe it. But some other prosecutor might."

"Meaning what?"

"Meaning this matter will need to be assigned to an independent prosecutor for investigation. Someone outside the U.S. Attorney's office. An independent counsel."

"Son-of-a--"

"I know. It's unimaginable the uproar this is going to cause. The papers will be all over it by morning, I promise."

"Oh, my God."

"You're big news, Michael, as of about one hour ago. There's going to be very little I can do to help you."

"Oh, no. I'm on my own, then?"

"Pretty much. I have a conflict of interest just being here. So we'll keep this meeting on the down low. Nobody needs to know I was here talking to you."

"Agreed. You don't need the heat."

"I don't need to have some reporter question my conflict of interest in seeing you. Let's just leave that one alone."

"I agree. We'll keep the lid on it."

She stood up then and reached across the table.

"We won't talk again until this is resolved," she said firmly. Her eyes met mine as she spoke and fixed me there. "You won't be coming to work until then."

"I understand," I said. "Just one thing. Please don't terminate me until we get to the bottom of this. I can promise you I had nothing to do with Tybaum's death."

"I know that. Michael Gresham isn't a shooter."

"Thank you."

For another hour I sat alone in that interrogation room just letting it all roll through my mind. There was a missing puzzle piece that I could almost see, but then it dissolved over and over. I had to admit that at one time I had considered getting part of Gerry's money for myself, but that was more a flitting thought than even an idea. I just wasn't built that way; I could never cheat someone or someone's kids out of their money. If it even was their money. I realized I still knew nothing about the legality of GULPs money moving into Gerry's private bank account. If it were legal, then the money clearly could be passed on to his kids, and no one could object. But if Gerry had embezzled the money then all the powers of attorney in the world wouldn't make its transfer to the kids a legal act. Plus, if he had embezzled, then the rightful owner was GULP, and that was way outside of my role as power of attorney. One thing was becoming clearer to me: I had a conflict of interest between my official job as an Assistant U.S. Attorney and my unofficial job I had taken on of trying to get the money to Gerry's children. If the job required me to transfer embezzled funds, obviously I couldn't do that. And just the possibility that was the case was enough to make me jettison my unofficial job. I needed out from under its burden, and I needed out like yesterday. On the other hand, if I didn't at least take a run at moving the funds over to the kids' bank account when the money was legally Gerry's then I was letting the kids and Gerry down.

My mind was playing these forces against each other over and over until finally, around ten o'clock, I was visited by a jailer who said I could leave.

"Leave?" I asked. "As in leave the jail? Go home?"

"That's right."

"Someone decided I shouldn't be held?"

"That's right."

"Who would do that?"

He shrugged. "All I know is there was some excitement here about an hour ago. Someone at the front desk took a call from the White House. Someone on Pennsylvania Avenue said to turn you loose."

"Are you serious? What the hell?"

The jailer shrugged. "Follow me, and I'll lead you back up front to the exit.

And so I did until I found myself suddenly outside, standing on Indiana Avenue in the miserable cold without a clue in the world what was going on in my life and without knowing how to make it stop.

But someone knew. Someone over at the White House.

It was time for me to obtain the VP's testimony by the grand jury--that is if I still had my job.

Back at the hotel I called Antonia and told her what happened.

"Funny," she said, "I got a call from the U.S. Attorney herself. She said you're to be allowed to return to work tomorrow. No explanation, just get back to work."

I was stunned. Criminal cases don't just end like that.

Maybe the vice president could enlighten me.

Tomorrow I would impanel my grand jury and subpoena him to testify. It wasn't just about solving Gerry's murder anymore.

Now it was about saving my own life, too.

28

W e had no clue who the shooter was. Mona's death was being investigated by MPD, but so far there were no leads. Except Holt and I had agreed with Special Agent Ames that as a working theory the man who gunned down the father also gunned down the daughter. We also had a motive: with the daughter and the other kids out of the way the Russia money was up for grabs. Maybe GULP even had a claim since it might be able to show embezzlement. GULP's involvement seemed more and more likely because of Mona's death.

Holt told me all about what he'd seen at the Tybaum's temp house the night Mona died. I resolved to go there and see Jarrod and Annie without further delay. So I drove my rental car out to Bethesda while Holt followed in his SUV.

Jarrod was very distant when he let me inside the house. Annie was nowhere to be seen.

"You know I hold you responsible for Mona's death," he said

to me. Which did and didn't startle me. He had never fully trusted me--or my methods.

"You think I missed something and she died because of my negligence?"

"That's right, Mr. Gresham. Why wasn't anyone following her when she picked up the vice president? Where the hell were the cops?"

"I've talked to the uniforms. It seems Mona gave them the slip at her work, made off without being seen, and rented the Subaru. She lost them. It happens. But I had nothing to do with that. I'm not the reason your sister's dead, Jarrod. She's dead because sometimes bad things happen. Some-times the police get fooled, and a terrible thing happens like Mona dying. But I can apologize to you and Annie. I'm sorry."

He looked back at me, the first time he'd actually acknowl-edged me since letting me inside. "I've been wanting to kill you for letting my sister die, you know?"

"Doesn't surprise me. But here's the thing. I need you to try to put that on the back burner for now. I need you to work with me so I can move you and Annie again. There's no guarantee Mona's murderer doesn't know where you live now. If he does, you and Annie are next on his list. And I can guarantee you now, there is a list."

"I realize that too. So how do we protect what's left of the Tybaum family?"

"We move you again and double the watch this time. Plus, your van isn't a vehicle you're going to leave us behind with. It's big and white and very slow. Plus, it's hand-operated so it's not like you can dodge us and go rent another and keep going."

"Why would I be trying to lose you?"

"I'm speaking hypothetically. For example, consider a situation where you decide to go after your sister's killer by yourself. That won't happen--will it?"

"Look at me. I don't have the ability to kill anyone. Plus, I don't want to. It's more important than ever, now, for me to be there for Annie."

"Agree. Where is Annie, by the way?"

"Out back making snow angels, last I saw."

"Can I go say hello?"

"Sure."

I went through the kitchen and out the back door. Sure enough, Annie was sitting on a swing, idly dragging her foot through the snow as she slowly went up and back without trying to get it going really. She was staring at the ground and singing as I approached.

"Hello, Annie."

"Michael," she said without looking up. I was stunned. I hadn't known she communicated. I wanted to run inside and share the incredible news with Jarrod, but I didn't. I tried another sentence with her instead.

"How are you, Annie?"

"Michael."

"Can you look at me?"

No response.

"I'm so glad to see you, Annie. You're my friend, you know?"

No answer.

"Well, I just wanted to make sure you are okay. I'm going back inside your house, all right?"

Silence.

So I left her there swinging up and back, up and back.

"Jarrod! She said my name!"

"Who said your name?" Jarrod asked from beside the coffee table where he was parked.

"Annie said my name!"

"She does that sometimes. Sometimes she'll even say a complete sentence. Maybe two."

"I had no idea. I'm in shock."

"I can see that, Mr. Gresham."

"I just love that little sister of yours, Jarrod. She's so vulnerable I want to wrap her in my arms and take care of her."

"She wouldn't like that. She can't stand to be restrained."

Ever the literalist, Jarrod missed my point.

Which had me thinking I didn't have a point to begin with. Sometimes she spoke, even saying a full sentence or even two. So I calmed myself down and thought about moving the siblings.

"I'll find a place on Zillow, get it rented, and get you moved today, Jarrod."

"All right. Make sure I can smoke inside, okay?"

"You've taken up smoking?"

"Yes. Why, you think it might make my cerebral palsy worse?"

"No, I'm just--just--"

"Just make sure I can smoke there."

"I'll make sure. Okay, I'm leaving now."

Holt had been waiting outside in his SUV, watching the cars that came and went on the street. There was another police presence there, too. Even a cop stationed around back in the alley watching Annie and watching the back door.

"How'd it go?" Holt asked as I climbed into his vehicle.

"Annie said my name. Twice."

"Yes, I heard her say something the other night. Something about her sister."

"You've heard her talk?"

"She said something like 'Michael Gresham is here!' Why?"

"Nothing, I guess. Forget it."

"Where to, boss?"

"Back to the office."

But she knew me and knew my name.

That much had been established.

29

As it turned out I was free to continue with the Tybaum investigation regardless of the murder weapon being my own gun. Forensics confirmed it was my gun that had killed Gerry Tybaum. I was in a precarious position, subject to much investigation and maybe even prosecution over Tybaum's murder. But after the call came from the White House I was mysteriously reinstated and no more was said about the gun. I was bewildered by the whole process and several times felt an urge to make some calls to people higher up the info chain than me. But I fought down the urge and instead decided just to move ahead with my work and accept it was a gift. A gift of some sort and I wasn't going to be privy to its source.

We got Jarrod and Annie moved to another house in Bethesda barely a mile away from the first house. The police presence was beefed up, leaving me feeling much better. Then it was time to proceed with the grand jury investigating the father's death.

A little background. The grand jury's principal function is to determine whether or not there is probable cause to believe that one or more persons committed a certain Federal offense within the venue of the district court. Thus, it has been said that a grand jury has but two functions--to indict or, in the alternative, to return a "no-bill."

This was my first-ever time with appearing before a grand jury as the prosecutor. I've defended upwards of a thousand clients who had been indicted by grand juries but now I was on the other side of the street. Now I was in the know.

I realized that an instrument of great power had been placed in my hands. I now had the power to investigate every last detail about Tybaum's death by placing anyone anywhere under oath and asking them questions in a grand jury session. The power elicited in me a great feeling of responsibility. Never would I abuse this incredible tool by bringing false evidence against any person of interest. My promise to myself and to the public at large.

After my grand jury's enrollment and swearing in at the Main Courthouse, they gathered at the U.S. Attorneys' Office (USAO) located on 4th Street, N.W. for the remainder of their service.

We met in one of the grand jury rooms, I made a short statement about the case and about their duties, and it was time to call my first witness. I sent Detective Holt into the outer room to see whether Vice President Vengrow had obeyed our subpoena and was waiting to testify. Turns out he had and he was, so I called him into the room with me and the grand jury. He was sworn and took a seat.

I had decided to go ahead and bring the vice president before my grand jury for two reasons. One, I wanted to find out as much as I could about his relationship with Mona. Two, he had refused to speak with Detective Holt when Holt asked for a few minutes alone with the VP to ask some of my same questions. That left me no choice but to do it the hard way, in front of the grand jury.

Vice President Vengrow was an imposing man of large bulk and a walk that reminded me of John Wayne's sideways swagger. His face was impassive and his eyes darted around the room once he was seated and had adjusted his necktie. He looked over at the grand jury, nodded and gave a slight smile, then looked back at me. The jury looked impressed. I know I was. Here sat the second most powerful man in the world who was submitting his power to my power just because that's the way it works.

"Good morning," I said, and the court reporter's machine began soundlessly taking it all down.

"Morning," said the VP.

"Please tell us your name for the record."

"Jonathan Y. Vengrow."

"What is your occupation--for the record."

"I'm the vice president of the United States of America."

"Directing your attention to January 15 of this year, were you vice president on that day?"

"I was."

"We're here about a shooting that occurred on that day, Mr. Vice President. Actually, as best we can tell so far, the shooting occurred around four or five that afternoon. Do you remember where you were that day at that time?"

"Not really. I know that that night I was watching *Homeland* on cable TV. I was in the rear of our living quarters in my bedroom at the Naval Observatory."

"Was anyone with you then and there?"

"No, sir."

"Are you married, Mr. Vice President?"

"Yes, my wife's name is Indio. But she wasn't with me while I watched my show."

"Where was Mrs. Vengrow?"

"She was off visiting her sick mother."

"Was anyone else with you that afternoon or evening?"

"No, it was one of those rare days when I had some time to myself. Nothing on the calendar so I could do whatever I wanted. I'm hooked on *Homeland* so I dialed it in. I watched while I worked on my stamp collection."

"Do you recall what time you started watching your show?"

"I don't recall. But I'm sure the cable TV people can help you with the time."

"Sure, sure."

At just that moment, I felt some of the awe at my role and its importance fall away and I realized I was settling into my job and using all my skills to get the VP's story out in front of the grand jury. It felt like I had trained all my life for this job. I had amassed the tools to do it not only well but exceedingly well. My day brightened at that exact moment and I lost my fear.

"Approximately three hours before your show started on TV, a man by the name of Gerald Tybaum was shot to death near the Lincoln Memorial. Do you recognize his name?"

"Sure. Gerry Tybaum was a friend. He was also a candidate for President of the United States put forth by the Climate Party."

"So you're aware of his murder?"

"Of course. Everyone is. Terrible thing. So that's why we're here? I was wondering."

"Do you own a gun, Mr. Vice President?"

Vengrow sat back in his chair. The fingers of his right hand drummed on the small desk in front of him. It was clear he was thinking and my guess was that the question surprised him as well. Truth be told, I had no reason to ask about the gun that killed Gerry Tybaum. It had already been established that it was my gun. But these questions were for future reference. Call it a hunch--when I'm in cross-examination I follow all hunches. It has proven a valuable instinct time and the again.

"How is my gun relevant, Mr. Gresham?"

"Please just answer the question, sir, and leave the relevance to me."

"Yes, I own a gun. It's the same gun I carried in the First Gulf War."

"What caliber is that gun?"

"Nine millimeter."

"If I told you Gerry Tybaum was shot six times by a nine millimeter on January fifteenth would that surprise you?"

"No, no surprise. But it wasn't my gun. I'm happy to make it available for testing at any time or place."

"Thank you for that."

"Sure. No problem because that gun didn't shoot Mr. Tybaum. In fact, it has never shot anyone."

"Fair enough. I'll send someone by your office later today for it."

"It'll be ready, Mr. Gresham."

"Have you been in possession of any other nine-millimeter guns the last three months?"

"No. Of course not. I'm surrounded by Secret Service day and night. No need for handguns on my part."

"Now I'd like to talk about a particular item of clothing. I'm talking about a belt buckle. The belt buckle I want to talk about is silver and about the size of a buckle the rodeo cowboys might wear. On the face it says 'Effingham 2010.' Below those words there is a crucifix, a cross with a figure hanging from it."

"Yes, I have a belt buckle like that. It was presented to me by the Christian Cowboys' Association. I don't wear it all that often, but it's a favorite of mine."

"So my description of the buckle is accurate?"

"Yes, exactly."

"Were you wearing that buckle on January 15 this year?"

"That would be the day Gerry Tybaum was murdered?"

"Yes, sir."

"No, I wasn't wearing that belt that day. I wear it more like for picnics and cookouts and that sort of thing where I'm wearing jeans and maybe making a speech, Fourth of July and fundraisers stuff."

"Will you bring that buckle by my office and leave it for us to examine?"

"Certainly I will." He smiled at me, which I ignored.

"Do you own a North Face coat?"

"I think I do. Yes, a goose-down coat that's very warm in the winter."

"Were you wearing that coat on January fifteenth?"

"Oh, I really can't say. You've got me on that one, counsellor."

"Would you make that coat available at the same time we come by for the gun?"

"Sure."

"It hasn't been cleaned recently?"

"No."

"Good. Please don't clean it between now and when we pick it up."

It was a long shot, the coat, but I wasn't willing to leave any stone unturned. It might turn out there was blood on the coat; hell, even without blood, if the two men struggled it might even have Tybaum's DNA on it. I would track down every possible item of evidence. You just never know.

"Now, Mr. Vice President, I need to go into a series of questions that are personal. I wouldn't be asking them at all and I'm not asking them to embarrass you but there's talk on the street, as they say."

The vice president spread his hands and shrugged. "Ask away, counsellor."

"Let me just get right to it. Was your wife having an affair with Gerald Tybaum?"

"Yes."

"You knew about it?"

"Yes, I did."

"And how did that make you feel?"

"It didn't make me feel anything. Indio--my wife--and I haven't been in love for a long, long time. She basically goes her way and I go mine. All I've ever asked of her is that she not embarrass me or cost me votes," he said, smiling at the "votes" comment.

"Did it anger you that she was seeing Mr. Tybaum?"

"No. Did you not understand what I just told you? We weren't emotionally invested in the marriage any longer."

"I appreciate that," I said. "On the other hand, were or are you having an affair? In particular, I'm wondering whether you were having an affair with Mr. Tybaum's wife."

"Not with his wife, no."

"You're qualifying your answer. Were you having an affair with any member of his family?"

"Yes. His daughter."

"What's her name?"

"Mona Tybaum."

"How long have you been involved with Mona?"

"She was murdered counselor. I'm sure you know that. So what does my relationship with her have to do with anything now?"

"Just answer, please."

He drew away from the microphone then. "Counselor, what does this have to do with the death of her father?"

"Please just answer my question, Mr. Vice President."

"Please repeat it, then."

"How long had you been involved with Mona?"

"A few years. We met at a political fundraiser in 2011. She was a precinct worker and I was the junior senator from Illinois."

"Where did this take place?"

"Where? In southern Illinois. Edwardsville, actually."

"Tell us what happened?"

"Counselor, I think I'm going to draw the line right here. What happened between Ms. Tybaum and me over five years ago just isn't relevant to this case. I used to be a prosecutor myself and I know a little bit about relevance. I won't answer the question."

"You realize I could hold you in contempt for not answering if the judge orders you to answer?"

"I'm willing to take my chances."

"Was Gerald Tybaum, Mona's father, at that fundraiser five years ago in Edwardsville?"

"Well, he was, actually. I'd forgotten that."

"And was your wife there?"

"Yes, she always stood on the dais with me. The money shot--me and later with President Sinclair and our wives."

"Did your wife happen to speak to Mr. Tybaum that night--if you know?"

"Yes, she did."

"What happened between you, your wife and Mr. Tybaum that same night?"

"Well, she didn't come back to the hotel room all night long. The Secret Service was following her because I was a candidate for VP. I managed to make them come clean. She spent the night with Gerald Tybaum in his hotel room."

"Was this during the time period you've described where neither you nor your wife cared what happened romantically with each other?"

"No, it wasn't. But that would take place not long after."

"Tell us about that."

"Her overnight tryst with Tybaum was the spark that burned our marriage to the ground. Things were never the same between us after that night."

"Do you blame Tybaum for destroying your marriage?"

"Hmmm. That's hard to say. I really don't remember if I blamed him or not."

"Did you blame him on the night he was gunned down at the Lincoln Memorial?"

"No, I don't remember that being a part of my thinking any longer."

"Mr. Vice President, did you shoot and kill Gerald Tybaum?"

He shifted uneasily in his seat. "No. But neither did I frown on it. I thought and still think it served him right."

"So there's anger there?"

"I'd call it resentment, Mr. Gresham. I resented the guy. But not enough to shoot him. He was a nobody and I was and am Vice President of the United States. We don't even exist in the same universe."

"Were you still seeing Mona Tybaum?"

"I was there when she died. You should already know that."

"What I know isn't what the grand jury knows. Bear with me while we get the story out to them."

"Sorry."

"You were still sleeping with her?"

He lifted his eyes from me and quickly surveyed the room.

"Is this confidential? It's supposed to be. Has the jury been admonished and sworn to secrecy?"

"If you were a prosecutor you know they have been, sir."

"Then I'll confess that Mona and I were heavily involved. We saw each other face-to-face at least every week. Sometimes more."

"Are you aware that Mr. Tybaum died having over twelve-million dollars in a Russian bank?"

"Not aware, no."

"Are you aware that he wanted that money to go to his children, Mona and Jarrod and Annie?"

"Like I said, I wasn't aware of the money at all."

"So you haven't been pulling strings to help her get that money into her own account?"

"Good grief, no. I can't have dealings with anything Russian, Mr. Gresham."

"One last question, Mr. Vice President, then we can open it up to questions from the grand jurors."

"Fine."

"Have you had anything to do with my job at the U.S. Attorney's Office?"

"I'm afraid I don't understand."

"Have you made any calls to anyone about me?"

"Not at all. Oh, wait. I did call the U.S. Attorney herself and ask about you when I received the subpoena."

"Did you say anything about my working there? Or about my continuing to work there?"

"No. I'm sure I did not."

"All right. We're going to take a break now while I collect any questions from the grand jurors that they want me to ask. We'll stand in recess for ten minutes. All grand jurors please bring your questions to me now."

Several jurors presented me with written questions. More than half of the jurors headed for the restrooms. Some just remained in their seats, writing or staring at the floor. Cell phones and laptops and tablets had been collected so there were no recording or photographic devices in the room. Which meant that no one could check their email or send a text. Alas.

Ten minutes later, the grand jury clerk told me everyone had returned and was seated as before. I was good to go.

I read the first grand juror question to the witness:

"Mr. Vice President, have you ever been convicted of a crime?"

"No, I have not. That's random."

"Next question. Do you and your wife have any children?"

"No, she was unable to have children."

"Next question. Are you going to run for president when Sinclair's term is up? I'm not sure that's relevant but let's have you answer anyway."

"I have no plans to run. I think this is it for me."

Sure, I thought, a man one step away from the presidency is

going to just turn his back on taking that role for himself? What politician would ever do that?

"Next question. Did you ever get Mona pregnant?"

"No. I'm sterile."

Silence in the room. Startled looks on just about every face there.

"I'll follow up on that with one of my own," I said. "Did your wife know about your affair?"

"Oh, yes. Mona stayed over with me when we could arrange it. This didn't happen all that often."

Again, full-on silence. This was good stuff they were getting to hear. But if any of it turned up in the papers heads would roll. I'd make sure of that.

"Mr. Vice President, those are all the questions. Do you have any further testimony you'd like to offer?"

"No, I've said it all. Just please admonish the jury."

He meant I should remind them that we'd met in secret and absolutely none of what they heard could ever be repeated out of the grand jury room. I went on to add that if any of it was leaked I would hunt down and prosecute the responsible party. I did this nicely, not as a threat but as commentary on my role there.

Then we were finished for the day.

30

J arrod called me that night. Annie wanted to see me, he said.

"What would she want with me?" I asked, curious but pleased.

"She wants you to take her somewhere."

"Why don't you do it, Jarrod?"

"I no longer have a driver's license, Michael. Besides, she specifically said she wanted you."

"Can I come by tomorrow around noon?" It was a light court day, and I could spare an hour or two with Annie. Most definitely.

"That would be perfect. I'll tell her you're coming."

"So she's talking to you about all this?'

"Not exactly. She has it set up like a game show. She says, 'Who do you think Annie wants to see?' and then I have to guess who. Your name was my second guess."

"Who was first?"

"Doesn't that go without saying? Mona, of course."

"Of course. Okay, Jarrod, tomorrow noon-ish it is."

"See you then. And thanks."

The next day, I rolled into the kids' driveway at half past noon. I parked, got out and looked both ways for five minutes, just making sure I wasn't followed. Then I went inside.

"Annie!" I said when she came to the door. "Were you waiting for me?"

"Take me to the Smithsonian, Michael. There's an exhibit for me."

"What is it?"

"*Divine Felines: Cats of Ancient Egypt.*"

"Annie, do you have a cat?" Of course she did; I was asking to gauge her response.

She only looked at me. I realized the construct of her actually having a cat was something she didn't or couldn't consider. I didn't ask about it again.

I told Jarrod we'd be back in a couple of hours and then walked Annie out to my car. She climbed into the passenger's seat and pulled the seat belt into place. She snapped and smiled. Something about that simple act had caused her some small happiness. I'd never know what it was. Neither would anyone else.

When we arrived at the museum, we parked and went inside, got directed to the cat exhibit, and stopped at the

entrance to the exhibit to read the placard. I read it aloud
to Annie:

Cats' personalities have made them Internet stars today. In
ancient Egypt, cats were associated with divinities, as
revealed in "Divine Felines: Cats of Ancient Egypt." Cat
coffins and representations of the cat-headed goddess Bastet
are among the extraordinary objects that reveal felines' critical role in ancient Egyptian religious, social and political
life. Dating from the Middle Kingdom to the Byzantine
period, the nearly 70 works include statues, amulets, and
other luxury items decorated with feline features, which
enjoyed special status among Egyptians. The exhibition,
organized by the Brooklyn Museum of Art, also dedicates a
small section to cats' canine counterparts.

I finished reading, and Annie took my hand. "Cats, Michael,"
she said. "Now, Michael."

And so we began our sojourn around the exhibit. Annie
carefully stood before each of the seventy separate works in
the exhibit and studied the item. She was memorizing what
she was seeing. When we had turned the last corner and
surveyed the last cats, she tugged at me to move out of the
traffic flow where we could talk.

Against the north wall, she paused and said, "The man who
killed my father had a cat."

"What?"

"They brought his clothes to our house. I examined them.
He had cat hairs on the back of his shirt."

"You're sure of that?'

"It was a match with the hairs on the video. The cat was orange."

"Isn't that a tabby?" I asked, exhausting my knowledge of the subject.

"It could be."

"Your father might have struggled with the man who killed him. Maybe there was a transfer of hair."

"Most definitely. The crime lab needs to look at the shirt again."

"I'll make sure they do."

"It's only right," she said. "So far they've missed it."

"Okay. Hey, I want you to look at something. I pulled out my cell phone and played the cat-reflecting-pool video from the night her father was killed. But I only showed her the cat portion. Then I replayed it three or four times. Then in slow motion. "What's this look like to you?"

"A yellow tabby cat."

"Tabby is its breed?"

"Tabby isn't a breed. It's a type of marking, including spots and stripes."

"Anything else?"

"No. But I'd remember that footage if I were you. You're going to find it important one day."

"What else do I need to look out for?'

She ignored the question. "I read the police reports online."

I didn't bother to ask how she'd come to access the police reports online. Maybe they were posted now; I honestly didn't know.

"I'll take the shirt with me when I drop you off today," I said.

"Oh, they took it back to the evidence room after they let me examine it."

"Why would they let you examine it?"

"Because I called the police chief and said I wanted to look at something on the shirt that might help them. It will."

"So what happens now? Does the crime lab take a second look at the shirt? Did they tell you?"

"They didn't say, Michael. But the crime lab has been remiss, please force them to study the hair and fiber."

I couldn't believe what I was hearing about her grasp of police crime lab inquiries. But there you were; hair and fiber--she had it down.

"I'll make them take a second look."

"Thank you."

I turned to say goodbye when I stepped out onto the front porch.

But she had already closed the door, and I was left standing there amazed with her. Where does this gift come from? I asked myself. I sighed and clumped out through the snow to my car.

Out of the mouths of children.

31

The senator had responded to the grand jury subpoena. He appeared promptly at nine o'clock the morning after my trip to the Smithsonian with Annie. I called his name for the court reporter to take down and Holt went into the waiting room to retrieve him to come testify.

Senator Stanley J. Jessup showed up wearing a box gray suit with a yellow tie and oxblood loafers with tassels that bounced as he walked across the room. He smiled at everyone in the place, including me. He was forever seeking votes and always would be, you could just tell. His smile was worth at least thirty-thousand dollars in the dentist's chair, his hair was haphazardly piled on top of his head, and he smiled broadly when he raised his right hand and was sworn by the clerk. He didn't look like the kind of man who would want to perform sex acts with a hooker in broad daylight on the steps of the Lincoln Memorial, but do such people ever look the part? I was always surprised when the next normal-looking person came along with yet another bizarre sex accusation causing a file to be prepared by my office and a prosecution undertaken by me.

Oh well.

He sat down in the hot seat, ran the palm of his right hand across the small desktop in front of him, cleaning it, and smiled winningly at the grand jury yet again. He refused to look at me, which was common among grand jury witnesses. Prosecutors scare the bejesus out of people--especially the guilty people.

Without getting up from the table, I launched into my inquiry, having him first give us his name and employment for the record. Then it began in earnest.

"Directing your attention to January 15 of this year. Did you have occasion on that date to be in the vicinity of the Lincoln Memorial in Washington, DC?"

"Yes."

"Please tell us your location."

"I was looking around the Lincoln Memorial."

"As you were looking around, as you put it, did you hear one or more gunshots?"

"At first I thought it was a car backfiring. But then I looked over and saw a man with a gun. Another man had fallen into the Reflecting Pool. I didn't actually see anyone getting shot."

"Were you with someone else at that time and place?"

"Yes."

"Give us her name, please."

"I don't know her name. Never got it."

"What were you and Miss No-Name doing?"

"We were having a kiss."

"Now, are you married, Senator?"

"I am."

"Were you married on January 15?"

"I was."

"Was the woman you were kissing your wife?"

"No, she wasn't."

"In fact, she was a prostitute, was she not?"

Just then his face turned red and he stared up at the ceiling. "Can we take a break? I want to speak to my lawyer."

We took a ten-minute break and the senator ducked into the hallway to meet with his mouthpiece. He returned within minutes and, when the jury was seated again, I started back into my questions.

"She was a prostitute, was she not? I believe that was my last question before the break, Senator."

"Yes. Yes, she was a prostitute. But I'm going to ask you to admonish the jury, counselor, that not a word of what is said in here gets repeated outside this courtroom."

"They know that, Senator. Thank you. Describe what you were doing with Miss No-Name when you heard the first shot. Or the first backfire, as you put it."

"I was engaged in a sex act with the woman."

"Halfway up the steps of the Lincoln Memorial?"

"About halfway up, yes."

"Please describe the sex act."

"Fellatio. She was fellating me."

"She had your penis in her mouth?"

"Yes."

"On the steps of the Lincoln Memorial?"

"Yes. I'm a Democrat."

My mind raced. What in the world did being a Democrat have to do--then I got it. Lincoln was a Republican. The Lincoln Memorial was not sacrosanct to Senator Jessup like it might be to Senators McCain or Graham or other Republicans.

"So you had no compunction about having sex on Honest Abe's memorial?"

"None whatsoever."

"Did you see the man with the gun well enough to identify him?"

He knew what my next question and my next would be, so he didn't play hide-the-ball. He just laid it all out.

"Jonathan Vengrow. The vice president of the United States."

"You thought it was the vice president who had just shot the man in the pool?"

"Like I said, I didn't see the actual shooting. But I did see the vice president holding the gun."

"How was he dressed?"

"I don't recall."

"What was he doing when you looked over?"

"He shot the gun into the pool several more times."

"How many more times?"

"I don't know. Maybe five. Six?"

"Have you told this to anybody before, that you saw the shots at the man in the pool?"

"No, I didn't. I was afraid to say because I didn't want my name in the paper. If word got out that I was there with a prostitute and that she was fellating me, there wouldn't be any more re-elections for me. My career would be over, kaput."

"Have you seen the vice president since that night?"

"Since that evening? Yes, he addressed the senate on the health care amendments last week. I saw him then."

"Did you speak to him?"

"No. I mean I might've said 'Hello, Jon,' something like that."

"First names, you and the VP?"

"Yes. We served in the Senate together at one point."

"Senator Jessup, what else can you tell me about that night?"

"After it was over I ran to my car. I didn't even know I could still run."

"Where did you go?"

"To my Georgetown townhouse."

"Have you discussed this matter with anyone else?"

"Detective Ronald Holt, Metro PD."

"Anyone else?"

"No. Well, there was one."

"Who would that have been?"

He looked skyward again. Then, ever so softly, "Miss No-Name."

"You've been with the prostitute since that night?"

"Yes."

"And you discussed what you saw that night?"

"Yes."

"You've paid her for sex again?"

"There's no payment now. We've progressed beyond that. We care deeply for one another."

"Senator, I think that's all the questions I have."

"Good."

He started to rise up. Then I said, "Please remain seated, Senator. The jurors might have questions."

For the first time since he took the stand, I looked over at the jury. Some were angry, some were astonished, some were stunned. Not one of them had on their normal face at that moment.

"Questions, jurors?"

"I have a question," said a woman in the front row wearing a knit houndstooth suit. "How do you sleep with yourself?"

At which point one of our stalwart grand jurors, always ready with a comment, said, "Didn't you hear him? He doesn't sleep with himself. He sleeps with Miss No-Name."

Laughter erupted and I finally dismissed Senator Jessup with the right to recall. He was finished and he all but limped from the room, bruised, broken, and defeated.

We then recessed.

Justice had been served that day.

And I had no stomach for anymore of it.

32

Annie attended a special school for special kids. While she left home every day and went out in public, she was entirely safe. She was safe because no one knew what she looked like and no one knew what school she attended. She called me Friday night after I'd returned to my hotel the day of Jessup's grand jury appearance.

"I have to go to my school play" she stated. "Jarrod doesn't drive. Can you drive me?"

"Sure," I said, "when is it?"

"Tomorrow night."

"What time should I come for you?"

"Six o'clock. I'm in charge of the lights. I need to get there early and get set up."

"See you then, Annie."

I puttered around on Saturday and almost forgot about Annie

once I began reviewing lab reports and ancillary police reports on the murders of Gerry and Mona. In fact, the forensic report from Gerry's shirt was back. Annie had been right.

Driving to the school, I mentioned it to her.

"You were right about your dad's shirt, Annie. It did have cat hair. How it survived the Reflecting Pool is anyone's guess. Probably came from the back of the shirt and maybe that never went under water though it did freeze. I don't really know. But it's cat hair."

"I know it. I saw it under my microscope."

"You have a microscope?"

"You've never been in my bedroom, Michael. I forgot that. I have a whole science lab."

"Well, you didn't have a cat when your dad was still alive."

"So we're looking for someone with a cat," she said, finishing my thought. "Or, if you want to parse it out even more finely, we're looking for someone who has been in the presence of a yellow cat. Maybe the killer picked the hair up in someone else's house."

"Or maybe your dad picked up a cat somewhere and got the hair on him."

"Wouldn't happen. Dad's allergic to cats. That's why I don't have one or two. Or three."

"So the killer either had a cat or held someone else's cat."

"That's a fair way to say it," she said. "What else do we know?"

"We don't know anything else. I know more stuff, but I'm not allowed to share it with you."

"How about you feed me hypotheticals, then?" she asked. "Then I can respond."

"Hypothetically speaking, what would you think about a GoPro camera found at the scene?"

"I'd think your killer was riding a motorcycle and forgot the camera was mounted on his helmet and it fell off somehow. That's a no-brainer, Michael. I'm sure you had that."

"I didn't. But I'm making serious mental notes here."

"What else?" she asked.

"What would you think if that camera contained four or five seconds of cat video?"

"I'd say you have your man. Cat, cat hair, video, motorcycle-- these are solid clues for you, Michael. And I'll tell you something else."

"Shoot."

"Your killer is the vice president of the United States."

My heart almost stopped. "What!" I exclaimed.

"He rides a motorcycle--check out his web page. And his wife loves cats. There's your suspect, Michael."

"There must be a million men who ride a motorcycle and have a cat in the United States. I don't get how you narrowed it down."

"Listen to your words, Michael. You said, 'In the United States.' This isn't the United States we're talking about. This is Washington, DC. Several other men might fit that description in our little town, but there's one more piece of the profile I haven't told you about."

"For heaven's sake, what?"

"Mona spent the night with the vice president. So there's your connection between the VP and my family."

"Whoa, whoa, whoa. How do you know that about Mona?"

"I have my ways."

"Spill the beans, Annie. I need this."

"All right. It's so simple. When she went out on dates, I would follow her cell phone with her GPS. On more than one night she spent all night at the Naval Observatory."

"The vice president's home."

"Bingo! Now you have your man, Michael."

"How do you track her cell phone?"

"That's easy. There's a setting, a switch, inside a cell phone that has to be thrown. Then there's an app I use to follow her. She never knew."

"Were you spying on your sister?"

"Just looking out for her, that's all."

"So you're saying your father and your sister were both murdered by the vice president?"

"Yes."

"But why?"

"What's his motive? That's one I'm going to leave for you to decipher, Michael. Isn't that what they're paying you for?"

"Don't get smart, miss."

She laughed. "Okay."

We reached the school and pulled around behind the auditorium.

Ninety minutes later we were on our way to Annie's house. She lapsed into her customary silence and didn't say two words on the drive home.

But there was no need. She'd already said enough.

I had a new suspect, but we had no motive.

I'm a quick study. Motive was up to me.

33

M axwell Atkins sold pharmaceuticals and cheated on his wife.

That's what I knew about him the morning of his appearance before my grand jury.

Detective Holt escorted the frightened man into the grand jury room, placed him before the clerk, who swore him in, then arranged him in the witness chair.

Atkins was a man of average height, average looks, with hands that visibly shook as he waited for whatever was to come. He had black hair combed back and slicked down with white wings of hair on either side of his head. All in all, he looked like a *Soprano's* thug, but after a series of introductory questions we in the grand jury room knew he was a Grantland College chemistry major with a masters in health sciences and we knew he'd been married three times.

"On January fifteen of this year did you have occasion to be in the vicinity of the Lincoln Memorial?"

"Yes."

"You were near the Reflecting Pool?"

"Yes, I was standing off to the side in the shadows behind the lights."

"Tell us what you saw and heard."

"Two men came running by me. They were so close I almost could have reached out and touched them. The first man was panting and running in large, staggering strides. The second man was wearing a motorcycle cold-weather onesie with one of those cameras mounted on his shoulder. It was a GoPro."

"Have you seen one of those cameras before?"

"Seen one? I have one, Mr. Gresham. I'm a snow skier--a Vermont addict. I wear a camera pinned to my ski coat."

"Tell us what you witnessed after the men ran past you."

"Just before the pool, the man behind suddenly stopped, raised a gun I hadn't noticed before, and fired a single bullet into the back of the first man. The first man was knocked face-first into the water and floated there, but the shooter wasn't done. He ran up to the pool and fired four or five more times into the man. That first bullet knocked him down like he'd been struck with a sledge hammer."

"What did you do?"

"I stepped farther back in the shadows. The shooter then ran past me the same way he'd come. I was having a melt-down. But either he didn't see me or ignored me. I then left the scene and drove home."

"Did you call nine-one-one?"

"I didn't."

"Why not?"

"I was scared. But I returned to the scene four or five hours later. Cops were everywhere, and they were cutting a man out of the ice. I guess the pool froze up while I was gone. Maybe it had been partly frozen when the guy was shot; I don't know. But it was cold enough to freeze hard without much effort."

"Why did you return to the scene?"

"I had calmed down enough to realize the security cameras in the area probably had shots of me. Arriving at the scene, as I had walked right past the pool myself. I didn't want them to think I'd been involved or anything so I went back and told my story."

"Who did you tell your story to?"

"A cop in a black business suit. I think he was FBI."

"Did he badge you?"

"Yes, but I was too nervous to make sense of it. As I said, I think it was FBI."

"Let's back up to when you first go to the scene of the killing. Where were you coming from?"

"I'm a pharmaceutical rep. I had dropped off some samples at the White House with the White House physician's office."

"What kind of samples?"

"The president has joint problems. These were anti-inflammatory drugs like Celebrex."

"What is the drug used for?"

"Pain and stiffness. Osteoarthritis symptoms."

"Were you parked nearby?"

"Yes. With a trunkful of samples, so I was nervous as hell. Sorry, can I say hell?"

I ignored that. "Why were you at the Lincoln Memorial at that time and place?"

"I was meeting someone."

"Someone who?"

"I'd rather not give names."

"Was she ever at the scene?"

"No 'she.' It was a 'he.' He was a physicians' assistant assigned temporarily to the White House."

"Why were you meeting this person?"

"Why? Do I have to say?"

"Please say."

"We were meeting to have sex."

"Did this physicians' assistant ever join you at the scene?"

"No, he stood me up. He was an hour late when the shooting happened. But I don't think it was intentional. I think he'd been called upon to treat someone."

"Why do you think that?"

"I'm not usually stood-up. Men like me. Lots."

"Okay, when you went home--who do you live with?"

"I was living with my wife. But that was fizzling out. She was lesbian, and we were together to present a front. It's an old-fashioned thing, but we've been together almost twenty years."

"Was she home that night?"

"No. I don't know where she was. But I can guess."

"Please don't guess. Answer only what you know to be a fact."

"Sure, sure."

"Now, think carefully about this next question. When the man turned and came back by you, did you see his face?"

"Yes."

"Did you recognize him?"

"No."

"Did he resemble anyone you know to hold an elected office in Washington DC?"

This time the witness took his time. I supposed he was running faces through his mind and comparing them to the person he'd seen.

"No. He was dark-complected and not very tall. Shorter than me. And he turned his face away when he saw me, so I only had a glance."

"Did he in any way resemble the vice president of the United States?"

"Not at all. Our VP is tall and light-complected. This man was undersized and very dark."

"Describe his facial features."

"I only had a glimpse. Anything I could say might mislead you, sir."

"That's all right. Tell us what you saw anyway."

"Aquiline nose, dark eyes, long black hair. He had a neck tattoo, too."

"Could you tell what the tat was?"

"Something green and yellow, hard to tell even with the light as he was running in my direction."

"Green and yellow tattoo? Was it an animal? A weapon? A name?"

"It was impossible to tell. It all happened so fast."

"But you're sure it was a tat?"

"Pretty sure. As I said, it all happened so fast. Maybe it was a collar sticking up from his onesie, a shirt collar underneath. I'm sorry I can't be surer."

"So now it might have been a tattoo, and it might have been a shirt collar against his neck?"

"Yes. I'm sorry, sir."

"You're telling your truth. That's all we ask, Mr. Atkins."

"Thank you."

"I believe that's all I have. Do any of the grand jurors have questions?"

A large man in the back row raised his hand. "What happened to the GoPro, if you know."

"I don't know."

"Was it still attached to his clothing when he came back past you."

"Now that's a good question, come to think of it. I don't remember seeing it."

"So it could have fallen off at the scene?"

"It could have."

"That's all my questions, Mr. Gresham."

"Thank you. Anyone else?"

No other hands went up, so I dismissed the witness after swearing him to secrecy.

Then we adjourned.

34

Rudy Geneseo stepped off the elevator on the ground floor of the U.S. Attorney's Office. He had staked out and followed Michael Gresham for several days now. It was only a matter of time before the lawyer led him to the two remaining Tybaum children.

Just like the three previous nights, Gresham came down at six o'clock. It was pitch dark outside. He headed for his car. Rudy followed him out of the parking lot, taking care not to tip off the marshals' vehicle following Gresham for protection. They drove and drove, up and down the freeways, making sudden jaunts off an off-ramp at the last possible second, up and down alleyways, and then back out to the Bethesda connection.

They arrived in Bethesda forty-five minutes after leaving the USAO. Rudy broke off the pursuit as soon as they entered a new neighborhood, one he hadn't seen before. He knew he'd be able to lurk around for ten minutes and then locate the Gresham rental home where the children were hiding out now. So he went straight when the Gresham and marshals' car went left. Two blocks up was a middle school. He pulled into the circle drive out front and came to a stop at the far end just where it would enter the roadway again. He turned off his lights, turned off his engine, and waited.

Ten minutes later, he exited his vehicle, the overhead light having first been turned off. The Lincoln's heavy door shut silently, and Rudy stepped back. He adjusted the laces on his running shoes, checked that his shoulder holstered gun had a round in the chamber, and began a slow trot back the way he had come. When he reached the street where the Gresham entourage had turned into the neighborhood, he made that turn and silently jogged up the street.

It was almost too easy. The government vehicle was departed; a single MPD marked car took up the driveway to the frame house, and Gresham's car was snugged up to the curb out front. Rudy stopped running and began creeping along the street-parked cars, making his way to the Tybaum driveway. From out of the shadows he crept up on the police car, left side rear to just behind the driver. Sure enough, one cop was sitting inside, texting on his phone. Rudy withdrew the gun from the shoulder holster and fired one silenced round into the man's head. Then he froze. There was no reaction along the street--no lights came on, no doors opened--and there was no reaction from inside the children's house. So he became emboldened. He opened the door to the cop car, pushed the dead cop over onto the passenger's side, and sat down to wait. Ever so quietly he shut the door.

Fifteen minutes later, Gresham stepped out onto the front porch. He paused under the porch light and checked his wristwatch. Rudy scrunched down in the seat. Then, when

Gresham was coming up alongside the police car, edging up the driveway to avoid the snow in the front yard, Rudy pointed the gun at him. He fired a single shot--silenced-- through the passenger window at the lawyer. The man fell forward, and Rudy came flying out of the car, running around to the opposite side. There he found Gresham stretched out on his belly, his face planted in the snow and ice just off the driveway, one arm thrown impossibly out to the side, unmoving. Rudy went back to the car, opened the driver's door, and removed the cop's shirt from his dead body. He pulled it on over the sweatshirt he was wearing, put the police hat on his head, and boldly strode up to the front door. He rang the bell and waited.

Five or ten seconds went by before the door opened on its security chain. Jarrod--whose face he recognized from earlier stakeouts--peered out at him.

"Yes, officer?"

"I need to use the bathroom."

Jarrod closed the door and Rudy could hear the chain lock being slid open. When the door opened, he stepped inside. There was nothing to be gained by waiting, so he immediately drew the gun from his backside where he was hiding it, pointed the muzzle at Jarrod's head, and squeezed off a single shot. The heavy caliber round caught the hapless young man between the eyes, knocking him and his wheelchair backward a good three feet. After that, the house was still, and Rudy knew he was alone with the little girl.

He began creeping down the hallway toward the bedrooms.

At the first bedroom door on his right, he placed his ear against the wood and listened. There was no sound coming from inside, so he turned the knob and looked inside. It was Jarrod's room, given the extra wheelchair and walker along the wall. So he moved on to the second bedroom, the last one at the end of the hall. The door was open. He stuck his head inside and swung his gun into firing position. Sure enough, the little girl was seated on her bed, two coloring books arrayed before her, coloring two pictures at the same time. The man watched her for several seconds; then he raised the gun to fire.

He never heard the blast coming, never knew a thing.

Suddenly the killer's head exploded, and the man behind him watched as the killer slithered to the floor, dead before he settled across the carpet, first on his knees then slumping onto his side. Michael Gresham lowered his firearm and collapsed on the floor.

Michael slumped back against the wall, the police officer's weapon in his hand. Across his forehead was a deep gash from which blood was oozing where he'd been grazed by the killer's single shot. Ever so slowly he slid down, back against the wall, to a sitting position. His head turned to the side, and he passed out.

The little girl had to have heard the massive blast of the un-silenced police weapon. But she didn't move. Ever so lightly she began humming, changing from the red crayon to the blue.

All of her art featured women with blue hair.

It was just how the world looked--it always had--to Annie.

35

J ust before midnight, the relief police vehicle swung
into the driveway. The driver exited his vehicle and
crept up on the driver's side of the first police squad
car, his service weapon clutched in his two hands. He swung
around to face the interior of the car, which is when he saw
Sidney Linney, a patrolman by rank, lying back against the
passenger door, shot on the left side of the head. The officer
knew Sidney was dead.

But he was here to guard the children inside. So he began
the long tiptoe up to the front porch. The door was standing
open. He went inside and all but fell over the wheelchair
still bearing the body of Jarrod Tybaum. The man was
slumped back. The entry wound between his eyes told the
whole story about him. The officer knew there was one
more to account for, a girl of about twelve. He headed for
the hallway leading back to the bedrooms.

Which was where he found Michael Gresham, unconscious
on the floor, a weapon still clutched in his hand.

He stepped over Gresham's legs and peered inside the last bedroom.

A little girl was asleep atop her bedspread. Two coloring books were on the floor along with a box of spilled crayons.

The officer keyed his shoulder mic.

"Need an ambulance stat! And I need backup," he told the dispatcher.

"Roger that, Officer Hardy. I'm dispatching an ambulance and backup officers now."

The policeman approached the sleeping girl. He laid two fingers against the side of her throat. Strong pulse there. So he went into the first bedroom and pulled the bedspread from the unmade bed. He returned with it to the little girl's room.

Ever so gently he covered her with the bedspread and went back into the hallway. He pulled her door shut so on the off-chance she woke up she might not get a look at the two men lying outside her door, one dead and one alive but unconscious.

He walked outside and checked more carefully on the officer inside the first police vehicle. He was obviously dead, which he had assumed when he'd first crept past. He locked the vehicle's doors with the electric button and stood back. Now that scene was preserved.

Then he went back inside and sat down in the hallway beside the unconscious man. The forehead wound had all but stopped losing blood. He put two-and-two together and knew the man beside him had shot the dead man closer to the girl's bedroom.

There was no doubt what it all meant.

He stood up and went back to the first bedroom and pulled a pillow up out of the tangle of bedcovers.

Returning to the second man, he lifted his head and placed the pillow underneath.

Now he'd done all he could do.

Sirens closed on his location. Tears came to his eyes.

It had been so close.

But she was alive.

36

M y recovery wasn't long and protracted; while the bullet had laid bare my skull there had been no significant or lasting damage done besides a concussion. Three days after I was taken to GWU hospital, where I underwent CT scans and two surgeries, my treating physician came into my room and discharged me. Antonia happened in to visit just then. Her face went pale when she saw me and saw the stitches across my forehead. "They told me it was a deep wound," she said, "but they didn't tell me it was four inches wide and would require four hundred stitches. Then she learned I was about to go home and bent over backward to help me. "One of my prosecutors," she said to the physician, "and he is going to have company when he's released and goes home. And he's going to have all the help he could ever need."

I was taken to my hotel and helped into casual clothes. A nurse and two aides were at me always asking how they could make me more comfortable, bringing snacks and coffee, and doing whatever they could to make my way easy.

My laptop was opened for the first time in days, and I immediately called Verona and the kids to check in. The kids were
at school, but Verona answered on the second ring. "You're
home now? You thought last night that it might be today."

"I'm feeling much better," I said, "for a man shot in the head.
It could have been much, much worse."

"Are you done with this case, whatever it was?"

"Not quite. But there's something I need to do."

"Can I help?"

"Yes. There's a young orphan girl. She's twelve, and she
needs a place to hide for the near future. Her name is Annie,
and I'd like to send her to you."

"Is she in danger?"

"She is."

"Will that put our kids in danger?"

"It could. But the marshals who bring her will provide all
possible protection from here on out. No one will ever know
where Annie is once I have her out of Washington. Can
you help?"

"Of course I will. Tell me more about Annie? Is she injured
too?"

"She's not. But she has just lost her sister and her brother.
Her father was shot and killed not long before that. She's all
alone now. But the upside is, Annie's different and that is, in
an ironic way, freeing. She doesn't notice she's all alone now.
Plus, she and I have become quite close. I think having me
in her life helps."

"So you're coming with her? I hope."

"Not quite yet. I have some final pieces of the case to resolve. But there will be FaceTime every day. That will allow her to see me and stay connected with her. Same with our kids."

"What's her long-term placement?"

"Her aunt is in Berkeley, California. She's already stepped up to take the girl."

"Why not just send her there now?"

"Because the aunt is in trial--she's a professor of law and part-time lawyer. She's hard at trial in a very taxing class action that requires her attention all day and much of her nights. It wouldn't work to put Annie with her just now only to have her ignored."

"I see. Well, send her to me. You know I'll take her in a heartbeat, and I'll love her just like one of our own."

This was new: "our own," and "our children." Verona had become closer to my kids than I could have hoped. They were now her kids, too. A miracle.

We talked for another few minutes and then said our goodbyes, agreeing we'd speak again on FaceTime that night when the kids could be included. I realized as I hung up just how much I was missing my family. I also resolved again to ask Verona to marry me. I loved her; she loved me; we had our kids. It brought tears to my eyes to think of all that had happened between us and how far we'd come. She was a fantastic helpmate, but she also had her own life. Her Green Card was just weeks away from arriving and then she could teach or enter industry--whatever she wanted to do. So her life was about to take on new dimensions as well.

I lolled around the rest of that day, going over office email and updating myself on several key cases. Other Assistant U.S. Attorneys had been assigned to my most active cases and were moving things along. I was incredibly grateful that I was now in a situation where there was all but unlimited resources. I could rest easy, confident my cases were being handled with the highest possible degree of competence and care.

The following day, Detective Ronald Holt came calling and brought with him Special Agent Jack Ames. They gathered around the dining table in my suite and opened their notebooks.

"Okay," I said, "here's what we're going to do next with the Tybaum case. Jack, I want you and your Special Agents to obtain all banking records from GULP. I believe we're going to find a smoking gun among those records."

"What kind of smoking gun?" Ames asked. He sat leaning forward, his grizzly bear of a body pressed against the table as he made his notes. He was waiting for me to explain.

"I'm looking for cash withdrawals from their bank accounts. And I'm looking to trace those funds from the PAC's bank to wherever they ultimately wound up."

"How do we do that? Cash isn't usually traceable, Michael."

"As a general proposition that's true. But I think you're going to find in this case that someone at GULP has left bread-crumbs along the way. Without meaning to, of course. Then, find out who the person was who withdrew the funds and find out who the person was who received the funds. When we have done this, we have our conspiracy."

"Conspiracy?" asked Holt. "How do you know this is what we're looking for?"

Ames answered for me. "Because, Detective Holt, our prosecutor friend here has narrowed down the players who have motive and proximity. The motive to kill Gerry Tybaum and his children and proximity to the Russian money and proximity to the GULP bank accounts."

"Bingo," I said. "Special Agent Ames has been reading my mail."

"Well...not literally."

"Oh, that's a relief," I chided. "All kidding aside, Agent Ames will obtain the bank records. In the meantime, Detective Holt, I'd like you to put a tail on the GULP CEO Paul Wexler with your people from MPD. My belief is that he sent this Rudy Geneseo to take out the Tybaum family so that he could sweep the Russian funds back into the hands of GULP. From there, the funds were up for grabs, and since he was the senior officer in the PAC, he could move the money wherever he decided."

"Where are you getting all this?" Holt asked.

I touched the side of my head. "I was a defense attorney for way too long. I've seen many cases just like this one before."

"Okay. Consider me tasked," Holt said.

"Same goes for me," said Ames. "But as long as we're kicking stuff around here, what name am I looking for at GULP?"

"Same guy. Paul Wexler," I said.

"He's my suspect?"

"He's your cash cow, I'm thinking."

"Got it," said Ames.

"Same goes for me," said Holt.

"Then we're done here. Now you gentlemen scatter and let me get back to watching *Ellen*."

They left, and I called the U.S. Marshal's Special Operations Group. It was time to do something about Annie, who'd been placed under the protection of a policewoman named Alice Munes since the night of the shooting. Annie was doing well; Munes was with the girl 24/7, but it was time to move Annie to Evanston and Verona and my kids.

The Marshal's Service SOG would move her by special air to Chicago by way of several intermediate destinations and plane changes that couldn't be traced because no flight plans would be filed. *Underground Air*, the government, called such sorties. They scheduled the flights for the next day, and finally, I could relax.

Reactive law enforcement was now a thing of the past. We had become proactive, and already I liked it better.

~

The next day I received a call from Special Agent Ames. The banking records were all but impossible to obtain through GULP itself. There was no one on the inside willing to cooperate. So we determined that we would obtain a subpoena and hit the bank itself.

We had the records forty-eight hours later.

And Annie was now in Evanston, surrounded by people

who would love her. And strong men who would protect her.

At last, I could sleep, and I spent all of the next few days in my room, calling up room service and moving pieces around on my mental chessboard.

There were only so many pieces, it was turning out.

And I had them all covered.

I was back.

37

Two days after getting home to my hotel suite, I was picked up by Agent Ames to accompany him to Rudy's apartment for a look around. In particular, we were looking for a cat on a kitchen table. I was virtually convinced we would find this scenario at Rudy's. As we drove along, Ames went over what we knew so far. He asked about the conflict between Jessup's grand jury testimony where he ID'd the shooter as the vice president and the testimony of the pharmaceutical rep who had the shooter looking nothing like the VP.

"It's a mystery," I said. "But Maxwell Atkins had a closer look as the shooter came running back past him so I'd probably put more weight on his story. Plus, Senator Jessup was engaged with his date for the night and wouldn't have had the same opportunity to observe as Atkins."

"It sounds to me like the senator has an ax to grind. He couldn't have made out faces from where he was standing. Plus, he was looking at a downward angle. My team has it all measured and the angles computed. He had a very difficult point of view to recognize a face down below."

"Good point. Yes, I'm fairly sure we're on the track of Rudy Geneseo, our dead guy."

"Did you show his picture to Maxwell Atkins?"

"No, I wanted his best recall. I'll show the picture if there's any court follow-up. Though I doubt there will be."

"How about if I take Geneseo's picture around to Atkins and ask him one-on-one whether he can ID?"

"Now that I like. Let's get it done."

"I'll do that later today."

We arrived at Rudy Geneseo's apartment. It was located in a rundown part of town, with a liquor store on one corner of his block and a Chinese restaurant/grocery store at the other. The sidewalks were cracked and askance and littered with trash, hoodlums apparent everywhere as we drove past their suspicious, hate-filled eyes. But evidently, they made us as more cops as Rudy's place had been overrun with police examiners and photographers since his shooting at Jarrod and Annie's house. Ames and I were johnnies-come-lately, truth be told.

The door to Rudy's apartment was manned by a police-woman who seemed to recognize Ames before he badged her. She allowed a nod of recognition and said, "So even the FBI wants in on this one. I'm impressed. Who are you?"

"I'm an assistant U.S. Attorney," I told her and flashed my ID. She pushed open the door and waved us inside.

The place was laid out in an L-shape, with the living room

and bedroom off to the side making up the base and leg of the L. Following the leg through to its other end, we came to the kitchen. But the table was a small white metal table, and there was no sign of a cat anyplace in the apartment--no kitty litter, no bowls on the floor, no cat food in the cupboards or refrigerator, nothing.

"This isn't it, Jack," I told Ames a few minutes after we'd entered. "We're still on the hunt for the cat."

"I'm surprised," Ames said, nodding with his eyebrows knitted in puzzlement. "I would've bet we'd find the cat or a cat setup in here. But Rudy evidently had no pets at all."

"Evidently."

"One more thing. Let me check his closet."

I opened the accordion door to Rudy's closet and riffled through the hangers until I found the belts. Three belts. Then...there it was. The Effingham belt buckle. But it stopped me in my tracks. Why would Rudy be wearing a belt buckle capable of implicating the vice president in a murder? It made no sense, especially if it was the VP who had enlisted Rudy to murder Gerry at the Reflecting Pool. For Rudy to then wear the buckle to the murder knowing that he was being captured on CCTV—it didn't add up. On the other hand, if the VP wasn't involved might Rudy have simply been wearing the buckle in order to draw attention away from himself? Had he planned to make us believe the VP was the shooter? But that made no sense: he wouldn't have known about the VP's belt buckle yet purposely obtained one and worn it. That would have been way beyond Rudy's pay grade to pull off something that sophisticated. I decided to put the issue on the back burner. I had a feeling that when we located the cat on the table—rather, *if* we located the cat on the table—that happy discovery would reveal much more to us, including the mystery of the belt buckle.

Driving me back to my office, Jack Ames said, "We need to follow the money, Michael. Following the money backward will lead us to whoever paid Rudy to kill Gerry Tybaum. And Mona. What do you think?"

"I think I'm taking Wexler's grand jury testimony soon. I'd like to hold this conversation until I'm done with that."

"Understand."

"But I do agree. The banking transactions are going to lead us to the guys who didn't pull the trigger. The guys who hired someone else to pull it for them."

"Agree," said Ames.

We wheeled into underground parking, and he let me out.

We still hadn't found the cat.

But we were still looking.

38

News of the deaths of Jarrod Tybaum and Rudy Geneseo reached Paul Wexler at GULP. He was just ordering breakfast from the cafeteria downstairs when his secretary buzzed. He answered the phone, and she told him Nivea Young had shown up without an appointment, demanding to talk to Wexler. The CEO said to bring her right in without delay.

Nivea came charging inside, her face a determined mask of single-mindedness. She brought Wexler up to speed on the shootout in two minutes. When she finished, Wexler sat back in his executive chair, rubbing his eyes with two fingers. Then he addressed what Young had come to tell him.

"The girl is missing."

"The youngest child has vanished."

"I'm paying you to find her. What's the hold-up?"

"I've run down every lead, everything I can come up with,"

she said. She was tense, a snake ready to strike but one without a target. Her hands clenched and unclenched; her blink rate had doubled, Wexler saw. It felt good to have her on his side and looking.

"I can pretty confidently guess where Gresham has the kid, this Annie Tybaum."

Nivea Young shook her head. "My guess is it won't be Bethesda again. What are you thinking?"

"Remember the dossier you prepared on him? Home in Evanston, Illinois? Live-in girlfriend, live-in ex-mother-in-law, two young kids? Wouldn't that be a natural place to stash Annie? I mean, who would think of looking there for her?"

Nivea studied Wexler's sharp features. His eyes were glowing as he made his projection, his educated guess about the young heiress's whereabouts.

"So you're sending me to Evanston?"

"I'm surprised you haven't left already, Ms. Young. I'm disappointed in you."

For the first time, the ex-CIA case officer smiled. "I'm already packing a bag as we speak. What about Gresham's kids? What about the others in the house?"

"What about them? We're not trying to save lives here, Ms. Young. There's too much money at stake for us to be thinking of anything but the result. I need this Annie problem to go away...permanently."

"I know that. Get ready for a big bang, Mr. Wexler; I won't be taking any captives."

He waved her off. "Just do it. Don't tell me any more. And when it's done, never contact me again. Your money will be waiting in your Swiss account."

"You won't hear from me ever again, Mr. Wexler. If this doesn't end it, you need to look elsewhere for my kind of help. I'm too exposed already."

"I would look elsewhere anyway."

She scowled at him. Then she left.

When he was alone, his breakfast arrived. Soon his mind was grappling with the notion of killing a young child.

With a sigh, he had to admit to himself: it wouldn't be the first time.

39

Two days later, Jack Ames reported back to me. Evidently, they set up their investigation HQ right inside the FBI's field office at 4th Street NW. There they had several computers on a LAN, and they were receiving Charter Bank and Mercantile of Boston account records for all GULP accounts. CBMB hadn't attempted to quash the subpoena; records were flowing into the field office the same day the subpoena was served at the home office.

They then began the arduous task of locating the smoking gun.

They searched the records for all GULP cash transactions. Less than forty-five records were returned as a dataset. The four agents divided them up and began poring over them, attempting to connect transaction values with new account values at CBMB. It was a shot in the dark, but it was what I'd wanted them to do.

At noon, Ames called me. "What would you say to fifty-thousand cash going out of GULP and a safe deposit box being opened by GULP the same day in the name of Green Laundry and Cleaners?"

"I'd say we need to crack a safe deposit box."

"That's on you, counselor. Let me know when the subpoena's ready and I'll walk it through."

We had the subpoena signed and delivered to Special Agent Ames two hours after his call. Then he was on his way to Boston.

Ames arrived in Boston after banking hours and settled into a hotel room a block away from the bank. At eight a.m. the next morning he was waiting at the door when the security service unlocked. At 8:11 he was inside the vault and the vault manager was unlocking the box listed in the name of Green Laundry and Cleaners. She pulled the box out and laid it on a velvet table-top for Ames to open.

Which he did.

"Cash," he said to the vault manager.

"Hmm, yes," she answered.

"I have to count it," Ames advised her and so, while she waited, Ames counted the money in the box It wasn't fifty-thousand; it was seventy-thousand. So Ames returned to his computers in Washington and looked for cash withdrawals of twenty-thousand dollars. Nothing came back. So he tried ten-thousand dollars, and two data files were returned. They were dated the same day, just after the fifty-thousand deposit.

Which was when Ames formulated his working theory, that Rudy Geneseo had been paid fifty-thousand dollars for the hit on Gerry Tybaum and ten-thousand apiece on Jarrod and Mona. There was not a third payment, he reasoned, because Annie was still alive. But she would have been next if I hadn't shot Rudy just as he was about to shoot Annie in the back.

It had been just that close.

Next, Ames and his team went to work on tracking down the identity of the person who had facilitated the cash payouts and deposits. He started with the most obvious choice, Paul Wexler. The bank's vault records proved that Wexler had visited the bank vault on the same dates as the cash with-drawals and that he had opened the account for Green Laundry and Cleaning. Access identities included, of all people, Rudy Geneseo.

Jack called me from Boston.

"I've got your man," he told me, trying to disguise the excite-ment in his voice that no FBI agent would ever evince to the world.

"Give me a name, Jack."

"Paul Wexler. You were spot on, Michael."

"Why doesn't the name Paul Wexler surprise me? I'm hauling his ass before the grand jury as we speak."

I issued a grand jury subpoena for Wexler. As I predicted, he immediately lawyered up. But then a strange thing happened. I received a call from a DC lawyer by the name of

Susan Kayye, and she had news about Paul Wexler that she could only share with me in private.

We met that afternoon in my office downtown, Susan Kayye, Jack Ames, Ronald Holt, and me.

At first, she didn't want to talk to the cops in the room, but I assured her that their presence was the only way this conversation was going to happen. She relented as I knew she would; this conversation was a must for her and I thought I knew why.

A lawyer has a duty to reveal to the authorities the planned commission of a crime that their client reveals to them. I believed we had snared Paul Wexler at the same time as he had another attempt on Annie's life in the works.

Sure enough, I thought as I heard out Ms. Kayye.

"I've met twice with Mr. Wexler. He doesn't know I'm here. But I'm here because the attorneys' ethical rules require that I divulge to you, the proper officials, Wexler's intent to commit a crime."

"What crime would that be?" I asked.

"Paul Wexler has hired a hitman to kill Annie Tybaum. He wouldn't tell me the hitman's name and believe me I cajoled and threatened and begged him for it. But then he became way too suspicious of me and why I needed the name, and he clammed up. For all I know, I've already been fired by him, which is irrelevant. I'm required by law to tell you and the authorities what I'm telling you, and now I've done that. I'll be confirming all this in a letter to you, Mr. Gresham, dated today and delivered before five o'clock this evening. Let there be no mistake. My duty is done here."

Just as quickly as she had appeared, Susan Kayye was gone. It wouldn't have done to try and coax more answers and information out of her. She was a true professional who usually litigated in the area of white collar crime with a top-drawer Washington law firm. While Wexler's conspiracy to commit murder case was a little off her beaten path of typical case types, it was something she had taken on because the man paid her one-million dollars to defend him.

After she had been gone, Ames and Holt and I put our heads together.

"Where is GULP's headquarters?" Ames asked.

I looked up their address on my computer and passed it to him.

"I know this building," Ames then said. "There's closed circuit TV everywhere."

"We're fishing now, I've got a feeling," Holt said.

Ames looked at Holt. "Yes, we are. Get ready for some long days and nights."

"You're reviewing closed circuit TV video?" I lamely asked.

"We are. We'll know every person who has entered Wexler's office over the past week. We'll also run facial recognition on them and get some names and backgrounds. Bear with me, Michael, I'm pedaling as fast as I can."

"You're looking to ID the killer."

"Looking to put a name with a face, yeah."

"I'm praying you can," I said. "Without a picture or name we're sunk."

I was uneasy. Someone was after Annie yet again--which we had already guessed anyway, but now it was confirmed. It was like a knife shoved deep into my gut. My first inclination was to jump the red eye to Chicago and head for Evanston and swoop the girl into my arms and protect her. But I was needed in Washington.

It was time to set Wexler's ass down in front of my grand jury and go to work on him.

40

P aul Wexler walked boldly into the grand jury room and raised his right hand. I knew he had been sandpapered by his attorney--whoever it turned out to be, and it wouldn't surprise me if he immediately took the Fifth and refused to answer. Five minutes later, I had my answer.

"Mr. Wexler, have you had any role in the deaths of Gerald Tybaum, Mona Tybaum, or Jarrod Tybaum?"

"I refuse to answer. Fifth Amendment, Mr. Gresham."

Just as I expected, he was going to sky out on me.

So I tried a different approach.

"Tell me the names of all people you know who are making any effort to murder Annie Tybaum."

"Same thing. Fifth Amendment."

He was wrong, I thought. The question didn't seek to incriminate him; it sought to obtain information about someone other than him. My position was that he should have to answer that. I also thought the Honorable Erasmus M. Samuels would back me up on this if I went into his court and sought an order directing Wexler to answer the question or go to jail for contempt of court.

"I want to talk to my lawyer," Wexler said, coolly and without hesitation.

"We'll stand in recess for ten minutes," I announced.

A witness has a right to step outside the grand jury room and discuss a pending question with their lawyer. Wexler had requested as much, and I had no way--or interest--in preventing that. I had no interest in preventing it because any criminal lawyer worth their salt would probably direct him to answer my question. Which would save us a trip to the U.S. courthouse.

Ten minutes later we were back on the record.

"Mr. Wexler, I again ask you for the names of people you know to be making efforts to murder Annie Tybaum."

This time there was no hesitation.

"Nivea Young."

"And are you in any way connected with Nivea Young in any conspiracy to kill Annie Tybaum?"

"I take the Fifth Amendment."

Which went on another thirty minutes and I then called a recess. I told Wexler's attorney to keep his man close by as he was subject to recall by the grand jury.

We now had a name--Nivea Young--and Special Agent Ames had a huge collection of pictures, the visitors to

GULP's building. But now he could go back to his facial recognition software and look for any hits with the name of Nivea Young. Which he did. He called me less than an hour later. We now had video of Nivea Young.

When I looked at her picture, I was shocked. She was the same woman who, my Chicago office's video system showed, entered my building the night Gerry Tybaum came to see me in Chicago. She was the person who had removed my gun from my desk.

Which also meant she might very well have followed me home to Evanston.

A cold chill shuddered up my spine.

She knew where and she knew who.

The race was on.

41

Nivea Young didn't fly. Airline databases were too easily accessed by the FBI, and she knew this. So she rented a car with a bogus credit card and lied about her destination. "Tampa Bay, Florida," she told the rental agency clerk and handed over her bogus driver's license. After she had secured the car and was out of sight of the rental agency, she headed west on the interstate for Illinois. There was plenty of food inside the car with her, as well as a thermos of coffee and a gallon jug of water. She started out on Interstate 270, connected with I70, then decided to take the southern route because it made the least sense if they did come looking in this direction.

If they even figured out who she was and where she was going. She guessed they would not.

She turned onto Interstate 65-70 and eight hours later was in Columbus, where she pulled into a truck stop and ordered the Truckers' Special breakfast. When she finished, she walked out to the parking lots where dozens and dozens of trucks were parked, idling, while their drivers ate and then slept. But she had a mission there, so she began knocking lightly on driver's windows and, as sleepy heads rolled down windows and gruffly asked what she wanted, she would explain what she needed and how much she was willing to pay.

"I'm looking to purchase a semiautomatic pistol in either nine millimeter or forty caliber. I have two thousand dollars to spend on one."

At first, the truckers were angry to be disturbed from their sleep. But when they heard "two-thousand" most became sweetly reasonable.

"No, but I've got an extra three-fifty-seven if that does the trick for you," said the driver of the second rig.

"Won't do it. I need a semiautomatic for magazine swapping."

"Got it. Then I can't help."

But she struck gold in the second row of trucks where, inside a Freightliner, she watched the driver roll out of the sleeper and put the window down.

"What?"

"I need a semiautomatic pistol, nine mil or forty cal."

"I've got an extra forty. How much you got?"

"Two thousand cash right now."

"Sold!"

He opened the console and pulled out a pistol held inside an IWB holster.

She passed the man her cash, and he passed her the pistol. "Got a second magazine with it, too. Wait one."

He went back to rummaging in the console then pulled out a second, loaded, magazine in .40 caliber.

"This do?" he said with a rough smile.

"Perfect," she said.

"The second mag is two hundred."

Acting reluctant, she fished out another two hundred dollars from her jeans pocket. "This is too much for one magazine," she told the seller.

"You'll make it back after you knock off a few 7-Elevens."

"Forget that."

"You're after a bank, maybe?"

"Forget that."

"All right. Good luck. I'm headed back into my sleeper. You don't want to join me for an hour or so do you?"

He was leering now.

"Have a safe sleep," she said making a finger pistol and pointing it at his forehead. "Bang," she said softly.

"Get out," he said and rolled up the window.

She found her rental and slid back into the driver's seat.

Now she was armed.

And dangerous. She didn't have to buy dangerous from anyone.

She came that way.

42

Before the day was over, I had flexed the muscle of my office. Now the FBI, the Special Operations Group of the U.S. Marshals Service, and the Metropolitan Police were formulating a search and arrest net for Nivea Young. Jack Ames had the FBI lead; Ronald Holt had MPD, and Rusty Xiang became my liaison with the Marshals Service. Ames knew there was always the possibility that Young was hitchhiking to Chicago to avoid any form of registration at an airline or car rental outlet or train. If it were him, he decided, that's what he would be doing. The FBI task force began scanning databases of car rentals, airlines, trains, and any other form of transportation that might produce a result. Another group of agents from the team contacted State Police authorities in many of the states she would have to pass through and had them setup roadblocks and examine vehicles one-by-one. It was a massive manhunt underway before the first day was over; if she were out there moving toward Chicago, the agents believed they would turn her up.

At the other end of the trip was Evanston, Illinois, my home. Federal marshals hardened the perimeter defense around my house and neighborhood. I knew they had an uncanny ability to blend in and leave the impression the route to the house was completely unguarded. If she walked into their setup, she would be taken down in a surprising show of force erupting from seemingly nowhere.

Then I had done all I could about the security risk posed by Nivea Young. When the dust had settled Nivea Young was a key witness in a federal murder case, and that was enough to activate all the services I had reached out to. Now it was time to turn my attention to the money sequestered in Moscow, Russia.

I called the bank number from the Internet, got passed around until an English-speaker came online, a man named Leonid, and he asked me how he could help.

"I have an account in Russia, and I want to transfer the money to the United States."

After the bank's previous resistance to my request to move the money, I was all but floored by this agent's response.

"Have you considered a wire transfer? That's your easiest way to transfer funds."

"Can you help me?"

"Of course. Give me your name, routing and account number, and your receiving bank information."

"That's just it. The money is in the name of Gerald Tybaum. I have a power of attorney giving me control."

"That should pose no problems. Can you email me a certi-fied copy of the power?"

I did as we were speaking. Leonid read it over.

"This looks above-board. I'm going to put in the file and mark it accepted."

"Just like that?"

"Of course just like that. We're a bank, Mr. Gresham. We have only distant ties to the Russian government and then only because we have a Kremlin charter."

"When can you get the funds to me?"

"I'm filling out the wire transfer as we speak. Wait thirty minutes then check your account."

We hung up, and I resisted checking my account balance for the full thirty minutes. Then I looked. My account now showed a balance of twelve-million dollars. Twelve to Annie and twenty-four grand of my own. Not bad for thirty-five minutes of work.

Annie was set. Her account was at my bank. I made a transfer between accounts at the same bank and her balance suddenly shot up to twelve-million dollars and change, and my own plummeted to twenty-four-thousand.

Annie had her money, and I was free of that responsibility to her.

All in all, a great afternoon.

43

"FBI located her on truck-stop closed circuit TV," Holt told me by phone. He was calling my room in the middle of the night from somewhere between Washington and the truck stop. "I'm headed to Columbus now."

"Columbus?"

"That's where she walked into the truck stop and got made by the FBI."

"Hats off to Jack Ames," I told Holt. "Tell him he's won my heart."

"He already knows that, Michael. He's the FBI, for God's sake."

"So she's headed for my home. How did she figure out where we had Annie stashed?"

"I think we've got a leak."

"Where is it? Only you, me, Ames and the U.S. Marshals Special Operations Group know where she went."

"Maybe someone in Special Operations. Maybe a pilot or co-pilot with a flight manifest. Or a clerk with the U.S. Marshals who has access to the manifest. There're lots of people who might know where we've got her."

"True, although I hate it."

"Or maybe she's just that smart that she did the calculus of where you'd stash the kid and decided you'd choose Evanston. There are enough smart bad people to balance-out the dumb bad people."

"I'm afraid that's true," I said. While I was speaking with Detective Holt, my mind was already headed for Evanston and the protection of my family. And Annie. Maybe it had been a terrible idea to take her there. In fact, it probably was a terrible idea because now my kids were at risk. I started kicking myself that night and couldn't get back to sleep.

Around four a.m. I finally got up out of bed and made coffee. I reminded myself that my family--and Annie--were fully protected by heavily armed federal agents, state police, and Evanston PD. There was no way Nivea would get through that.

"You're whistling past the graveyard," I finally had to admit. "You've screwed the pooch this time. Terrible plan, Gresham."

At six o'clock I couldn't wait any longer. I dialed Verona and waited.

"Hello, Michael," she said on the second ring.

"You know my number," I said.

"It's early, Michael. What's up?"

"Are you all okay?"

"Of course we are. We can hardly get in and out of the house to get to school or go shopping there are so many policemen around. There are guns everywhere, coffee thermoses, requests to come inside and use the bathroom. It never stops."

"That relieves my mind. I'm calling because I'm distraught. They've got a world-class killer headed your way, and I'm horrified I've put you all in jeopardy,"

"Nonsense, a prosecutor's family is already in jeopardy. Bad people don't care who they hurt."

"That's one way of looking at it."

"Look, Annie isn't talking. Hasn't said one word since she got here. Can I get her and see if she'll talk to you?"

"Of course. I'll wait."

Five minutes later, I could hear a stirring on the other end of the line, then hear Verona's voice calling into the phone, "Say hello, Michael."

"Hello, Annie, this is Michael. Is that you?"

"Yes. Where are you? I miss you."

"I'm in Washington. I'll be coming to see you before much longer."

"I don't like it here. I want to be with you, Michael."

"Well, what about being with your aunt in California? How does that sound to you?"

"I don't know her. I know you lots better."

"We'll have to talk about that. Now, tell me what you've been up to, please."

"The WI-FI is adequate here. I can get on my computer and not look up until bedtime."

"What about my kids, Dania and Mikey? Do you play with them at all?"

"I don't like kids, Michael."

"That's okay. There's no rule you should."

Long pause. Then, "That's one thing I like about you, Michael. You don't let all the stupid social rules run your life. I don't either, in case you haven't noticed."

"Believe me, Annie, I have noticed."

"Who are we worried about this morning? I can hear it in your voice someone is coming to kill me."

"Her name is Nivea Young. She's a hired gun."

"Hired by who?"

"Guy named Paul Wexler."

"Oh, him."

"What do you mean, 'oh him'?"

"My father talked about him a lot. He hated my father."

"I think that's right. There was no love lost by your dad, either. It was mutual."

"So I'll get online and do what I can with this Nivea Young and Paul Wexler. Do you have a number where I can call you?"

I was astounded. Annie had never talked so much or even hinted she liked me or would do something like get entangled enough to call me up. But I gave her my cell phone number, and she immediately committed it to that massive memory bank in her head.

"All right, Michael. What other questions do you have about the cases?"

I decided to go for it. My decision was based on nothing but her past ability to help me.

"Vice President Jonathan Vengrow. Can you look into any connection he might have with Rudy, Wexler, or Nivea Young?"

"We've talked about this before. Vengrow is very involved, Michael."

"Now I need you to come up with connections that I'll try to trace back to him."

"Of course. Like I said, I'll call you."

We left it at that, and I hung up without speaking again to Verona.

In one way I felt much better, but in another, I was more frightened for my family and Annie than ever. I began making plans to go to Evanston.

This case had outgrown its Washington DC playpen.

It was time.

44

When she reached Indianapolis, Nivea turned off the interstate and began driving the back roads. It was all part of the plan she had been conceptualizing to lose any pursuers. Not a trace of her after Indianapolis, where she pulled into the first Exxon-Mobil and topped off her tank. Then at Lafayette, she changed her mind and pulled into a huge truck stop. She parked the rental at the far end of the endless rows of massive eighteen-wheelers idling and coming and going. Then she again began knocking on windows.

"Hi," she said to the first trucker to roll down his window. He was a good old boy wearing baggy jeans, red suspenders, a too-small flannel shirt tight around the middle and a year's growth of unruly whiskers. He was just shifting into first gear when she knocked, but he paused for her anyway.

"Hello," he said. "I'm not looking to get laid if that's what you're selling."

"Naw, I'm looking for a ride to Chicago. I'm looking for a

good buddy who wants to earn a thousand bucks by taking me along on a straight-through to Chi-Town."

"Show me the money."

She passed him ten one-hundred-dollar bills.

"Go around and climb in. It's unlocked."

And just like that, she began the last leg of her trip to Chicago. Up Interstate 65 they went to Gary, Indiana, where they hit Interstate 90 and jogged west then north toward their destination.

On arriving in Chicago, they continued north a few miles until they reached Skokie. The driver pulled into a Wal-Mart lot and stopped.

"Time for you to hop out, sugar."

"Would you take another thousand to lie to anyone about ever seeing me? Would you lie and tell them I was never seen anyplace along your route?"

"Pass me the money. Let's count it."

Again Nivea counted ten one-hundred-dollar bills into the driver's hand. As she counted his head nodding became more and more pronounced, and she knew she had just bought his silence.

Then, out of the cab and walking away, done with the long part. But now began the difficult part, getting up to Evanston without being discovered.

Back out to the road, she trudged in the slushy snow. Across the four lanes and down a half-mile stood a Jadon's Restaurant, Chicago's answer to the mid-priced restaurant crowd of diners. She ran across the road when the traffic let up and checked her watch. Five a.m. Then she began hiking a quarter-mile to the friendly, glowing restaurant sign.

As she had guessed there would be, several motorcycles were parked in front. Good riders, she thought, capable of negotiating a film of snow on the main roads that would come and go throughout the night. In the daytime, the rime would melt away, and normal driving speeds would be attained. She counted: four bikes. So she was looking for four men wearing leather.

Sure enough, inside the doors seated in the second booth on her left with four bikers in black leather and a passenger wearing red leather. Nivea sidled up to the table and waited patiently until the topic being discussed was abandoned. Now they were all looking at her. "What?" said a middle-aged man with long stringy hair and a mouthful of gold. "Are you looking for us?"

She smiled. "I'm looking for a ride up to Evanston on back roads. I have one-thousand dollars to pay for the ticket."

"Two thousand," said the same man. "Two thousand and I'll get you up to Evanston by way of Iowa if that's what you need."

"No, just back roads will do."

She began counting out yet another sheaf of hundred-dollar bills. At twenty, she stopped and looked up. "We good?"

The man held out his hand, and she paid him. "Let me finish my coffee," he said.

"I'll be out by the bikes," she replied and nodded graciously before turning and walking back outside.

Two-and-a-half hours later they pulled into Evanston on a side road, found the inner highway and the driver dropped Nivea at the portico of a Red Roof Inn. Without a word to her driver, she hurried inside and paid for a room.

Upstairs, her tiny backpack's contents arranged on the bed, she took inventory. There was a KBAR knife, PlastiCuffs, pepper spray, and throwing darts. Plus, there was the gun. But, she decided, the caliber was too small if she were shooting at armored law enforcement officers. So she decided to re-group and add to her armaments.

At nine o'clock that morning she called a cab and rode to North County Pawn. She climbed out and asked the driver to wait and slipped him a hundred-dollar bill. He nodded and said he'd be there, no hurry.

Inside the pawn shop, Nivea went back to the glassed-in showcase module, where she could view the guns.

None of them leaped out at her. Most were six-shot revolvers, most of those being .38 caliber, a worthless gun for what she had in mind. A man approached from behind the bulletproof glass and slid open a window.

"Help you?'

"I need a semi with at least a fourteen-round magazine. Best is .40 caliber."

"No such thing on our shelves," the man said with a sweep of his eyes along the display case. Let me go inside the office and speak to the owner."

"I'll wait."

Several minutes later, he returned. He was carrying a gun-sized box with blue sides and a white top.

"Here's what you need," he said and opened the book. He removed a fat gun and placed it in Nivea's hand,

"Nice," she said, swinging up the firearm and sighting along its barrel. Forty-five ACP. It holds fourteen in the magazine. How much?"

"Five thousand dollars."

"Whoa, hoss. That's robbery."

"No, what you have in mind is robbery. When you pay me five grand, I hand you the gun and three loaded magazines without any paperwork."

The part about no paperwork turned her head.

"Really? No paperwork?"

"None, nada, zilch. We won't ask questions, and you don't tell us any answers. No need."

Nivea lay the gun on a shop rag on her side of the window counter. She reached inside her coat and pulled out a zippered bag. Then she counted out five-thousand-dollars. She passed the bills under the glass, where they were eagerly scooped up by the clerk. "Nice," he said. "Be right back with the magazines."

Minutes ticked by. Nivea worked the gun, field-stripping it and examining it for dirt or grime. But the gun was perfectly clean and went back together in a snap. She was pleased and happy with her purchase.

He returned holding three magazines hanging between his fingers. "Here we go, Miss--I didn't catch your name."

She took the magazines and dropped them into her coat's left side pocket. "Right," she said. "Now I need a silencer for this gun."

The clerk's head snapped up. "Silencers are illegal."

"That's why I'm willing to pay five thousand dollars for one. Go talk to your owner, please."

The clerk, a grim look on his face, left the room. Several minutes later he returned. He was carrying a long box about the size of a pocketknife box.

"Five thousand first," said the clerk.

"Nivea counted the bills onto the counter and pushed them under the glass. The clerk snatched them up, recounted, and, satisfied, pushed the box under the window.

"Try the fit," he said.

Nivea easily twisted the silencer onto the muzzle of her weapon. Now she was ready. She turned and began her walk to the front door, leaving without a word.

"See you around," the clerk said as she walked up the aisle toward the entrance.

"No, you won't," she said, suddenly spinning on her heel and aiming a finger pistol at the clerk. She smiled and turned away.

Minutes later, she was outside and climbing into the back seat of her waiting taxi cab.

Then she was gone.

~

Nivea stood in the showroom of the local Harley-Davidson dealer just blocks from Northwestern University. It didn't take long. She made her selection, paid for the bike with a fake American Express, and took the bike in the same name as the credit card. They offered to give her a lesson. She only looked at them blankly and shook her head. At last, the keys were handed over, the bike was rolled outside, and Nivea pulled on her helmet and straddled the bike. She stuffed her few belongings into the saddle bags and closed the covers.

The first ride was a short one--down to the end of the block and a filling station.

Then she began riding toward Michael Gresham's shore-side home. He lived in the north part of town, just off Ashland Avenue. Several blocks from his house, her next target came into view. It was a mail lady sitting in her door-less van, studying a clipboard propped up in her lap. Nivea parked a hundred yards away and began walking. As she drew abreast of the unaware mail lady, Nivea pulled the silenced gun from her pocket, closed the last ten yards, crept up to the driver's door, and fired at point blank range one bullet into the worker's head, just behind the ear.

Death was instant. Nivea climbed into the van and quickly undressed the corpse. She then undressed and pulled on the USPS's uniform. She reached back behind, then, and found the mail pouch with its shoulder strap. She dropped her gun into the bag and climbed out. Back at her motor-cycle she climbed aboard and closed to within two blocks from Gresham's home. She had studied the place on Google Earth and would have no trouble identifying her target.

She parked the bike on the edge of a small local park, a place of green grass and great old oak and hickory trees, leafless in the winter. Then she shouldered the bag, removed the key from the ignition, and began hiking to the end of the block upon which Gresham's house stood. Her pulse was picking up its rhythm when she made the Gresham street, but she was steady as she always was at such times.

The dream state was taking over, and Nivea became one who saw herself in the third person, operating as if in a dream. She had become detached. She had become death walking.

Feigning mailing deliveries all along the street, she at last threaded through several government vehicles occupied by government agents and stepped up to the front door of the lawyer's house. She pushed the doorbell and waited.

An older woman answered, opening the door a crack and being greeted with the green card fastened onto an envelope representing a letter the woman must sign for. She opened the door a crack wider and reached for the letter and pen being held toward her by Nivea.

"Can I use your restroom?" Nivea asked. "It's been a very long morning, and I have to go."

"Of course you can, dear," the woman said, and she stood aside, allowing Nivea to enter. Once inside, Nivea plucked her gun and fired a silenced round into the woman's face, just between her eyebrows. The force of the shot knocked her backward several feet where her arms flew out to the sides, and she came to rest on her back, cruciform, on the wood floor.

Nivea ignored her, heading for the long hallway and the bedrooms she knew would be there. Sure enough, there were four bedroom doors along the hall, two on each side. At the second door on the right, she peered inside and encountered a little girl of maybe twelve, sitting at her desk, rocking up and back, up and back, in that common repetitive movment Nivea knew indicated a troubled mind. Standing at the doorway, she heard voices coming from the direction of the slain woman, voices growing in volume and now shrieking. It would be only a minute until the agents came charging inside. Nivea placed the barrel of the gun across the wrist of her other hand and squeezed off two quick shots, striking the girl midline on her back. Her head flew forward, hitting the desk and bouncing, and then she fell to the floor and came to rest on her side.

Nivea was already gone, looking for the back door. Just through the kitchen she found a closed door, threw it open and was facing four steps leading down into the garage. She quickly jumped the steps and found the garage door opener, a switch on the wall. She punched the switch, and the door began crawling up. At three feet, Nivea was ducking under and coming upright and running for the alley that would lead back to the end of the block. Coming through the gate, she encountered two agents with automatic weapons running right at her. Rather than turn and run, she stood her ground, assumed a sidewise stance with the gun steadied in a two-handed grip, and she expertly fired off four rounds, knocking both marshals to the ground. Then she was running beyond them, headed for the cross street just a hundred feet away.

It was a short dash to the Harley and an immediate starting up of the two-cylinder engine as soon as she turned the key and hit the starter button with her thumb. Then she turned around and shot away.

So far, so good. No vehicles appeared to follow her.

She smiled. The girl was dead, she had done her job, and now she was free to go wherever she wanted in her exfiltration. At the corner, she paused, clicked open the hard-shell saddle bag behind her on her right, and pulled a powder blue sweatshirt out. It would offer some protection against the cold and would cover the gray waistcoat of the USPS. She pulled on the leather Harley coat, pulled on her gloves, and put her helmet on again.

She pulled onto Michigan Avenue for two blocks and then turned west on the back roads.

They were looking, but they didn't know about the motorcycle and didn't know about her gender as she rode with her helmet in place.

She laughed and kicked her legs out to the sides.

Freedom was everything!

45

F rom my office in the U.S. Attorney's Office in Washington, I called the U.S. Marshals' Service and asked for help. I was transferred to the Special Operations Group, that highly-trained tactical unit that, among other things, is tasked with protecting court witnesses and employees. I told them I had a witness, Annie Tybaum, presently in Evanston, Illinois, and that I needed to reach her without delay to prepare her testimony for an upcoming trial and that I needed the SOG to transport me there surreptitiously.

They responded beautifully and inside of two hours I was airborne in a SOG aircraft to O'Hare in Chicago. Several SOG officers accompanied me as security for my witness. We touched down a little after noon and headed for the government terminal. Inside, there were no questions asked, but our group one-by-one flashed ID and badges. Then we were out the other end and climbing inside two waiting black Lincoln Navigators with one-way windows.

Jackie James, the group leader, turned to me from the front

seat of vehicle 2. "What are we doing when we arrive? Just falling in with the perimeter boys? Or do you want us to go inside with you? Or just wait in the vehicles?"

"Hook me up with a headset and wait in the cars. How's that work for you?"

"That works just fine."

James rummaged around in the console, located another headset, and passed it back to me along with the transceiver. I immediately put the send/receive mic and earpiece on my head and adjusted the volume. "Can you hear me on the net?" I asked into the boom mic.

"Loud and clear," Jackie James came back. "Dial back your gain a quarter turn, and we're good to go."

I did as he said and then tested again. This time I got a thumbs-up from every marshal in the SUV. I was good to go.

Then our ear phones crackled to life. There had been a shooting at my house. Two people were down. Plus, law enforcement officers had been shot, too.

The marshals on either side restrained me as our driver floored the gas pedal. We were thirty minutes south of my home, but we covered the distance in half that time, running Code 3 with lights flashing angrily and siren angrily screaming.

Pulling into the circle drive at my house, the SUV screeched to a stop, the lights and siren turned off, and I was jumping from the back door even before the man nearest the door could exit. I ran for the front door, pushed through the agents guarding the entrance and froze in my tracks. Danny's mother lay on her back on the floor, arms flung out, clearly dead once I spotted the large bullet hole between her eyes.

"Michael!" I heard Verona cry from beyond the first knot of agents, "Annie's been shot!"

I pushed people aside and broke into a run for the bedrooms. The EMT cart stood at the far end of the hall, half of it inside what must be Annie's room. Down to the door, I flew, grabbing and door frame and twisting inside, just in time to find Annie being lifted by four EMT's onto the cart.

"What--what--" I cried.

"You're the father?" asked paramedic across her body.

"Yes," I shot back.

"She's alive. The marshals had your daughter wearing a bullet-proof vest. It saved her life."

"Where are you taking her?"

"To the ER to get her checked out. You're welcome to ride in our truck."

I moved around to the head of the gurney. Annie's eyes were open and staring at the ceiling. She wasn't evincing any pain though I knew the pain must be great. "Hey," I said and pushed a lock of hair from her forehead. "I'm here."

At first, she didn't respond to me. Then she evidently identified my voice and immediately raised up both arms and reached out to me. I bent down to her and wrapped her in my arms and hugged her. "It's okay, Annie. I'm here, and I'm going to take care of you."

She then relaxed completely and fell back against the gurney's padded surface. Seconds later she was being rolled from her room and flying down the hallway.

We rode to the hospital in the back end of the EMT's truck, Annie and I. She was awake but quiet and refused to answer my questions or respond to my comments. We turned into the ER service lot at Evanston Hospital, and the EMTs had Annie headed inside on the gurney in under a minute. Then the ER staff took over, allowing me to enter the curtained room with her. The EMTs waited patiently with her while the hospital staff gathered and began examining the child. When they had cut away her shirt and had her sitting up, we were able to see two silver-dollar bruises where the bullets had impacted against her vest. That vest had saved her life, but she was definitely in a lot of pain. Even with a vest, gunshots can break ribs and damage internal organs. So the staff was taking all due care.

After the physician had examined her, she was put on a slow drip, and it was explained to me that medications were being administered that would ease Annie's pain and help her sleep. I stayed with her during all of this, holding her hand as I was able and speaking softly and reassuringly to her.

An hour later she was asleep and I placed her arm and hand back on the examining table. As I did so, she opened her eyes dreamily and reached for my hand again. I wasn't going anywhere, I could see. So I held her and did what I could to soothe her until she was once again sleeping. A nurse brought me a coffee with cream, thank goodness. I drank with one hand, holding onto Annie's hand with my other. At long last, she lapsed into a deeper sleep, and I was able to free my hand and take one of the chairs at her bedside.

Nurses kept coming in to take vitals and check on her every ten minutes or so. Finally, the same physician returned and advised me they would be admitting her. They wanted to see not only her physical status return to normal but her emotional status to. "These little guys can deal with trauma in not-very-healthy ways," the ER doc told me. "We're going to keep her here so we can avoid some of that initial reaction."

"Whatever you say, Doc," I replied. "Is she going to be okay, though?"

"Oh yes. Those bruises will disappear in a month. She'll be feeling no pain the rest of the day and tonight. By morning, she'll be pretty much pain-free."

"Can I stay with her?"

"You're her father?"

"Yes."

"Then of course. That's just what she needs is her dad around just now."

"All right."

I pulled out my cell phone then and called Verona. She was a strong woman, but I could hear the tears in her voice. "Your mother-in-law died instantly, Michael. She's with Danny now."

"She is," I said. Verona, Russian by birth and raising, surprised me in her spiritual belief just then. But she was always surprising me.

"How are the other kids?"

I knew they'd be fine. They were at school when the break-in happened.

"They're fine. I've checked and re-checked. The marshals are out collecting them up as we speak. We'll not let them out of our sight again until this horrible killer is caught. Who is it, Michael? Do you know?"

"It's a she. Hired by a man in Washington. He's already successfully had Annie's two siblings, and her father killed, as I've told you. Now Annie is all that stands between him and twelve-million dollars. Too much for him to resist, evidently."

"You're staying with Annie tonight?"

"I am. You stay with my kids, please. I want to see you, but we can't do that just now."

"I know, I know, damn the luck."

We talked for a few more minutes before hanging up.

Annie was moved upstairs to a private room thirty minutes later.

At six p.m., Annie's eyes blinked open and she began weeping. She looked around wildly for me until I stood and made it to her bedside. I hugged her and kissed her forehead and made myself available to her.

"I want you with me, Michael," she finally said. "Please don't leave me alone again."

"I won't, I won't."

Which was a lie. Her aunt in Berkeley expected her as soon

as Nivea Young was tracked down and locked up. The woman called me every other day or so always asking "when."

But now I was uncomfortable with that. Annie wanted to be with me, and I felt the same way. She'd been through enough, and if she was happy being with me, then that's how it should be. Except the aunt had the legal right to have Annie with her and the aunt was a lawyer and already knew this. For now, I would leave that on the back burner. For one thing, Nivea Young hadn't been located, and for another thing, I could see Annie's eyes and how they pled to stay with me.

That changed the complexion of the entire thing.

46

A nnie made the trip back to Washington DC with me. I got her a connecting room at the Hyatt. Then we began looking for an apartment in Georgetown. We must have looked at a dozen places before we found one that suited Annie in the ways unknown to me that it takes to suit her about such things. The one she selected was no different from the ten or eleven others we'd already inspected; still, the one with the hydra-jet tub in her bathroom was the one she wanted. I had to hand it to her: I'd never seen a hydra-jet tub turn anyone's head before or make a house lease happen, but there was a first time for everything--especially with Annie.

The place was a four-bedroom, which gave us room enough for my own two kids when school let out, and they could join us. So the townhouse was the right place. If things kept going as well for me at the U.S. Attorney's Office as they had been, our growing family would look for a permanent home in a couple of years.

Then Aunt Geraldine called me at work. Aunt Geraldine

was Gerry Tybaum's sister. Which gave her first choice as Annie's legal placement ahead of me. Geraldine was a hugely successful class-action lawyer in Berkeley, and she'd never married. The idea of her taking Annie away from me when the woman had no experience with child raising at all was more than I could accept.

So I returned her call that night when I was home.

"Geraldine, Michael Gresham here. I'm calling about your niece, Annie Tybaum."

"The government contacted me, the Special Operations Group, to advise they had intervened in her welfare. By law, they have to notify me because I'm her guardian."

"Sure, so you know the whole story. But what you might not know is that Annie and I have become very close through all this. Now she wants to stay with my family and me."

"Your family consists of who?"

"Two younger children and my fiancée Verona Sakharov. We are very functional, loving, caring people. We all love Annie and are praying she remains with us. I hope you can support us in this."

"Ordinarily I would say yes. But where there has been so much killing I'm afraid I want to see Annie get a fresh start. Someplace away from old memories, places, and things. No, I want Annie here with me, Mr. Gresham. Has the mad woman who was stalking her been arrested?"

"It was more like tracking her--hunter and quarry. No, she's still at large."

"Then, by all means, let's get her placed with me without

delay. She'll never be found on the other end of the country."

"I wish I could agree," I said, "but I don't. Annie is very safe here with us. She and I are surrounded by three-deep security all day and night. No one can get through to her."

"I wish I had your certainty, Mr. Gresham, but I don't."

"Then we have to agree to disagree."

"Do I need to file a motion with the court, Mr. Gresham? Maybe a motion alleging unlawful restraint by you?"

She had me there. She could do that, and there was nothing I could do.

"No, no need to file. I'd like to remain in touch with Annie, and I want no hard feelings between you and me."

"Good. Then let's talk airline arrangements. Is this week too soon for you? Say, have her fly out Saturday morning? Or is Sunday better?

"Saturday. I'll make the arrangements and let you know.

I felt deflated. As I said, she had the legal right to custody. I had nothing. Even the argument that she would be safer with me wouldn't withstand judicial scrutiny.

Annie was on her way to Berkeley.

That night I tried to discuss the new arrangements with Annie. But she only sat at her desk in her room, refusing to turn and look at me when I told her I'd been in touch with her aunt about her living arrangements. So I plunged ahead.

"Your aunt has legal custody of you, Annie. She knows the judges in Berkeley, and she's been to court and gotten papers. There's nothing I can do to stop her."

Silence. Except for a steady tap-tap-tap on her computer keyboard as she retreated inside her shell.

"Papers were served on you here at the house some time ago before you left for Chicago. I just didn't tell you then. She served me, too. We were too busy with your protection to take a side trip to Berkeley, so legal custody of you was awarded to her without objection. I'm so, so sorry."

Still, the keyboard tapping continued. Annie refused to look at me although I asked her several times.

It was unsettling, and I was despondent. I could only imagine how she must feel. But I tried once again.

"What if I ask your aunt for visitation every summer? A month with me back here? Does that help?"

Her fingers stopped typing, and I thought I'd struck a chord. But, just as fast they started up again. She was going to be resolute and untouchable. Annie could do that to you. It wasn't the first time she had completely shut me out. She was gone, hiding somewhere deep inside herself, non-verbal.

That weekend, I had her and her two suitcases aboard the United Saturday morning flight to Berkeley. She wouldn't even look at me as I walked her onto the plane and helped find her seat. She buckled in without a word then turned her head to stare out the window.

So I was lost. There was no way of forcing communication with Annie. I was standing in the aisle with other passengers trying to squeeze past me, so I soon had to clear out.

"Goodbye, Annie," I said to her just as I was leaving. "I'll call you."

Nothing. No goodbye, no go-to-hell, nothing.

But I loved her all the same and knew I always would.

Then I walked off the plane, back up the jetway, and put on my sunglasses before it became evident to all who looked at me that I was crying.

Even tears didn't ease my sadness, however.

My tears were disconnected from my feelings.

Just like my precious Annie.

47

I told his attorney that he was subject to recall, so Paul Wexler shouldn't have been surprised when I gave notice of his continued grand jury appearance. So far the case was entitled *UNITED STATES OF AMERICA vs. JOHN DOE*, but the JOHN DOE name was about to be supplanted by PAUL WEXLER. I was sure I was very close to having enough evidence to indict him.

Once he was settled on the witness stand, I began.

"Mr. Wexler, describe your contract with Rudy Geneseo."

"Who?"

"The man you hired to murder Gerald Tybaum. Tell the grand jury what your contract with this Rudy person meant to accomplish."

"I don't understand."

"We know that you and Rudy Geneseo conspired to murder Gerald Tybaum. Do you deny this?"

"I deny it, sir."

"Then please allow me to show you some banking records."

"Oh."

"First off, the blow-up of the GULP account in Charter Bank and Mercantile of Boston."

I displayed the blow-up. It showed where the money had left one account at Charter Bank and Mercantile of Boston and then emerged in the account of another at Charter Bank and Mercantile of Boston.

I then showed a blow-up depicting the movement of funds. Jack Ames and his team at the FBI had gone to work on tracking down the identity of the person who had facilitated the cash payouts and deposits. He started with the most obvious choice, Paul Wexler. The bank's vault records proved that Wexler had visited the bank vault on the same dates as the cash withdrawals and that he had opened the account for Green Laundry and Cleaning. Access identities included, of all people, Rudy Geneseo.

"Now do you recognize these transactions depicted on the second blow-up?"

"I don't recognize them, no."

"Mr. Wexler, you're telling the grand jury you've never taken the time to look at the transactions that moved your company's money around to the tune of twelve-million-dollars?"

"I didn't say that. You asked if I recognized it. I don't. This doesn't mean I haven't seen it before. If I did, then I just don't recognize it at this point because I didn't think it proved anything."

Next, I produced a blow-up of the bank's records that facilitated the movement of PAC funds from the PAC's account to the account for Green Laundry and Cleaning.

"Tell us about this transaction. You did it at both ends: you transferred PAC funds totaling seventy-thousand dollars from the PAC bank account to the Green Laundry account the same bank. Why did you do this?"

"As I remember, Green Laundry was a campaign contributor that demanded its money be returned after Gerry Tybaum lost the election. It happens. I returned their seventy-thousand dollars."

"What about this signature transaction where Rudy Geneseo came to the bank and wired the seventy-thousand to a Swiss account? Can you tell us why a campaign contributor would hide its money in Zurich?"

"I can't speak for a campaign contributor's business purposing, Mr. Gresham. Sorry."

He spread his hands and looked over at the grand jury. They returned blank stares. He then smiled. They did not react. He turned back to me.

"Mr. Wexler, isn't it true that you used seventy-thousand of your PAC's money to hire Rudy Geneseo to murder Gerry Tybaum?"

"Untrue!"

"You don't deny that Geneseo was shot dead in Gerry Tybaum's youngest girl's bedroom as Geneseo was aiming his gun at the back of her head?"

"I don't know about that."

"How do you expect us to believe the seventy-thousand dollars wasn't used to hire Geneseo to murder Gerry Tybaum and his daughter? How dumb do you think we are?"

"I don't know about that. I don't know what Geneseo was doing."

"So you deny all knowledge of Mr. Geneseo?"

"Yes. I don't know the man."

"All right. I think we're finished here, Mr. Wexler. Does the grand jury have any questions?"

A grand juror whose name I can't reveal raised her hand. She looked rather fragile in her late-winter dress, and she looked wan. She asked, "Do you honestly think we're so stupid we don't see how you paid this man to kill Gerry's daughter? And probably Gerry?"

"No, I don't think--"

"Forget it!" said the grand juror and sat down in her chair, throwing knife looks at Wexler.

I then dismissed the witness and asked the clerk to read the indictment I had prepared. It charged Paul Wexler with conspiracy to commit the murders of Gerry Tybaum, Mona Tybaum, Jarrod Tybaum, and the attempted murder of Annie Tybaum.

"All in favor of indicting Paul Wexler on the terms stated, please raise your hands.

It was unanimous.

Wexler was now officially indicted.

He belonged to me.

48

It hadn't been quite a full month when I got the phone call from Annie's aunt in Berkeley. I was sitting in my office, reviewing the plea of not guilty filed by Paul Wexler's lawyers, when the call came in.

"Hello, this is Michael Gresham."

"Michael, this is Geraldine Tybaum," she said, using her maiden name.

"Hello, Ms. Tybaum. How's our favorite twelve-year-old doing these days?"

"We need to talk, Mr. Gresham. I've had Annie to my own psychiatrist's office three times. She refused to speak to Dr. Witham, but she did write him a letter."

"And she said in the letter?"

"The gist of the letter is she misses her family. Enough that she cries when no one's around. But most of all--you're going to love this--she misses you and wants to be with you."

"We were very close, Ms. Tybaum."

"She hasn't spoken to me even one time since she's been here. If you hadn't sent her list of favorite foods, she'd be starving by now. It's hopeless. And I love her enough to grant her wish. I'm sending her back to you, Michael. And I'm signing over custody so that you can sign papers for her and so forth as any parent can."

I was stunned.

Annie was coming home!

"One requirement before I agree, Ms. Tybaum."

"Which is what?"

"You will consent to me adopting Annie. I want to make her my child."

"Will I be allowed visitation if she's open to it?"

"Absolutely. I'd never try to cut you off from your niece."

"Then I'll waive any rights I have. She's already your daughter, Mr. Gresham. Make it official with my blessings."

"I'll be dictating the paperwork today."

"I'll send her to you this Saturday when I'm off work. Does that work out for you?"

"I'd come in the middle of the night for Annie," I said. "Saturday is great!"

"Goodbye, Mr. Gresham. And good luck."

Two hours later, I received confirmation of her flight and arrival time. Annie was coming home Saturday at three o'clock precisely four Saturdays since I had put her on the plane to leave. I couldn't have been happier and immediately called Verona with the good news.

"The kids and I will have her bedroom ready," Verona said. "Maybe I'll even get bunk beds so Dania can sleep in with her big sister now and then. She talks about that when her sister comes back, you know?"

"No, I didn't know."

"Oh, the kids have been telling me all along that the aunt wouldn't keep Annie. They said Annie would outlast her. Now look; she has."

At noon that next Saturday we all journeyed to Reagan International to collect up Annie and give her our all-in welcome. Sure enough, coming up the jetway, on seeing me she doubled her gait and then was running, her computer bag banging against her hip. She ran into my arms and wrapped herself around me. Then she was soundlessly crying, and I started crying too.

We carried on like that for several minutes before Verona got us herded up and headed for the parking garage.

On the ride home, I said into the rearview mirror, "Welcome home, Annie."

For the first time in a month, she spoke. "Thank you for taking me back, Michael. I love you."

"Well, we love you too, and we're all delighted you joined us."

"I'm ready to work with you some more, too, on my dad's killer."

"He's just been charged with the crime. A man by the name of Paul Wexler."

It went silent for a minute, then, "I thought I told you. The vice president killed my family."

"Well, the evidence at the grand jury just doesn't support that, Annie."

"Then you haven't found all the evidence yet. I'm telling you I'm right, Michael."

"Well, we're still looking."

"Number two in what I have to say. I want you to teach me how to shoot a gun."

I looked at her in the mirror. "You want to learn to shoot--why?"

"Is Nivea Young still on the loose?"

"Yes."

"Then wouldn't you want to know how to shoot too if you were me?"

"Probably. Yes."

"Please find a teacher for me. I'm ready now."

"All right I think I know who we'll use."

"Good. Name?"

"Rusty Xiang."

"Your other son?"

Silence from me. How could she possibly know this?

"How did you know?"

"I knew you were in Moscow last year on a trial. So I looked it up on TASS. The whole thing is on there. Reading between the lines, you wouldn't have been there at all if it wasn't your son you were defending."

"Who is Rusty, Dad?" asked Dania.

"He's my son."

"When do we get to meet him?"

"Very soon now. This week, probably."

"Let's make sure that happens, Michael," said Annie, more demanding than I'd ever heard her before.

"All right."

"I'm very serious about taking steps to protect myself. I need that firearms training without delay."

I agreed. Annie deserved to know how to defend herself, given the severe breach of the defenses around her in Evanston. She had every right to be worried.

We all did.

That next day, Annie went shooting with Rusty.

"This is the magazine, this is the muzzle, this is--"

Annie looked impatiently at her guide. "Show me how to aim and shoot. Isn't that why we're here?"

They were at the firing range at National Guns & Ammo in

Annapolis. It was the most popular gun range/firearms outlet in the DC area. Rusty always was bumping into CIA agents he knew by name and police officers and detectives he was meeting now that he worked with the USAO.

"This is a very popular place," Rusty told Annie. "I'm hoping it's not a long wait for a target."

"You come to this one to keep sharp?"

"I do. This place is also anonymous. They give everyone a number, so real names don't appear on their sign-in sheets and the like. I wouldn't be anyplace else."

"Works for me too, then," said Annie.

Their number finally came up, and they hurried to their firing range. Then he provided shooting eyewear and earplugs. He went through gun safety with Annie.

Finally, it was time to shoot. Rusty positioned his new sister--papers had been filed for the adoption--at the firing line, adjusted her stance, and helped her aim the gun at the human silhouette target.

"Now squeeze the trigger. Exhale first, then squeeze. Good, good."

Annie's gun erupted and the target showed a hit about the centerline of the chest.

Rusty knew--figured--the girl's accuracy was luck. He told her to fire a second time.

A hole appeared in the target's head, just above the right eye.

"Not bad, Annie, not bad."

"I want to empty the magazine on him now. Is that cool?"

"It is. Empty away."

Annie squeezed off a dozen more shots before dropping her arms and placing the gun on the shelf before her.

"What?"

"She's dead," Annie said. "I'm saving the rest of my bullets in case anyone else came with her."

"Smart lady," Rusty agreed. "Now let's learn how to strip and assemble this weapon. Then we'll run another couple hundred rounds through it and call it a day."

"If I want to fire my most high-percentage shot, where would that be, Rusty?"

"You're talking smack in the middle of the chest, then. The reason is, the head can move around. The chest cannot. So disable your target with that chest shot and then walk up and put two in his head."

"Her head."

"Her head, then."

"Let me try a few hundred chest shots then. Let's make this perfect."

"You're on."

49

Time with Michael went by too quickly in the evenings, for Annie Tybaum. But time alone during the day was interminably slow now that she was under police protection again and unable even to walk outside without some burly marshal directing her around behind the house to the treehouse and adult swing set. Two months had passed by, and Annie fitted in well enough with the family. There were inconsistencies the other kids had to learn how to deal with, and there were times of extreme moodiness with Annie and emotional ups and downs and times of rocking up and back, up and back, for an hour or more when everyone knew just to leave her alone.

But there were also times to snoop around the house. She was excited when she discovered Michael's gun. He had never talked about it, but she knew that his Chicago gun was marked as evidence in the Gerry Tybaum murder case. But this one was new, a small pocket Glock 26 in .40 caliber.

Now all she needed was a way to get to Annapolis. So she started a campaign for a bus pass, ostensibly so she could tour the Naval Academy and its environs. The pass was acquired--against Michael's and Verona's better judgment--, and Michael sat down with her several nights and studied the bus routes and which one got you where. When she was alone, Annie memorized the routes in one sitting. The trip to Annapolis was easy enough on Route 220 of the Maryland MTA.

It wasn't long before she was being dropped at the bus stop, but always there was a U.S. Marshal shadowing and protecting her. Until one day over the Fourth of July when she managed to escape her overseer and jump on Route 220.

She walked up and down the bus twice, looking for the Marshal. He hadn't made the connection that Annie had made, scrambling from the front of the bus to the rear door exit, where she jumped ship. An old ploy but it worked this time.

She had decided that if Nivea Young were still in the area, she would sooner or later go shooting to keep her skill-level top-drawer. And what better place than National Guns & Ammo?

National Guns & Ammo shooting range was within easy walking distance of the bus drop. Wearing her backpack with the new gun inside, Annie headed for a confrontation she had in mind.

It was a long-shot and Annie wasn't kidding herself about that. But it was proactive, and it was the first time she'd had the chance to address her greatest fear: facing Nivea Young from the wrong end of a gun again. This time, the way Annie planned it, the gun would be in her hand, and Young would be at the wrong end. Such is the faith of children.

Such is the unrelenting focus of someone suffering Annie's diagnosis. She just couldn't let it go.

She took up a point of surveillance inside the shooting range in a customer waiting area. Her location gave her a perfect view of the customers as they came and went. She passed five hours on her perch, scanning and discarding the faces as they came and went. She knew her chances were less than five percent, but still she persisted. That night, she was confronted by Michael for losing her protection.

"It's serious when you do that," Michael said. "I feel like I should ground you for two weeks."

"Meaning what?"

"Not letting you leave the house."

Annie began crying and rocking up and back, up and back. She pulled her arms around herself and hung on as if hugging another. Michael reached across the table and gently touched the side of her face. But nothing helped; they were not going to have a serious discussion that night about the rules of the road. He could see that. But the next time she went on the bus, she made no attempt to break away from her protection.

Annie's first stakeout at National Guns & Ammo was on a Saturday. Now she needed a Sunday, which she managed by telling her guard that she wanted to people watch at National. He had his suspicions, and he had his doubts, but in the end, he figured that if he were with her, nothing could go wrong.

Wrong.

Sunday morning just turned out to be Nivea's day to

sharpen her firearm skills. She showed up for her nine-fifteen reservation and was firing her gun when Annie arrived. Annie told her marshal she needed to use the restroom and gave him the slip just before she walked into the shooting range and began checking faces.

Sure enough, the killer was emptying her gun--a huge Beretta--at a silhouette target when Annie appeared. Annie's heart leaped. She pulled the small photograph out of her wallet and compared pictures. No mistake.

From a distance of thirty feet--entry door to last shooting position along the range--Annie removed her backpack, drew her gun, and began walking toward her target.

Just as she came to the killer, she spoke her name: "Nivea!"

The woman didn't jump or act surprised. Instead, she was wheeling on Annie and swinging her gun around at belly-button level to protect herself. Just as she raised the gun to fire at Annie, Annie shot first. In the din and clamor of the shooting range her own gun's bark was meaningless, falling on deaf ears. Luckily, the shooters were inside their shooting stalls, a small wall on either side, and no one caught sight of what had just happened.

Annie's bullet caught Nivea in the throat. A second bullet entered just above her eyebrow-line. The woman crumpled. Then she suddenly flopped forward, arms spread, smashing her face into the floor. She didn't move. She wasn't breathing.

Annie calmly slipped the gun into her backpack and slowly picked her way along the shooters, never drawing attention to herself even one time.

Then she located her marshal and told him she wasn't feeling well, that she wanted to go back home.

The bus ride was without incident. Annie was long gone by the time the police were called.

She sat comfortably beside her protector, scanning the Internet with her broadband iPad.

Not a word was said to her after that. Michael didn't mention Nivea's death; no one said a word to her about it.

But *Good Morning, Washington*, the early bird TV show, did. They reported the death, reported no suspects, reported a video system that only caught the head of someone wearing a Washington Senator's baseball cap and silverized sunglasses as she entered the scene and captured the same view as she departed the scene walking backward.

The noon follow-up reported the victim's identity and reported the victim had been sought under a federal warrant seeking her in connection with multiple murders in the Washington area.

"Huh-uh," Annie said under her breath to the dead woman's picture on TV that night. "She's not the top dog. But we're getting there. We're getting there."

50

I learned the most disappointing rule about being a prosecutor, which was this: If you get most of the bad guys and put them in prison that's about as good as it's going to get. Which left me sad because I wanted to heap lots and lots more punishment on most of their pointed heads. And, the really bad guys, the guys who live and work in the tall buildings and ride in chauffeured cars and spend holidays on their yachts--you were never going to get those bad guys.

But what I had done in indicting Paul Wexler and solving the Tybaum murder case, was to be celebrated Friday afternoon at the vice president's home. Other Assistant U.S. Attorneys were scheduled to be recognized there too, so it wasn't just about me.

But it made me happy that someone was paying attention to my efforts.

At the last minute, the look coming from Annie--that jealousy look that only your kids know--made me realize she needed to get out, too. While she was anything but social, her doctor said that attempts at socialization should always be being made. So I told her she was going with me and she was immediately ecstatic. A friendly judge had all but personally walked through the adoption, and now Annie was mine. Or maybe I was hers, I have never been sure. But now she was known as Annie Gresham.

After I had said I wanted her to accompany me to the celebration, Annie headed for her bedroom. She went to dress and came out wearing jeans and a GWU sweat-shirt. Verona looked her over and led her back to her room to change into a more celebratory look. This time she came out wearing a navy summer skirt and a white blouse with a blue necktie. Now we were getting somewhere.

A marshal drove us to the Naval Observatory--the vice president's home, a tri-story, white edifice with a circle drive out front where we climbed from the car and went inside. The marshal stayed right with us.

Annie and I were greeted by the vice president and his wife as we came up the front steps and entered the foyer, then we shook hands with several more dignitaries in the line of greeters. Once we were inside, we melted into the crowd, and I began trading shop talk with Antonia Xiang--my supervisor--who was there without Rusty. He was working a stakeout, she told me. But she was there to enjoy herself and was proud of what her staff had accomplished the first half of the year. As we talked, Annie wandered off, and I remember hearing a female voice asking her if she'd like a tour of the vice president's residence.

Other AUSA's came into our circle and joined in our talk

and then we went into the vice-presidential dining room. Annie had attached herself to me by then and was trying to get my attention as we were seated. She raised her hand and cupped it to my ear so she could whisper to me.

"Check out the kitchen," she said.

"What for?"

"You'll know it when you see it."

"Such as?"

"Don't be pushy, Michael. Check it out for yourself."

"I will." I nodded, and she drew away. We'd drawn no attention to ourselves as drink orders were being taken.

Then the appetizers arrived, followed by salads, followed by a poached salmon entrée and a substitute of New York strip. The vice-president's youngest daughter was seated to Annie's right. The poor girl attempted to strike-up conversation with my child but was largely unsuccessful.

I, on the other hand, spent the meal sharing *voir dire* techniques with a young attorney, a man by the name of Herb Marling, who was currently serving on my staff. Herb was preparing for trial Monday next and was picking my brain in the meantime. I was glad to help and unloaded what I knew on him.

"Never forget the primary aim of *voir dire* is that you qualify the jury. Ask questions such as, 'If you were the government here today, would you want a juror with your mindset on the jury? Could you set aside any bias and try the case only on the facts adduced in court?'"

Herb understood already and ran a few sample questions past me. By the time we finished our little instructional, dessert had come and gone. Now Annie leaned over to me and cupped her hand to my ear a second time.

"Michael, we're going into the kitchen now."

With that, she stood and took my hand and pulled me along behind her. She led me back through the connecting hallway that opened in the kitchen. There, in an alcove off to the side, stood an old six-legged table. But that wasn't all.

Lying on the table, its tail whipping up and back, side-to-side, lay a large yellow cat.

"That's the tabby on your camera," she said. "I memorized the marks."

My mind was racing, and I was gulping down air. This couldn't be--it couldn't.

"You're sure...certain?" I asked.

"Michael, am I ever wrong about trivia like this?"

"Never."

"Well, this is the same cat as on your phone camera. Look at the 'M' on its forehead. A perfect likeness."

"Oh my God!" I whispered, shuddering while the words came rolling out.

She wasn't finished. "And check out the table. That's your table exactly with the same salt and pepper shakers."

I pulled out my cell phone just then and looked up the video. I replayed the cat portion several times. She was right. The mark on the forehead, the silver salt and pepper shakers, the other markings--everything was a perfect match.

Whoever had taken the GoPro to the scene of the murder of Annie's father had photographed this cat and table first. Which meant they had stood in this kitchen and probably planned the hit with the vice president. Why else would a killer's camera be in this room?

There was no other explanation.

My mind raced ahead. I could indict the vice-president. I could take him to trial. His motive? Gerry was involved with the vice-president's wife. Jealousy? Alternatively, I could see where the VP's wife's dalliance with Gerry Tybaum could embarrass the White House. President Sinclair would not allow that, not even for a second. So maybe the order to end the affair between the VP's wife and Gerry was given by Sinclair himself. I was sure I'd never know. But I was sure of one thing: someone living here had killed or hired a killer to end the affair. My mind was racing by this point and I turned blindly away from the table and the cat.

Then I stopped moving. Annie was at risk. I could lose Annie's twelve-million dollars with a renewed claim by GULP's PAC for the money. Because if Wexler and Rudy Geneseo had met with Vice President Jonathan Vengrow and conspired to kill Gerry Tybaum, then the PAC wasn't involved, only Wexler. Which meant the PAC could show "clean hands." Then it could renew its claim for the money against Annie's claim.

My prosecution of the VP could result in Annie losing her money. Money that she was going to need to help care for her after I was gone. She had no siblings, no parents--except

me--and would be alone in the world save for what relationships she had developed with Mikey and Dania, who I
couldn't count on to support and care for Annie. No, she
needed the money to stay right where it was.

So I took her by the hand, then, and we left the kitchen.

On the way outside to our car, I shook the vice president's
hand. Then I closed the space between us and said under
my breath, "I've got you, but I'm moving on."

He continued smiling and shaking hands, never breaking
away from his hosting duty.

But when I climbed in the backseat of our marshal's car, I
turned and had a last look at the vice president. He was no
longer in the line. Then I saw him, hurrying toward my car. I
rolled down my window. Then he spoke.

"Thank you, Michael. This can only help you in your job."

"If it does, I just might change my mind, Mr. Vice President. I
would come after you."

"All right, then," he said and thumped the side of our car to
send us on our way.

Several blocks away, Annie looked over at me.

"You've got him cold, but you're thinking about my money.
How close am I?"

"Have you ever had to punt on a profile, Annie?"

"Never. That won't ever happen."

"I know," I said, the puffed-up pride I had felt in the VP's
house rushing out of me.

That was the last time I would ever feel that pride. I was in bed with the devil, and that couldn't be good.

We turned at Wisconsin Avenue and headed south toward Georgetown.

I was tired, and I needed a nap.

THE END

ALSO BY JOHN ELLSWORTH

THADDEUS MURFEE PREQUEL

A Young Lawyer's Story

THADDEUS MURFEE SERIES

The Defendants

Beyond a Reasonable Death

Attorney at Large

Chase, the Bad Baby

Defending Turquoise

The Mental Case

Unspeakable Prayers

The Girl Who Wrote The New York Times Bestseller

The Trial Lawyer (A Small Death)

The Near Death Experience

Flagstaff Station

SISTERS IN LAW SERIES

Frat Party: Sisters In Law

Hellfire: Sisters In Law

MICHAEL GRESHAM PREQUEL

Lies She Never Told Me

MICHAEL GRESHAM SERIES

THE LAWYER

SECRETS GIRLS KEEP

THE LAW PARTNERS

CARLOS THE ANT

SAKHAROV THE BEAR

ANNIE'S VERDICT

DEAD LAWYER ON AISLE 11

30 DAYS OF JUSTIS

THE FIFTH JUSTICE

PSYCHOLOGICAL THRILLERS

THE EMPTY PLACE AT THE TABLE

EMAIL SIGNUP

If you would like to be notified of new book publications, please sign up for my email list. You will receive news of new books, newsletters, and occasional drawings for Kindles.
— John Ellsworth

ABOUT THE AUTHOR

For thirty years John defended criminal clients across the United States. He defended cases ranging from shoplifting to First Degree Murder to RICO to Tax Evasion, and has gone to jury trial on hundreds. His first book, *The Defendants*, was published in January, 2014. John is presently at work on his 25th thriller.

Reception to John's books has been phenomenal; more than 2,000,000 have been downloaded in 60 months. All are Amazon best-sellers. He is an Amazon All-Star every month and is a *U.S.A Today* bestseller.

John Ellsworth lives in Arizona in the mountains and in California on the beach. He has three dogs that ignore him but worship his wife, and bark day and night until another home must be abandoned in yet another move.

johnellsworthbooks.com
johnellsworthbooks@gmail.com

Printed in the USA
CPSIA information can be obtained
at www.ICGtesting.com
LVHW051335291024
795101LV00016B/763